Items should be returned to a library by closing
time on or before the date stamped above,
unless a renewal has been granted.

SWINDON
BOROUGH COUNCIL

# ERIC MALPASS

# The Cleopatra Boy

HOUSE OF
STRATUS

This edition published in 2001 by House of Stratus, an imprint of
Stratus Holdings plc, 24c Old Burlington Street, London, W1X 1RL, UK.

www.houseofstratus.com

Typeset, printed and bound by House of Stratus.

A catalogue record for this book is available from the British Library.


ISBN 0-7551-0198-7

# CONTENTS

# Contents

# DRAMATIS PERSONAE

*Richard Burbage*:  Friend of Will Shakespeare. Not only witnessed the birth of, but was also the first man ever to act, Richard III, Hamlet, Macbeth, Othello, Lear. Was probably far too busy ever to appreciate his good fortune.

*Robert Catesby*:  Onlie begetter of the Gunpowder Plot, he had his thunder unaccountably stolen by a very minor character called Guy Fawkes.

*The Devil*:  Caused less general mayhem than God, but made up for this by being a constant thorn in the flesh of King James.

*Helen Fox*:  A lady who enjoyed nothing so much as the company of pleasant gentlemen.

*Nicholas Fox*:  A boy player. Her son.

*God*:  A very partisan Deity. His obvious detestation of the Catholics was a great comfort to the Puritans. The fact that he *must* be on the same side as the Pope fortified the Catholics.

*Philip Henslowe*:  A rival theatre owner. His piety was an example to us all.

# DRAMATIS PERSONAE

*James Stuart*: Theologian, writer, huntsman. His attempts to combine these activities with ruling England and Scotland led to some difficulties.

*Ben Jonson*: Though not for want of trying, this turbulent fellow could never feel any real animosity towards his rival, gentle Shakespeare.

*Mary, Dowager Countess of Pembroke*: Sidney's sister, mother of Pembroke. Wrote plays: a remarkable, though not altogether seemly, achievement for a lady.

*Annette Peyre*: A silversmith's widow.

*Matthew Peyre*: A boy actor. Her son.

*Anne Shakespeare*: Wife to William. Loyal and loving, she had little scope for exercising either virtue, ninety miles away in Stratford.

*William Shakespear Gent*: A poet manqué. In the fell clutch of circumstance he became, instead, a writer of popular plays; and, God save the mark, a Groom of the Chamber.

*Henry Wriothesley*: Third Earl of Southampton. Originally friend and patron of the young poet Shakespeare. Later followed his friend Essex to the Tower, while the cautious Will made his excuses. After this, their ways parted.

Courtiers, Soldiers, Citizens of London, Messengers, Friends, Romans and Countrymen.

*To Heather Malpass with my love*

# PROLOGUE

Death himself, it seemed, had died with the winter days. Life was everywhere, vociferous and abundant. Clouds sailed and shone, dogs ran, snapping at the breeze, the washing danced and jigged in Stratford gardens. The winter was dead, and Death with it.

No. Death had not died. In the dank shade of Stratford church he skulked. 'Hamnet Shakespeare. Born 1585. Died 1596.' A small stone, for so small a span. A short inscription, for so short a life. An old sorrow, half forgotten yet always remembered. Death had not died. The grave still had its victory.

A still-young, soberly dressed man gazed down at the stone. A breeze of morning stirred his grey cloak. A breath of spring ruffled his chestnut hair. He wept a little. But he was a man who wept easily: an old sorrow, an old song, the sweet anguish of passing beauty. All these could start a tear.

He sighed. He turned away. He mounted his horse. He took, yet once again, the road to London; not because he wanted to, but because he could not help himself. He went as the swallow heads north in the springtime, and the deer returns to the far forest.

# CHAPTER 1

## HALLOO YOUR NAME TO THE
## REVERBERATE HILLS...

Those early spring days were as harsh and exhilarating as sea water flung into the face.

And it wasn't only the birds and insects that bustled. To the Foul Fiend who, as everyone knew, spent some time each day perched on a pinnacle of Paul's (having been seen by many), the spider web of roads out of London must have looked alive with horsemen. And, flying north, he would have seen the great highway from Edinburgh to London acrawl with coaches, waggons, horses, soldiers. For it was not only a new spring. it was a new reign. And not only a new reign. The English and the Scots, who had so gamely slaughtered each other through bloody centuries, were of a sudden bed-fellows.

It would, thought many, be a restless night.

But William Shakespeare was not thinking overmuch about the new reign as he jogged towards London. His two years of quiet living at Stratford had taught him many things. He had been able to stand outside himself, see his London life for what it was – turmoil, a man striving for baubles like a

1

silly child, a life as false and hollow as an actor's crown. Two years of country living had matured him, strengthened him, given him a clearer sight; so that even as he rode the long dichotomy of his life was suddenly resolved. For the first time he knew where he wanted to be: Stratford. His roots, his emotions, his love, his comforts, were all in the quiet world of Warwickshire; where sunrise and sunset, and the cattle returning for milking, and the lightening of the lamps at evening, were your only exits and entrances. London had been excitement, discomfort, danger; to be borne in his youth; but a man nearing forty liked his comforts and his peace of mind. So, he would see to it that his future visits to London were short. A new play for the Chamberlain's Men, perhaps, a bit of acting. (Could a man who had once played upon the groundlings as upon the jacks *ever* forget the excitement, the intensity; mounting to break in a sudden roar of anger or laughter?) He would make sure the lads were keeping to his rules of acting, none of Ned Alleyn's ranting, by God! And then – back to Stratford, and Anne, and his lovely daughter Susanna, and poor, scared, curranty-eyed Judith, dead Hamnet's twin. Well, old conscience, how do you like that? he murmured, it being the first time he had taken this road without conscience riding him like a black dog. Before, he had always left Stratford as one leaves a prison. But now he was an older, wiser, *better* Will.

Or so he told himself.

Richard Burbage, notable actor and friendliest of men, was near breaking point.

No acting; it would have been unseemly with the old Queen not yet in her grave. More important, such disrespect would have given the Puritans another stick to beat the poor players withal.

So, since neither he nor any of the popular Chamberlain's Men ever wasted a moment – life was too teeming busy for that – he was devoting himself to trying to recruit a boy player; and was fast coming to the conclusion that every boy in London with a roof to his mouth had already joined the Children's Companies, those bands of acting boys so beloved of audiences, so hated by the *real* players.

His ruff was chafing his neck. His padded clothes, caught tight at knee and waist and wrist, were sticky with sweat. His skin, after a winter of salted beef, pricked and burnt as though the devils of Hell were at him with their needles. All he wanted was to get home, and put on a loose gown. He might even, so great was his irritation, risk taking a bath.

What a day! As if interviewing ten brats – and their doting mothers – hadn't been enough, he'd met his rival Philip Henslowe outside Henslowe's own theatre, the Fortune.

No escape! Philip's claws had grabbed his arm as though it were a money bag. Philip's sallow, pious face had been thrust close to his. 'Terrible times, Master Burbage, terrible times! They say the new king will close the theatres for ever.' He raised his eyes in dumb beseeching to heaven, giving Richard an unappetising glimpse of their white, bloodless rims.

'It may not be true,' said Richard, just to keep his spirits up.

Henslowe looked at him earnestly. 'Pray God you be right.' He shook his head. 'For myself I go down on my knees and thank our gentle Saviour nightly for my bearpits and my brothels. I would not like to be dependent on my players, in these terrible days.'

'No,' said Richard, who had neither bearpits nor brothels, and *was* dependent on his players. He tried to move away, but those claws still gripped his arm. It would be unjust to say of so devout a Christian that Philip Henslowe had more salt to rub in a wound. Say rather he had more sympathy to dispense from his overflowing heart. He drew Richard even closer. Richard smelt the pickled herrings of his last night's supper. Henslowe lowered his voice. 'Tell me, Dick. I have been most troubled. Will Shakespeare – he is not ill?'

'No. No.' But that accomplished actor, Burbage, sounded much less unconcerned than he had intended. 'It is just some rather lengthy business in Stratford, I believe.'

Henslowe looked very relieved. He lifted his eyes upwards, but this time in thankfulness. 'I am glad to hear it, Dick. It is so long since London had a new play from him that I had feared – '

Burbage gave him a smile of pure loathing, and passed on. He hadn't fooled Henslowe, he told himself. Damn Henslowe! And damn Will, he thought for good measure. Hiding himself away in Warwickshire. The best man they ever had. Johannes Factotum. Despite the fact that he had long been a sharer in the Company, you could still rely on old Will to step into a part at a moment's notice, blow the opening trumpet, even sell quinces if the housemen were all sick. He'd written some good plays too. In fact Dick was prepared to agree that the lucky accident that one of their players had the knack of writing plays, *and* seemed to know just what the groundlings wanted, had as much to do with their success as Burbage's acting or Heminge's management.

After a cup or two of sack, he would have said more; that Will's plays were like onions – every time he acted in one of them he peeled off a skin and found another skin beneath; that Will, who had already shown him so deep into the labyrinths of the human heart and mind, might yet be capable of taking him even deeper; that they all, and Burbage especially, had a tremendous affection and respect for old

Will; and that he, Burbage, was secretly a little hurt that Will had deserted them for so long.

But now it was time to go home. To leave this airless, cluttered room at the Globe, which all day had been noisy and restless with children, and go home to Halliwell Street, where, God save the mark, there were eight more children, eight little Burbages.

He began tidying up, restacking the swords and pikes – why did the little devils always go for the weapons? Since they were applying to be apprenticed to play women's parts – though there wasn't one today he'd touch with this pike, save to prod him – why didn't they play with the wigs and farthingales? It would have shown more dedication.

He picked up a square of paper: 'Make me a willow cabin at your gate,' he mimicked. God! To think there had been a time when he quite liked that speech from Will's *Twelfth Night*. Today he'd heard it ranted, piped, squeaked, mumbled until it had lost all beauty, even all sense. Children! They were destroyers. They destroyed peace, and order, and seemliness. And now he was going home to eight more.

There was a knock at the door. Richard stood, stiff and taut. If he didn't get his clothes off soon he'd suffocate. Had there been a back door, he would have slipped through it, and away.

But there wasn't. 'Come in,' called Richard Burbage belligerently.

She was overdressed, even for the present fashion.

Her skirt was as yellow as a canary bird. Her ruff would have made a wheel for a dray. Rings covered her fingers like golden mittens. Yet she was pretty, handsome even. And somewhere under that carapace of brocade and cane hoops,

Richard found himself thinking, there was an ample woman's body. 'I have brought my son Nicholas,' she said, 'to be prenticed as an actor. I am Mistress Fox – Helen Fox, though friends call me Nell.' She looked as though she thought it unlikely that this stout player would ever be allowed in *that* circle. 'Say your piece, Nicholas.'

Nicholas struck an attitude – up on his toes, calves flexed, left arm curling round and over his head. Like a damn lamp bracket, Burbage thought sourly.

Nicholas now lifted his right hand and held it, palm outwards, fingers spread, before his horror-stricken face. ' "What outcries pluck me from my naked bed?" ' he cried. ' "And chill – " '

'Wait!' shouted Burbage. How dare they burst in here and start ranting that fellow Kyd's old stuff?

The boy maintained his pose, but looked hurt. The mother said, 'But you must hear more, sir. When he comes to "Alas, it is Horatio, my sweet son", I vow you will weep uncontrollably.'

Burbage thought it unlikely. He scrabbled about on the table, found that much-thumbed piece of paper. 'Read this,' he said shortly.

The boy climbed back on his toes. ' "Make me a willow cabin at your gate," ' he began.

It would have been fine for some deaf old creature at the back of the theatre. In that small, overcrowded room it was shattering. Burbage flapped him angrily into silence. The boy looked more than hurt. He began to sulk. 'Where in heaven's name,' said Dick, 'did you learn *this* preposterous way of acting?'

'By watching Master Alleyn at the Fortune,' said the mother. Dick wondered two things: why mothers never, never, *never* let their sons answer for themselves; and why she hadn't taken her precious brat to the Fortune to be apprenticed. Henslowe and Ned Alleyn would both have appreciated him. He said, 'Why, mistress, did you not take your son to the Fortune?'

'I did. They had no places for boys.'

So. The Fortune had all the boys they needed. That was bad. It became more important than ever to fill the Globe's ranks. He said, stretching his patience like a bow, 'Now, boy. Try again. And remember, you are not crying your wares in the market place. You are a girl, disguised as a man, wooing on behalf of her master a woman who is in love with you, the girl, thinking you a man, of course.'

'Well, did ever you hear such a gallimaufry?' said Nell Fox.

But the boy had heard the word 'wooing'. It was enough. He sank down on one knee, lifted imploring arms. ' "Make me a willow cabin at your gate," ' he began again. Now his voice was full of treacle.

Burbage stopped him, beckoned to him to rise. The mother, who had been looking hard at Dick, said, 'You are not, surely, Master Burbage?' He nodded curtly.

'I had thought you taller,' she said.

'Had you indeed, madam?' Short, tubby Richard would have given his right arm to be six inches taller. His figure was a terrible handicap for a dramatic actor. He didn't welcome comment on it. 'Now, boy,' he said. 'Stand up. And just – '

'Master Alleyn has a fine, commanding figure,' said the lady. 'But then,' she added, for she was a woman who always prided herself on her tact, 'height is not everything. And I liked well your Edward II, Master Burbage.'

'I have never played Edward II, Mistress Fox.'

She looked unbelieving. 'Nay, but I vow – '

'I assure you, madam, it is not a point on which I would be mistaken. Now boy, read this. *Quietly.* Slowly.'

'But with expression,' said the mother. 'Nicholas always reads with expression, don't you, Nicholas. Nicholas absorbed expression with his mother's milk, if you will pardon the somewhat homely expression, Master Burbage.'

There was no doubt about it. Now that she had decided that this player was not just any player, but someone really quite well known, though not in Edward Alleyn's class, of course, she was becoming much more affable. 'Is not Master Shakespeare of your company, sir?'

Would she not let him test the boy? But he was always generously pleased to find that Will was becoming known in his own right. He said warmly, 'Yes, indeed, Mistress Fox.'

'I thought so.' She folded her hands in her lap in a gesture of satisfaction. 'There, Nicholas. Satisfy the gentleman, and you may well belong to the same company as Master Shakespeare.'

Dick Burbage was a good fellow, but he was human. And he could not forget that this woman seemed to know nothing of *his* acting. Jealousy began to prick him with its daggers. He said, 'And why are you so interested in Master Shakespeare, madam?'

'He is Mistress Mountjoy's lodger, sir.'

'I see,' said Dick. 'Now, Nicholas.'

'Such a pleasant, quiet gentleman, she says he is. Never a bit of trouble.'

'He wouldn't be. Now, boy.'

'And undemanding. A bit of beef for his breakfast, a pickled herring for his supper, and he is quite happy. Not that Mistress Mountjoy doesn't give him her best, of course, when he is in London.'

'Of course.'

' "Make me a willow cabin at your gate," ' began the boy. ' "And call upon my soul within – " '

'Stop,' said Richard quietly, and in a voice suddenly unsteady. For he was facing the door. And the door had opened. And a man stood in the doorway: a still-young man with a trim, chestnut beard and laughing eyes. 'W – ' began Richard, but tears swamped his voice and filled his mouth. He groped his way forward. ' "Halloo your name to the reverberate hills," ' cried Nicholas, swept on by his own momentum.

The two men were hugging each other like bears, laughing, crying, 'Will!' 'Dick!' Weeping.

Nell Fox gazed at the newcomer with interest. She was always interested in personable gentlemen; and this gentleman, with his warm colouring, his neat, good clothes, was very personable indeed. Familiar, too, in some way. And then, suddenly, she realised who he was. 'Why,' she cried with satisfaction, ''tis Mistress Mountjoy's lodger.'

'London, thou art the flower of Cities all,' he had murmured wryly as he crossed London Bridge, and he had smiled to find himself quoting a Scots poet. For, ever since the death of the old Queen, Holinshed's tale of Banquo and Macbeth had been flickering in his mind like firelight. Could it be that he, William Shakespeare, Gent., followed fortune as instinctively as a hound follows a scent?

Being a man who saw himself very clearly, and who sometimes did not like what he saw, he thought it very possible. Why, already he had decided it would flatter the new Scotsman king if the play stressed his descent from Banquo, and not from the cruel Macbeth. But was he being too severe on himself? Was it not rather that he simply enjoyed pleasing people?

His emotions were in a whirl. Two years ago he had fled from London for his life, his noble friend Essex dead, his noble friend Southampton in the Tower. Two years of comfort in Stratford had softened the bleak horror of those February days. Now his mind was back in those days – the empty, hushed streets, waiting for no one knew what; the sleet falling out of a hostile sky; the usual portents: stars wandering from their courses, the moon running blood. He shivered. In those days he had learnt a great deal he would have preferred not to know about the shortcomings of William Shakespeare, Gent. Two years as master of New Place had glossed over the hateful discoveries. But now – Stratford was ninety miles away, and he was back in the crucible; and already the gloss was beginning to crack.

After New Place, his lodgings had looked chill and squalid; the rooms above the tire-maker's shop in Cripplegate smelled as though they had been shut up since he left; as, indeed, they had. And not all Mistress Mountjoy's huffing and puffing and firelighting and dusting could bring the life back to them. And the Mountjoys themselves: like most Londoners they had probably not taken a bath since he went away, and another two years of grease and grime were embedded in their wrinkles. The sunless chasms of the streets were still ankle deep in glutinous filth. At his feet a dead dog heaved and crawled with maggots. London, thou art the flower of Cities all!

He looked up. Even the heads on London Bridge did not seem to have changed. One traitor looked much like another after the hungry birds of winter, and the rain. Even – and his throat filled with sudden bile, his mind with stark horror – even my peacock-beautiful Lord of Essex. London, thou art of townes A per se!

Just now, from the windows of New Place, the sun would be tangling with the high elms, and boys running from the Grammar School like driven leaves in autumn (but not *one* leaf, withered by summer suns, already trodden in the loam, poor Hamnet – he would have run and boasted and high-cockalorumed with the best). Anne, the kitchen work done, would have changed into her best blue kirtle, and would be sewing or darning or mending. Sweet Anne! In the last two years a wonderful gentleness, and tenderness, had grown up between them. In the beginning, he knew, he had loved her because she loved and admired him; and because, fearfully, clumsily, selflessly, she had given him the wonder of her woman's body. Often, since then, he had hated her: with the impersonal hate of a man for his prison walls. But now, the prison had become a home, the jailer a worthy helpmeet. His marriage had gained the one vital quality it had lacked: a husband's deep respect for a wife.

God! He would give much to be in Stratford, enjoying with Anne the quiet closing of another day. The pain of longing was almost physical, tight and heavy in his chest, pricking behind his eyes. But then he saw something that drove Stratford out of his mind, and really brought the tears. He was on the South Bank now; and there it stood, silhouetted against the bright west, towering above the houses like an octagonal medieval keep, the birthplace and the home of so many of his characters – the Globe Theatre itself.

He went inside.

A vast, echoing, empty shell. He shivered. Would it ever again, he wondered, be uproarious with Falstaff, noisy with Agincourt. It was said the new king would close all theatres.

He heard voices. They came from the tiring-room.

He opened the door and went in.

Dick was there! And he didn't need to look at him twice to know that old Dick was seething like a pan of beans.

Then Dick glanced up and saw him.

The delight, and happiness, that flooded into his tired face was something Will would never forget. To be so loved! And not, this time, by a wife; but by a man, a companion, a noble actor, a great leader of a band of brothers. 'Dick!' 'Will!' They hugged each other, slapping backs, patting shoulders, laughing, weeping. 'Will, Will. I thought you had become Stratford shopkeeper,' Burbage said in an unsteady voice.

' "Cry out, Olivia," ' concluded Nicholas on a high, wavering note.

They turned and looked at him, both bewildered. What had this prating child to do with them? 'Now, Will. You have a chest-full of new plays? You have not been idle?'

'No plays.' Burbage's face fell. 'But ideas, Dick. Holinshed has a tale of two Scotsmen, Banquo and Macbeth. It could please the King well. And – and how would you like to black your face, Dick, and be a Moor, crazed with jealousy? There is a tale in Cinzio… '

Nicholas said, 'I can also recite from Master Marlowe's *Faustus*.'

'Some other time, boy,' Burbage said absently. Marlowe wasn't one of their authors. Besides, a black, mad Moor! That would be something to set the groundlings quivering.

But the gentle Will was growing uneasy. There was a lady here, and a boy. He and Dick were being discourteous. He said quietly, 'This boy? Good?'

'Dreadful. An infant Alleyn.'

' "Was this," ' demanded Nicholas, ' "the face that launch'd a thousand ships, and burnt the topless towers of Ilium?" '

'Oh be quiet,' snapped Burbage.

Will said hurriedly, 'Dick, Dick! We've so much to say, to talk about. But first let us deal civilly with this lady. Then – ' He turned to Mistress Fox. He bowed. 'Madam, you must forgive us. My long absence had made us forgetful of our manners.'

'No offence at all, sir.' She positively glowed.

He bowed again, and turned to Nicholas. 'Now boy. Begin once more, if you will.'

The boy blew out his cheeks in a sigh, and let his shoulders sag in exaggerated weariness. Saucy little devil, thought Burbage. But Will prompted gently, 'Was this the face –?'

The boy began again.

It was terrible. But Will heard him out; carried away, despite the swooping voice, the outrageous gestures, the eyes rolling heavenward, by poor Kit Marlowe's poetry.

Then he sat – for he had flung himself into an X chair – hand on mouth, thoughtful, silent. He looked at the boy. Pale, with a narrow, mean face, only a thin nose to keep apart two crowding eyes. Well, Harry Condell could work wonders with a bit of grease paint. And as for the ranting: if he didn't have this boy – what was the phrase he'd once used? – roaring as gently as any sucking dove, his name wasn't Will Shakespeare.

But he suddenly realised that Burbage was saying, 'Thank you, madam. We will let you know.'

He shouldn't interfere. But he was a sharer, wasn't he? 'Dick,' he called quietly.

Dick came. 'Are we short of a boy?'

'Yes,' said Dick coldly. 'But not as short as all that.'

'Then take him, Dick. We can soon – '

'I'm damned if I will.'

The woman was waiting, straining her ears for every word. So was the boy. Will said, 'Very well. Edward Peers will soon make something of him.'

Mistress Fox's hearing must have been as keen as her animal namesake's. 'Begged and prayed of me to let him have Nicholas for the Paul's Children, Master Peers did. But no, I said, the real theatre for Nicholas. He will not always be a child, I said.'

The storm that had hung about in Dick Burbage's head all day, burst with a sudden clap of thunder. 'God's death, Will, you desert us for a couple of years, lording it in Stratford. You condescend to come back, and you haven't been back five minutes before you're trying to teach me my side of the business.' He stood foursquare, breathing heavily, glaring furiously at the old friend he had so recently been embracing.

Will turned to Mistress Fox. Another bow. 'Madam, I beg you to leave us and return in the morning. We have matters of business – '

She went, purring. She couldn't wait to tell Marie Mountjoy about her meeting with such a proper man.

Richard looked at Will, scowling.

Will looked at Richard, smiling. Two years ago this outburst would have hurt him. He would have crept off to a miserable evening in his lodgings, like a scolded boy. Not now. A Grant of Arms, a fine house, the love of friends had given him another skin. And tomorrow, he knew, Dick Burbage would be so eager to make amends for hurting his feelings, that the boy was as good as prenticed.

He clapped a hand on his friend's shoulder. 'Oh come along, Dick,' he said, rallying him. And then, a sound at the door drew his attention. He looked. For a fraction of a second his smile flared with joy like the last, sudden holocaust of a setting sun. Then his face was grey, and desolate, and ashen. He licked his lips, swallowed. 'I took you for another,' he whispered.

The two men stared at the doorway.

Dick Burbage saw a woman, with a boy.

Will Shakespeare saw a boy, with a woman.

She was a woman to disturb a man.

Not that she flaunted her beauty, or even her womanliness. She was dressed, simply, in black. Her face was oval, framed in dark hair, her brows exquisitely arched. Above her silken bodice her flesh was flawless, almost dusky. A drop or two of the South got into this wine cask, thought Dick Burbage with interest. French, Italian even.

Will Shakespeare would notice the woman later. Now all he could see was the boy.

(Stratford, and the river meadows, and a small, friendly hand in his, and a boy's boastful prattling in his ears. 'When I am grown-up, Father, I vow I will be an actor, and act your plays better than any man.' Stratford; and Anne, frozen of face, a cold clout about her heart. 'You should have been home, not in London, Will, when your son was sick. Belike, then – he had not died.'

Belike he had not died. Nearly seven years that thought had been with him; a sour apprentice indeed. But this, he knew, was an apprentice who would never take his freedom, who would cling to the very grave.)

And here *was* Hamnet – grave, sturdy, with a fresh, open face; yet, in his face, Will searched in vain for the sure, serene confidence of Hamnet, who had died before he could discover doubt.

He motioned to the boy. The boy left his mother, and came and stood before him, looking up at him shyly. 'What is your name, boy?'

'Matthew, sir. Matthew Peyre.'

The voice was not Hamnet's. Hamnet's, like his father's, had been warm with the ploughlands and the meadows of Warwickshire. This was a London voice; and shy; yet it spoke with something of the clear, cold precision of one to whom the language is not native. 'Peyre?' said Will. 'That is not an English name?'

'No, sir. We are of French extraction. My father was a silversmith.'

'Was?'

'He died, sir. Last year.'

'I am sorry, Matthew.'

'Thank you, sir.'

So. An English Hamnet, a French Matthew. So alike, in their boyhood. And hateful death had not been able to keep his hands off either. Oh, you are too busy, death. He said, smiling, 'And you want to be an actor?'

'Yes, sir.' The face was eager, now.

'It is hard work. The discipline is strict. You will have to work longer hours than it is good for a boy to work – learning, rehearsing, acting. Does not this frighten you?'

The boy shook his head firmly, lips tight, eyes smiling.

'You will have to learn to speak, to move, to dress, to *think* like a woman. Does not this distress you?'

'No. Since my mother is a woman, I see no shame in acting a woman.'

'Brave imp. But you must also learn to dance, to sing, to fence, to caper. You will have to leave your mother and work with men who will seem harsh and rough to you. The theatre is entirely a man's world, Master Peyre.'

Will noticed the hesitation, the touch of tongue to lip. Then bravely, 'I am not afeared, sir.'

'You will go on tour, sleeping in waggons, putting up stages at dawn, taking them down at midnight. You will be cold, often hungry. And you are still not afeared?'

'No, sir.'

Will laughed, and put a hand on his shoulder. He found a well-thumbed paper. 'Now, Matthew, read me this. And remember – you are a girl, disguised as a man, wooing a lady... '

Richard bowed the woman into a chair.

She walked to it and sat down; all, it seemed, in one smooth, uninterrupted movement. Even the swift inclination of the head, the flicker of a smile, were a part of the movement. She sat there, hands in her lap, relaxed, composed; yet never taking her eyes off her son.

Burbage looked at her gratefully. She was as cool to look at as a summer pool. As restful. He felt his irritation melting away in her serenity. He said, 'May I commend you, mistress?'

The look she gave him was not encouraging. Her 'why?' had more than a little of contempt.

Beautiful, and a widow, she had already discovered that a man, any man, had only ever one object in mind; and knew only one opening move to gain it: flattery. It was wearisome. Nowadays she left her verbal pawns where they were, and simply tipped the board up.

'Because, madam, you are the first mother who has ever let her son speak for himself.'

She softened. She even laughed. 'It is he who wants to be an actor, not I, by the Rood.'

By the Rood! A strange, old fashioned oath for this quiet woman to use. One did not hear it in these days of watered-down religion. So, decided Richard, who missed very little, she was probably Catholic.

Now Richard didn't care greatly what religion people were, so be they were not Puritan. In fact, he thought privately that the world would have been a much less disagreeable place if the Almighty hadn't put this religious bee in men's bonnets. Nevertheless, things being what they were, and with a Calvinistic king on his way from Scotland, one couldn't ignore these things. There had been times, and there might still be again, when even to *know* a Papist could bring one into the hands of the tormentors.

He said, 'The work is hard. But we look after our boys well. Each is apprenticed to one of our married sharers, and is treated by him like one of his family.'

'That is good. Since his father's death, Matthew and I have grown very close. Too close, I fear – so far as the boy is concerned,' she said sadly. 'But – '

'But, madam?'

She said, 'If it were possible, sir, I would wish him to be apprenticed to Master Shakespeare.'

Despite the courteous phrasing, it was a command. Richard's hackles, which had been so pleasantly soothed by this lady, rose again. 'It is *not* possible, madam. The law insists that these boys are apprenticed to family men. Otherwise, you understand, there would be embarrassments.'

'And Master Shakespeare is not a family man?' Those exquisite brows arched.

'Not in London, madam. His family are in Warwickshire.'

'He is not a Londoner? You surprise me. I would not have believed such wit could grow in country loam.'

Burbage was silent. Then he said, 'It is unlikely we shall have a place for your boy.' He added, with an irritation he could not conceal, 'Master Shakespeare engaged a boy only ten minutes ago.'

But now Shakespeare and the boy were walking over to them. Will was smiling broadly. He said, 'Dick! He *is* Viola. At the first reading. It's unbelievable.' He turned to the lady. 'Mistress Peyre, I will take the boy as my apprentice. It is not usual in these cases to draw up formal articles, but if you wish for something to be written – '

She inclined her head. 'I am grateful to you, sir.' She did not look at Burbage. A lesser woman could not have resisted a glance of triumph.

But Richard Burbage looked at her, *and* at the boy. And at Will. By an almost superhuman effort he kept his voice low. 'Madam, things are by no means settled. Master Shakespeare and I have much to discuss before he could offer your son apprenticeship.'

'I understand, sir.' With the same supple, controlled movement as before, she rose and went to the door. 'Come, Matthew.' She inclined her head to the two gentlemen. To Burbage she gave her smile – swift as the flicker of a cat's tongue. But to Shakespeare she gave a long, thoughtful stare that this well-married man found curiously disturbing.

# Chapter 2

## He's fat, and scant of breath

Matthew Peyre and his mother knelt beside his bed.

He wore a nightrail of smocked linen, frilled at the wrists. His mother still wore her black.

They rose from their knees, crossing themselves. He jumped into bed, pulled the clothes about him. 'Why must I to bed so early, Mother? 'Tis not yet dark.'

'Father Grainger is coming to hear my confession.'

'Why should he not hear mine?'

'Knave! You have nothing to confess.'

He grinned. 'I have great sins, Mother.' He hung his head, drew down his lips in mock penitence, clasped his hands over his fair hair. '*Miserere mei, Deus.*'

'Do not make game,' she said, smiling, yet stern.

He patted the bed. 'Will you not stay and talk, Mother? I liked Master Shakespeare well.'

She sat down with her own peculiar, effortless grace. 'That is good. He is a man of great wit. He can teach you more about acting than any man in London.'

'He –' The boy gave his mother a keen look. He knew sorrows were best left buried; but was this sorrow ever buried? 'He reminded me of Father. Kind. Courteous.' He looked at her in surprise. 'A grown man is not often courteous to a boy, Mother. But Father was. And Master Shakespeare is also. Is that not strange?'

'Yes,' she said shortly. She rose. He lay down, knowing the ritual. She made the sign of the cross over him. 'God give you good night and wholesome rest, Matthew.'

'I pray God that it so be with you, Mother.'

She bent down and kissed him with a sudden, desperate hunger. Then she went downstairs to the living-room where the thin, evening sunlight, pouring through diamond pane windows, splashed the wainscot with golden wine. God, she was restless! These light spring evenings always made her restless, tempting her outside with a pretence of summer warmth, only to drive her in with a whiplash of old winter round the shoulders.

But tonight there was more to make her restless.

Today she had taken a step that meant appalling loneliness for herself – few had the courage to be friends with a Papist – and, she feared, months or even years of misery for her sensitive, vulnerable son, flung from a home of quiet piety into the turbulence of the London theatre. More. Today, for the first time since Robert died, she had stepped out of her boy's and woman's world to meet two men – two clever, courteous men. And she always liked intelligence. That was partly her lack, nowadays. Since Robert died she had met precious little of it. Matthew was intelligent – and kind, and thoughtful, a good son. But a boy could not take the place of a man, however loving. And Father Grainger – intelligent, true; but no more than a black ghost flitting with the moth and the bat in the half-light.

She pulled on a cloak, and went out into the little garden; a square of gnarled apple trees in a shivering pool of daffodils; high walls of old brick, smouldering in the last of the sun.

Father Grainger was coming. And that meant danger.

Danger! It was always present, like the chill spring wind about her shoulders. But now, more so. The old Queen had, as she herself said, refused to put windows in men's souls, except when their faith became too political. Oh, there'd been times when to be a Catholic had been to carry your life in your hands; but, on the whole, being a Catholic had been better than being a Jew or a dog.

And now – a new, unknown king was hurrying down from Scotland. A Calvinist. A man who took his religion very seriously. What might not such a man do to those who insisted on clinging to the old faith? She was afraid. If the rack and the hangman's knife had not been used lately, they were still there – still oiled and sharpened.

The high garden walls were sunless now; dark, forbidding, like the walls of a prison. She shivered, and went indoors. She lit a fire against the evening chill. Then she sat in the window facing the street, and waited for the coming of Father Grainger.

The street, with its overhang of houses, had long been sunless. Now it began to fill with shadows.

The shadows deepened. Behind a window a candle flame would flit like a bright angel, followed by a ghostly face. Curtains were being drawn against the night. Each family was spinning about itself a cocoon of privacy. There would be talk, and music, and laughter. Or, so she thought, for she was a woman who saw clearly, quarrelling, hatred, strife. But, for herself, a quiet room, waiting for bedtime…

Across the street, the shadows were deep. A shadow blacker than the rest detached itself, floated across the street.

Hastily she drew the curtains, went to the door, candle-less. The black shadow was on the doorstep.

'Father!' she genuflected in the darkness, put out a hand, wrist uppermost. A cold, emaciated hand gripped her wrist. It was like being gripped by a skeleton. She brought him into the living-room, made sure the curtains covered the windows, lit a taper at the fire, lit a cluster of candles.

The golden light brought its own comfort. But she said, anxiously, 'What news do you have, Father?'

'Little good, my daughter.' With an instinctive glance at the window, he threw back his black hood. Now she could see the round, kindly face, so much at odds with those skeleton fingers. 'Little good can come to our people from this Scotsman. In his writing he has called the Holy Father' – the priest crossed himself, and brought the word out in a long sigh – 'antichrist!'

Annette Peyre was silent. The Pope could stand being called a few names, in his position. That did not trouble her. It was for Matthew, and her friends, and herself that she was anxious. 'Will there be trouble for our people, Father?'

He looked at her; the eyes glittering and intense in the candlelight. (The eyes and the hands. They went together. It was the kindly face that was odd man out.) 'If there is,' he said slowly, 'some of us will know what steps to take. Remember that, my daughter.'

She stared at him, not understanding, yet shivering with a horror she could not overcome. Upstairs, Matthew cried out in his sleep, and a log settled in the hearth as the sparks flew upward.

After Annette Peyre and her son had left, Burbage came back into the room, scratching himself viciously. He scowled at Will. 'God's teeth!' He flung himself into a chair. 'As if I hadn't had enough! A dozen brats and their idiot mothers. Meeting that kite Henslowe. *He* wanted to know where you'd disappeared to, by the way. I trust dear Will Shakespeare is not sick? Oh no, say I, just lording it in Stratford.' He sprang to his feet. He banged the table in an explosion of anger and self-pity. 'Well! If you'd stayed in Stratford we shouldn't have that posturing jackanapes Nicholas Fox on our hands.'

Will Shakespeare grinned. 'Since the good Master Henslowe is so concerned for my health, perhaps the good Master Alleyn might like to black his face and play my mad Moor. Or clap a bonnet on his head and be my Macbeth.'

Dick Burbage looked at him. He began to pull on his cloak. He fastened it carefully at his throat. All this time his eyes never left Shakespeare's face. And slowly his own face changed. At last he said, 'Oh Will, Will, it's good to have you back. Things have not been the same without you. Come to the tavern. Harry Condell will be there, Augustine and John.'

So they went to the tavern. And the word ran like wildfire that Will Shakespeare was back in London. And soon all the Chamberlain's Men were there: laughing, back-slapping, hugging. For without Will there had been an emptiness, a diminution of wit.

Yes. There was laughter, and singing, and bawdry. Will loved every minute of it. The deep, free-running laughter of men! The honest, uncomplicated friendship of men! Women were all very well, but they straitened life, they bound one with slender, silken threads of love until, suddenly – 'Oh! the oak and the ash, and the bonny ivy tree', roared the players in unison and 'Hold thy peace, thou knave'. This made his daughter Susanna, with her lute, singing her father's, 'Come away, Death', seem thin gruel indeed. And he could fill up his glass without feeling his wife's anxious eyes on him – not that he really liked the stuff, it always made him queasy.

But: 'They flourish at home in my own countree', they sang of the bonny trees, and of a sudden homesickness was gripping his heart again, like a tight fist.

It was late, that night, when the last of the players aimed himself carefully at the tavern door, and lurched through into the night. But Annette Peyre still lay awake, staring wide-eyed into the darkness. And Helen Fox lay and gazed without enthusiasm at the sleeping face of tonight's gentleman, and thought about Mistress Mountjoy's personable lodger. And New Place, Stratford upon Avon, stood dark and silent.

Only the rustle of mice, and the cry of the night owl.

This time he noticed the woman, as well as the boy.

She was, he thought, exquisitely made; but it wasn't the dark pools of her eyes, the delicate bone structure of face and hands that he noticed. It was the repose that wrapped her like a cloak, the resigned sadness of her lips. He bowed her to a chair with deep respect; for Master Shakespeare, Poet and Gent., respected grace and beauty even more than he respected rank.

There was respect, too, in the inclination of *her* head as she took the chair: a battered throne that had, in its time, supported Henrys and Richards and great Caesar; none of whom, thought Will, took it with more grace.

'You are comfortable, Mistress Peyre?'

That quick, flitting smile. 'I find a throne more comfortable, if we are to believe your plays, sir, than many kings have found it.'

He was delighted. 'You know my plays?'

She nodded. 'I know your plays, Master Shakespeare. I think them the most wondrous things ever written. After Holy Writ, of course,' she added dutifully.

What a discerning woman! Oh, he knew his plays were popular. The Court loved them, the Inns of Court loved them, the groundlings loved them; but as something to pass an afternoon, or to fill an hour 'twixt supper and bed. Few realised that there was a difference between a Marlowe or a Greene or a Shakespeare play; while the groundlings neither knew nor cared that the plays *were* written. They thought the actors made it up as they went along. He said, not meaning a word of it, 'Madam, you do me too much honour.'

She shook her head, smiling. He lingered, hoping she would say more. But she didn't. She was not a woman to elaborate.

He turned to the boy; and was delighted and moved to see the eagerness in that clear young face. He smiled. 'How would you like to sing me a song, Matthew?'

The boy, flatteringly, sang Will's own 'Who is Silvia?' Sang it well, and with feeling.

Shakespeare let the notes die on the air. Then, clapping his hands: 'Now, boy, turn me a cartwheel across the floor. Quickly. And another. And another.'

The boy revolved, arms and legs flying. He came upright, grinning, thrusting back his hair. And found a foil thrust in his hand. 'Now! on guard!' and a point was at his throat.

He took up the first parry, beating away the point. The point moved swiftly to his thigh. He switched to the second parry, circling Will's point to pick it up and carry it back to the guard position.

Will tried to envelop the boy's blade; failed. He made a feint. It failed. A false attack. It did not deceive the boy.

Will was out of training, and out of breath. He took the foils, tossed them into a corner. He sank into a chair, panting. 'Let me see you dance a galliard.'

Matthew danced, joyously, gaily, kicking, jumping. 'Saut Majeur,' he cried, and 'Saut Moyen', and 'Petit Saut', at each leap. He finished. 'Oh, it is good to dance,' he cried, eyes shining.

'Yes,' said Will. But he wasn't listening. Here was a boy who could act, dance, sing, tumble, use the foils, good to look at, pleasantly spoken; who was, in fact, all that Hamnet might have been. And with a most discerning and fascinating mother thrown in for good measure. He said, 'Mistress Peyre, I will teach your son everything I know. And if I do not make him one of the most notable actors of his day, the fault will be mine, not his.'

Again the inclination of the head, the flitting smile.

He said, 'He shall lodge at Mistress Mountjoy's, under my personal care.'

'Thank you. He has seen little of the world, sir. I'm afraid – he may find things difficult for a time.'

Oh, but that sadness in her smile! It brought out all the chivalry and sentiment that is never far below the surface in a happily married man. He stopped thinking about himself and the Chamberlain's Men. 'But *you* will be lonely, madam.' His voice was deep and warm with compassion.

She rose. 'That will be nothing new, sir. And now it will be to good purpose.' She floated towards the door (there was no other word to describe her movement, he thought). And there she paused, and looked him full in the face. And this time the formality had gone from her features. Her lips were open, her eyes shining. Almost she looked like a young girl. Strangely, for a woman, she shook his hand. Her grip was firm, and cool. 'I cannot tell you, sir, what this means to me. My husband and I saw all your plays, sunned ourselves in your genius. And now, you are taking Matthew as your apprentice. He, Robert, would have been so proud.'

Genius! It certainly wasn't a word he would have used himself. Oh, he had a talent for knocking a play together, he knew that. And those poems of his youth, *Venus, Lucrece,* he really had been puffed up about those. But that was the way of youth. No. Genius was too big a word for him.

Nevertheless, on the lips of a beautiful and intelligent woman, the word had a heady flavour. He bowed. 'I am no genius, Mistress Peyre. But I am happy to help Matthew in any way I can. He is – what I would have wished my own son.'

'Thank you.' She was looking down at the floor, now. The words were a whisper. 'Come, Matthew,' she said.

The boy turned and looked up at Will. 'Thank you, Master Shakespeare, most kindly.'

Will grinned, and ruffled his hair. 'When I'm less scant of breath, boy, we'll try the foils again.' He turned to the mother. 'I will make arrangements with Mistress Mountjoy. Then you must see the boy's lodgings, see that all is as you would wish.'

'That is kind.' But now she was looking at him again. And for the first time he saw her not quite sure of herself. 'Sir, there is one thing. I – should have told you before, before you said you would take the boy. We – Matthew and I – are of the old religion.'

Will was silent. To him one religion was as good – or as bad – as another. *His* religion was – what? The beauty of earth and sky, the nobility of man, love: the love of a mother for her babe, a man for a wife, a son for a father; even, perhaps, love and worship for a noble, suffering Saviour: God's order and degree, in family, in State, in the universe.

But certainly not the Pope's religion; nor, from what he had heard of it, King James'.

Nevertheless, Papists walked always in a certain shadow. And the shadow fell on those who walked with them.

Had the boy appealed to him less; had the woman been less attractive; had he committed himself less; had it been a few years ago, before the Essex rebellion taught him that fear *could* be outfaced; then he might have made his excuses. But now –

Seeing his hesitation, she said, 'Yes. I should have told you before. I shall quite understand if – '

'You must see that he attends Mass,' Will said quietly. 'I will release him if you will let me know when it is possible.'

'Thank you.'

What have I done? he thought, left alone. Taken a Catholic chicken under my wing just when that crowing Calvinist cock James is flapping down from Scotland. I must be mad.

Standing there, in the cluttered little tiring-room, he had a nightmare vision of a tall, raw-boned Scot rampaging about London, closing and burning theatres, racking and burning Catholics.

Catholics – and all who were friendly with them. It seemed to him then more than likely that Will Shakespeare, that poor player, had reached the end of the road...

And yet, less than two months later, the High and Mighty Prince, James, of England and Scotland King, had appointed his trusty and well-beloved William Shakespeare, Gent., a Groom of the Chamber. So blind, so foolish, so fearful, are our attempts to peer into the dark glass of time.

# Chapter 3

## Resembling sire, and child, and
## happy mother…

'The queen of Scots is this day lighter of a fair son,' Elizabeth had cried. 'And I am but a barren stock.'

But that had been thirty-seven years ago.

Now the Queen of Scots was lighter of her head; and Elizabeth of England lay at Whitehall shrouded for burial; and the fair son was making for London as eagerly as the Israelites for the Promised Land.

Eagerly, but not hurriedly. He wanted cousin Elizabeth buried first. Not that there was anything personal in this; but when someone has cut off your mother's head, attending that someone's public funeral would be a delicate matter. He was better away, thought Jamie.

So he took days off from travelling to enjoy his favourite pastimes: hunting hares and witches (the hares brought live in baskets in the great baggage train, the witches always in plentiful local supply) and hearing sermons from bishops. He scattered knighthoods in every county, and emptied the gaols of all except murderers, traitors and (ominously?) Papists. He was a happy man. Behind lay Calvinism, raw as Scottish winter; the dark, treacherous stairways of Edinburgh, stones black with age, sweating with the cold; Father blown to bits at Kirk o'Field, Mother beheaded (that, he thought smugly, could have caused a diplomatic incident, even war, if he'd listened to his rash advisers. Not that he'd ever regretted making his formal protest. It had given him a due sense of filial piety and hadn't, as he might have feared, robbed him of the English throne).

Yes. He was a happy man. Ahead lay – what? An English summer, Merrie England, the gaiety of London, a nobler throne; and – though this did not appeal in the least, but one was expected to show a certain interest – women. Not thrawn Scots creatures with scraped hair and scrubbed faces and – och, dearie me! – hellfire under the mattress. But sonsy English lassies who would laugh in the Deil's face as they tumbled in the warm English hay. And you never knew; it might be that he would come to like the creatures.

Nevertheless, not everything was perfect. His dear Annie was not with him. And though he was able to bear her absence with considerable fortitude, it did make it more difficult to convince the English of his connubial bliss.

For Queen Anne was suffering from a – for her – not unusual combination of bloody-mindedness, deviousness, and pregnancy.

Despite the fact that her parting from James had taken place in Edinburgh High Street, it had been so tender that their loyal subjects, gathered round in their thousands, had wept copiously. The Queen, tears streaming down her face, had watched him out of sight. Then she had gathered together a band of loyal gentlemen and had made a bee-line for Stirling Castle where her son Henry lay in the charge of the Earl of Mar.

With both the Earl and her husband heading for the delights of London, she felt it would be easy to regain the son who had been taken from her. But, like so many before and since, she had forgotten how formidable a really formidable old lady can be. The Dowager Countess of Mar's flat refusal to hand over Prince Henry so enraged Anne that she miscarried, thus terminating the pregnancy that had prevented her from accompanying her husband to London.

James found it all very tiresome. He was a dutiful king if not a dutiful husband, and would do his husbandly duty whenever his ministers suggested a new heir would be desirable. But what was the point if the stupid woman went on having these miscarriages?

He wrote her an aggrieved letter, and sent the Duke of Lennox to bring her to London. He had enough on his mind without the Queen's tantrums: affairs of State, his unrelenting war with the Devil. He began to feel very sorry for himself. After all, he wasn't *only* a king; he was also a writer. And writers needed time for thought. Did she but know it this woman, with her demands on his time and thought, was robbing posterity.

But he had one consolation. To the Scottish nobles, to be able to write anything more than one's name had been sheer affectation. But in London there were many who not only could, but did, write: poems, plays, moral tracts, a veritable galaxy of writers.

He spurred on his horse. That galaxy was very soon going to acquire a sun.

It was a great relief when they finally got the old Queen buried. Dead she might be. But so long as she remained above ground, no one ever felt quite easy about Elizabeth of England.

The horses that drew her coffin were draped in black to the fetlocks, and stuck with flags both fore and aft. The nobles who accompanied her coffin were draped in black to the ankles, and carried banners. Her black-draped women wept. But it meant nothing. Only one man would have mourned her fittingly: Leicester, her sweet Robin. But he had taken this loneliest of all roads so long ago. Perhaps, who knew, he would be at the gates of heaven to greet her, outsplendouring the archangels.

So they buried her, who had become too big for them, since they had grown too small for her. For England had changed. The old swagger had gone. Swashbuckling was out of fashion. And she, the greatest swashbuckler of them all, had had her day. So they shrugged off a glorious, but just too long reign, and went to cheer for Jamie as he rode into his capital.

Will did not go to see Queen Elizabeth buried. He had feared, but never liked her. She was altogether too strong a personality for gentle Will.

But he was very tempted to go and watch the arrival of James. Tempted, yet repelled. He loved the pomp and circumstance that surround a king. He hated becoming, even for a morning, a part of the milling, guffawing, gaping crowd which only increased the loneliness that so often descended on him since his return to London. Alone in his lodgings he was never really lonely. He had noble companions – Seneca, Ovid, Plutarch, Othello, Macbeth; but surrounded by men happy with wives and their pretty bantlings, he was lonely indeed.

No. He would stay at home. Belike his Scotsman would impinge on his life soon enough, without his going to meet him.

He fastened his doublet, went into breakfast. Matthew was waiting to serve him, bright as the May morning.

A million motes, stirred up by Mistress Mountjoy's duster, danced in the sunshine that tapestried the gaunt room. It was a gay and beautiful morning; and for a moment it was as though the strong old Queen had gathered all the sorrows of all her people, all the duties left undone, all the weaknesses and failures, and had taken them down with her into the earth. Life, on this May morning, was beginning anew, all debts cancelled, sins remitted. 'Matthew,' said Will. 'How would you like to leave your lessons, and come with me to see the King?'

'Oh, sir!'

'Good. Then wash well the back of your neck, and put on your purple doublet. If the King looks from his carriage and sees you, you would not wish him to think you one of the crowd.'

'But shall I not *be* one of the crowd, Master Shakespeare?'

He wanted to say, No, boy, you will not. Because you are the son of a gracious mother, and are accompanied by William Shakespeare, Poet and Gent. But such thoughts were not for uttering. He said, 'Of course you will, Matthew. And so will I. But that does not mean we must go unwashed and stinking.'

On which high note he tackled his breakfast beef with unusual relish. It was one of those rare moments – not merely of contentment, or well-being, or absence of care – but of sheer happiness. He had borrowed a son – to care for, to watch over, to bring to manhood unscathed by the crafts and assaults of the Devil.

Matthew presented himself: purple doublet, feathered cap, yellow stockings, pointed shoes, grubby fingers. 'How did you wash your neck without washing your hands, Matthew?'

'With a damp towel, Master Shakespeare.'

'Inventive youth! Now go and do it with water from the ewer.'

'Bur Master Shakespeare – Master Shakespeare, could my mother accompany us to see the King?'

'Your mother?' Will looked up from a mess of manuscript. The thought of a May morning's outing with the boy had filled him with happiness. But to have that calm, beautiful woman as well! To be responsible for her among the cut-throats and ruffians! 'Yes. Of course,' he said.

'I will go bid her prepare herself,' cried he boy. And was gone.

All London was on holiday, this exquisite bright morning.

Annette Peyre looked from her window. People were already setting off, the men strutting like peacocks, wives and children gay with ribbons and posies. Usually this light-hearted, chattering turn out would have meant a hanging. Today a new king.

Annette Peyre would not go. This was one of those days that recurred time and again, like the threat of thunder in a hot summer, in every Catholic's lifetime; when one stayed at home, the doors bolted, drawing as little attention to oneself as possible.

Besides, since Robert died, public holidays had been a torment stabbing knives into her loneliness; all London, it seemed, one big family, and herself as it were gazing in at the merriment, her nose pressed against the cold glass of the window.

The weather was so lovely. It would be warm later. She would take a chair, sit in the garden with her embroidery, watch the sun drag itself, oh so slowly, across the branches of the apple trees.

There was a loud hammering at the door. For a moment her hand went to her mouth. She had a nightmare fear that Protestant James had begun arresting Catholics in person.

She pulled herself together. She did not actually laugh at her fears. A Catholic could never say that a fear, however ridiculous, might not be justified. But she put on the mask of calm with which she always greeted the world, and opened the door. 'Matthew!' she cried.

It was so *good* to see him, sturdy and proud in his purple doublet and yellow stockings. Was the day not to be lonely after all? Had Master Shakespeare given the boy a holiday so soon? She held out her arms. 'Matthew! Come in.'

He ran into her arms. 'Mother! Master Shakespeare and I are to see the King ride by. And he sent me to bid you too.'

She held the boy close, struggling against her tears. One moment, a lonely day in her garden; the next, an outing with Matthew, and with a man Robert had taught her to regard as one of the great men of his time. A famous actor. People would turn, after they had passed. 'Was that not Will Shakespeare, of the Chamberlain's Men?' She would not walk alone, the Widow Peyre. For this one day she would walk proud again, a man on her right hand, another on her left. She would go, and shame her fears.

But why had Master Shakespeare sent to bid her come? Kindness, pity? With most men she'd have had none of that. But Master Shakespeare had had an air of such kindness, such understanding and compassion, that she did not care. 'I will be ready in five minutes,' she said, kissed him, and ran upstairs like a girl.

In twenty minutes she was down again, in a kirtle of heavy black velvet, and a widow's veil, the veil so fine that it served only to enhance her warm, dark beauty.

His doublet was rust-coloured, his breeches yellow, his hose brown, his hat tall and round, without a single feather. All very sober. His chestnut beard was short and pointed. He had a fresh, outdoor complexion. He was sturdily built, yet had an actor's suppleness. He looked at Annette Peyre's beauty with considerable appreciation; and wondered, irrelevantly, what Anne was doing at this moment in far-away Stratford.

He bowed: an actor's, courtier's bow. 'Mistress, this is an honour as great as it is unexpected.'

She curtsied, graceful as any boy actor. 'Sir, I am grateful for this invitation.'

He took in the house, as well as the woman. A good house, well built and seemly; not as grand as his own New Place, but not in any way mean. Just the house one would imagine, in fact, for a silversmith's widow.

They joined the thronging crowds.

There was an air of tremendous excitement. And Will Shakespeare, with a beautiful woman's fingers resting on his arm, and a handsome boy jigging by his side, was more excited than most. But regretful, too. So might he have walked with Anne and Hamnet. And never did. Why? Because poor Anne was no Mistress Peyre? Because he had not appreciated Anne until long after Hamnet's death? Because, he thought with sudden bitterness, he had once deserted his wife for a London whore, and God had, very understandably, punished him.

But the remorse didn't last long. The here and now was too sweet. There was the happiness in Annette Peyre's face. There was music, chatter, laughter. A hot sun, a dancing breeze. There were men crying ribbons and suckets and roast chestnuts and hot pies and beer. And, at last, the procession: tumblers, dancing bears, musicians, soldiers, horsemen, my

Lord Chamberlain, my Lord This and my Lord That; and finally, fenced with pikes and halberdiers, a great gold litter in which sulked James, whom God Himself had appointed King. James, who did not like the common people, who could never understand the tenacity with which they clung to their unattractive poverty, who despised them for wanting to make a show of the Lord's Anointed.

Matthew Peyre regarded him with great disappointment. No crown, no sceptre; a lolling, untidy figure. Why, Master Burbage made a better king any day.

Will Shakespeare and Annette Peyre regarded him, their new overlord. And each, for a different reason, trembled. The man who, by closing the theatres, might yet drive him back to Stratford and the glover's shears. The man who, by destroying the Catholics, might destroy her and Matthew.

Not that he looked a tyrant, thought Will, who was near enough to see the foolish face with its round, credulous eyes and its beard like a badger's tail. But Will knew that that meant little; for when it came to creating human suffering, folly could outstrip evil as the hare outstrips the tortoise.

The crowd too looked at the Scotsman with disappointment. They had expected something bigger and shaggier. And when they remembered the old Queen – by God, she'd been something to tell your grandchildren about! They had an unformulated feeling that England might have gained Scotland but had lost its own soul.

It had been a happy, friendly day. They had talked easily: of the theatre, and the new reign, and the days, already lit by a golden afterglow, of the old Queen. Annette had told him, laughing, of the King's instruction to the Council to send a thousand of Elizabeth's dresses to his Queen in Edinburgh; of the Council's refusal; of the King's anger. He had enjoyed seeing her rare laughter. Her teeth were white and even, enclosing a red, darting tongue.

She had asked him about his wife, and family. He had two marriageable daughters, he said. Susanna was beautiful and gay. Judith had always been a poor, frail creature; and, since the death of her twin she seemed to spend her time searching, listening for a ghostly voice. Did she ever hear it? Yes, he thought she did. Annette noted the compassion, the warmth. He is a good man, she thought.

But of his wife, she learned nothing, save that her name was Anne and he spoke it with affection. So, womanlike, she set about imagining this creature, married to and apparently loved by Will Shakespeare, yet who chose to live in Warwickshire. But she could not imagine her. She, to whom widowhood was such an emptiness, would have followed her man to the ends of the earth; especially, she was alarmed to find herself thinking, if that man was Will Shakespeare.

And now they had reached her house. His smile was open and friendly. 'Mistress Peyre, it has been the happiest of days.'

'For me too, sir.' Her smile was as open as his.

He said, with great understanding, 'You will be lonely, madam. Matthew shall stay with you.' He turned to the boy. 'But be early at my lodgings in the morning, knave. There is work to do.'

Matthew put an arm round his mother's waist (a slim waist, Will noted. A boy could encompass it). 'Oh, sir. Thank you.'

She slipped an arm about her son's shoulder, smiled down at him. So had Will seen Anne and Hamnet stand; long ago, it seemed, in another life.

Annette thought: if he goes now, it will have been a pleasant incident, no more. When we meet again, it will be almost as strangers. But if he comes into my house, then we set out upon a road that would lead either to heaven or to hell, no one can say. Which did she want? She thought she wanted no involvement. In fact there *could* be no involvement, for he was a married man and she was a woman of honour. So she was surprised to hear herself say: 'Sir, will you honour us by taking a glass of wine in my house?'

Will thought: she is dark, yet I cannot help but find her beautiful. And my heart is full of compassion for her, so that I could cradle her in my arms and comfort her, as one does a daughter. But pity is a treacherous emotion. And I have a wife I have come to love. I am a man punished by God. I have learnt my lesson. And she is a good and honourable woman. Yet to step into that house would be to step into quicksands for both of us. I will have none of it. Nevertheless, he said, 'Mistress Peyre, that would be a perfect end to a perfect day. It is I who am honoured.' He stepped inside.

They sat, one on each side of the carpeted table, very stiff, very formal. Matthew brought the wine and served it, mincing, with a cloth over his arm, like a servant in the tavern. They laughed at him more than his mimicry deserved, for they were suddenly silent, shy, lost for words, she thinking: he has taken Robert's chair and I do not resent it; he thinking: how well she holds herself, she is nearer in breeding to my lady mother than to my wife.

The visit was not a success. Yet, when he left, they smiled at each other with great friendliness. And when he turned, she was still standing in the doorway, her hand on Matthew's shoulder, watching him.

He waved. She did not reply.

So. The new reign was getting into its stride, forming its patterns. Anxieties and fears and hopes were rising, falling, turbulent as the waves of the sea.

The Chamberlain's Men, thanks to Will Shakespeare's over-generous nature, had two new boys, one of whom no one could stand. Dick Burbage had Mistress Fox looking in every day – bringing Nicholas a clean shirt, some moral precepts, or a pie for supper – and Mistress Fox always had time for an arch glance, a coy whisper for Master Burbage. Mistress Fox's gentlemen were all, of course, gentlemen; but an eminent actor like Master Burbage would have been a fine feather in her cap.

Will was possessed – by a mad Moor. Cinzio's little tale had begun simply enough. Now his characters had him by the hair, dragging him along through a torrent of poetry and jealousy and evil. He could not leave it alone. He ate, pen in hand. He attended rehearsals, encouraged Matthew, discouraged the posturing Nicholas; but all the time eager to get back to his quill. His fingers itched to hold it again. Othello and Iago, nobility and Lucifer, Lucifer triumphant. *Wash me in steep-down gulfs of liquid fire. Farewell! Othello's occupation's gone!* He couldn't write fast enough. He was swept along, on a gigantic surge of poetry that left him exhausted, but exultant. The thought that, if the King closed the theatres, the hideous clash between Iago and Othello might never see the light of day, troubled him a little. At this stage, his spirit's struggle was as single-minded as that of the child tearing itself from the womb.

Matthew Peyre loved every moment of his new life, when Master Shakespeare was there. It was hard work, up at dawn, attending on Master Shakespeare, then rehearsing, dancing, fencing, singing. Then, in the evenings, reading his Ovid or his Seneca while his master did his interminable writing. He would do anything for his master. Will had gone to his heart straight away. He was already merging into the gentle, kindly father the boy had so mourned.

But the times when Master Shakespeare was *not* there were hell. He was afraid of everyone, from the quick-tempered Burbage at the top to the sly pinchings, the secret arm-twistings, of Nicholas Fox at the bottom. The Chamberlain's Men were a band of brothers, a company of hard-working, decent friendly men; but it never occurred to any of them that shouts and curses and cuffs were not perhaps the best of upbringings for a sensitive, fatherless boy of twelve.

Yet Matthew bore it all, and had only one regret. He would never be able to act like the other new boy, Nicholas Fox. Not only had Nicholas told him so – he'd seen it for himself. Nicholas had his own way of doing things, and it was great and splendid. No one needed to tell Nicholas what to do (though, surprisingly, they *did* tell him all the time).

Nicholas Fox was happy too. Of course, it was a bad company. The Chamberlain's Men didn't know a thing about acting, and that old fellow Shakespeare had some quite idiotic ideas on the subject, but Nicholas would soon show them. He was happy to bide his time; and, in the meanwhile, young Matthew Peyre seemed quite willing to be used as a servant (and if he wasn't willing, by God, Nicholas would soon make him). His joining the Company also meant that Mother was meeting some very pleasant gentlemen. Mother enjoyed meeting pleasant gentlemen. And pleasant gentlemen often enjoyed meeting Mother.

King James was in the Palace of Whitehall, and he was relieved to be there.

King James feared three things: cold steel, gunpowder, and the Devil.

Understandably; for his mother had died of the first, and his father the second. And all Scotland knew that Satan, wearing a tall black hat and a ferocious expression, had announced from the pulpit of North Berwick Kirk that James was his arch enemy; an honour that the nervous James found flattering but would have preferred to be without.

Despite the swords and pikes that protected him, James had been very conscious that among the London crowds he could be in danger of all three. His experienced eyes saw many in the crowd who could have been Satan's witches; but without searching their bodies for the Devil's mark, or finding whether a hair from their heads would turn a scissor's blades, there could be no proof. And such tests were not practicable during a royal procession.

And now, here he was at Whitehall; unscathed, and not *feeling* bewitched; and none knew better than he the symptoms of bewitchment: the rotting away of the flesh, the blood boiling as in a cauldron, intolerable stink. Here he had none of these distressing symptoms. Satan's arch enemy he might be, but there was no doubt whatever that *God* was on his side.

He revelled in his new surroundings. He had exchanged the grim stones of Edinburgh for the new, fashionable red brick of London; Scottish nobles, swaggering in their skins and furs, for English nobles, swaggering in silk and satin; great rough men who believed in saying exactly what they meant, for men to whom flattery was an art they had given their lives to perfecting. In Scotland he had been accepted, grudgingly, as primus inter pares. In England he was a king, of high and most noble descent, full of those royal virtues, justice, clemency, learning, wisdom. It *must* be true. Everyone said it, over and over. It only confirmed what James had always suspected about himself.

In fact, only one thing hurt him: the cool reception of his brilliant and sensible plan to have Elizabeth's old dresses sent to his wife in Scotland.

It was so obvious. Everyone knew what a spendthrift Anne of Denmark was. (So of course, was James, but that was different.) His mind boggled at what she would deem a suitable outlay for making her appearance as Queen Consort of England – especially with her husband four hundred miles away. Why, it had cost £50,000 to keep her in jewels for the last ten years, when she'd only been Queen Consort of Scotland. Leaving her, he hadn't been able to sleep for the problem. And then, suddenly, he had this brilliant idea.

But no one liked it. The Queen said coldly that she did not wear cast-off clothes. And James' letter to the Council, asking them to send northward not only dresses, but also Elizabeth's litters, coaches, horses and jewels, was felt by the Council to be in somewhat questionable taste, and was not acted upon.

Yes, the new reign was taking shape. Only one actor was not yet present: Anne of Denmark, James' Queen, was still in Scotland, digging her toes in.

Nevertheless, once she had got everything arranged entirely to her satisfaction, she set out for London.

She had bought a new Edinburgh-built coach, and wore a mantle of white satin and purple velvet. Prince Henry also wore purple velvet, and Princess Elizabeth Spanish red taffeta. Anne was a most amiable woman when dealing with anyone but her husband, and now she had a splendid time doing all the things she most enjoyed: wearing expensive clothes, charming everyone she met, and exasperating her husband almost beyond endurance without even having to meet the fellow. At Berwick she refused to accept the ladies of the bedchamber whom James had thoughtfully sent her. At York she was given an outing to Heworth Moor, a silver banqueting cup, and a glass of beer, and after four days of feasting the Lord Mayor and Corporation escorted her out of the city. At Nottingham she was greeted by young girls strewing her path with flowers, shepherds, a flock of sheep whitened with flour, huntsmen, and a herd of deer whose horns were tipped with gold. No one seems to have thought of a partridge in a pear tree. As she came south ladies and gentlemen, eager to join her household, hurried to meet her. It was a triumphal procession of two hundred and fifty carriages that finally reached Windsor, where a reunion took place between James and herself quite as touching as their parting in Edinburgh. The King, in fact, seemed altogether beside himself with joy and pride in his family, going from courtier to courtier saying did they not think his Annie looked passing well; and, enthusiasm getting the better of his tact, he gathered up the Princess Elizabeth in his arms and cried, for all to hear, 'She's no an ill-favoured wench and may outshine her mither one of these days.'

Queen Anne gave him a smile of quiet venom.

In all this coming and going, this feasting and flattering, this scheming and fawning, perhaps one item had more significance for Will Shakespeare than any other: on a lovely summer's evening, at Althorp, Queen Anne attended the masque *Satyr*. It was in the open air, on the edge of woodlands now magically alive with elves and satyrs. The

Queen would never forget the beauty of movement and music and colour in that brilliant evening light. After the uncouthness of her Scottish Court, the grace and sophistication moved her almost to tears. From that evening, Queen Anne would be devoted to the masque until her death; and she would see that the Court was too.

The masque *Satyr* was by a promising young writer called Ben Jonson.

# CHAPTER 4

## DOST KNOW THIS WATER-FLY?

'Tell me, Dick. How went *Hamlet* when I was away?'

They sat on the edge of the stage, swinging their legs, contented, relaxed for once. They were still catching up on two years of the Company's history: takings, new costumes, failures, successes, trouble with the Puritans, trouble with apprentices, trouble with the plague, the unending war with Philip Henslowe.

But for Will this question was different from all the others he had asked. Hamlet had been part of his life for twenty years. This black-clad alter ego had walked with him, spoken for him, shouted his rare rages, brooded over his doubts and fears, bared his self-loathings. Yet he, Will Shakespeare, had never seen the play acted. For years the Company had refused to show any interest, and then, when at last they did produce it, he had been skulking in Stratford. So: 'How went *Hamlet*?' he asked.

Burbage was silent. Will's heart sank. Then Burbage said, 'The groundlings liked it well.'

Will's heart sank further. 'But?' he prompted.

'The better sort liked it. The players liked it.'

'But?' Will persisted.

'No buts. Takings were good. It's only that – ' he turned, still sitting on his hands, and stared at Will – 'it frightened me, man. It's *too* big. Playing Hamlet I thought: *could* old Will have written this? Could *any* man have produced this – this *infinite* creature?'

It was Will's turn to be silent. At last he said, 'What are you suggesting, Dick? That I sold my soul to Kit Marlowe's Mephistophilis, in exchange for Hamlet?'

'I'm suggesting nothing. I just mean – God's teeth, Will, how do you *know* all this?' he suddenly exploded.

'All what?'

'How a man feels, and thinks. Deep, deep down, in his innermost being.'

'I *am* a man, Dick.'

Burbage said swiftly, 'Yes, but not a prince who's seen his father's ghost, who's vowed to kill his uncle, who knows his mother for an incestuous adultress.'

'But I can *imagine* what he would feel.'

Burbage looked at him in awe. 'I believe you can. *And* what Gertrude feels, and Claudius, and poor young Ophelia. Oh, Will, it *sounds* like witchcraft.'

Will smiled, shook his head. 'No witchcraft, Dick. Just our common humanity. A king, a prince, a young girl, a Warwickshire glover' – he suddenly grinned – 'we share the same fears and pains and doubts. But Dick – before the King closes the theatres – could we not put on *Hamlet*?'

Burbage looked at him in mock alarm. 'What? Relearn that great part, just for an afternoon?'

'I have never seen *Hamlet*, Dick.'

'Oh, very well. But it will take at least a week. If Scotch Jamie shuts the theatres before then, what a waste of effort!'

'Thanks,' he said wryly.

'Oh, of *course* you must see your play. Will you take part? Be the Ghost. Then you will be almost free after the first act.'

''Tis a tedious long speech.'

'Long? What about *my* part?'

They grinned. Then Will said gravely, 'No, Dick. I will be Horatio, the loyal friend.'

'You will not be o'erparted.'

Will was silent. In fact, he was doing the old trick Burbage knew so well – going a thousand miles away in the flicker of an eyelid.

He came back. A thousand miles. 'Perhaps I *am* Horatio,' he said. 'Honest, down-to-earth Horatio.' He laughed ruefully. 'And I once thought myself Hamlet.' He sighed. 'I do not fly so high, old friend.'

The Globe was crowded, packed, seething, boiling like an ant heap.

The theatre was filled with the volatile emotional release that infects a family after a funeral. Elizabeth was buried, the succession had been accomplished without bloodshed. So far no one had said anything about closing the theatres, life was getting back to normal. The crowds packing the Globe did not consciously think: even *she* could not cheat death, yet *I* have, so far. But they did revel consciously in the life that was still theirs; in the smell of sawdust and sweat, the press of shoulder against shoulder; the shouts, the clash of arms that they could expect from the stage; the excitement crackling like lightning in the charged atmosphere.

The groundlings breathed noisily. From the stage it sounded like the drag of shingle. The gallants fidgeted their stools at the sides of the stage, cracked their nuts, guffawed.

But so long as no one started brawling, thought Dick Burbage, they mustn't complain. This excitement was one of the things the audience paid for; and to the actors it was as heady as wine.

Annette Peyre looked down from the gallery, high under the thatch. She had paid her penny at the theatre door, another penny at the door leading to the gallery, and a third for a seat with a cushion. Expensive, even for a silversmith's widow. But worth it, she thought, looking down at the heaving yard. Besides, when Robert had been alive they'd always had the luxury of twelve-penny seats. She wasn't prepared to sink too far.

From the roof, a trumpet sounded. Once. Twice. Thrice. A tremor, a frisson ran through the entire audience. A few latecomers were packed in, like coats into a tight wardrobe. Silence fell, as at the shutting of a door. From behind the stage came the slow, insistent beat of a drum – a sound to stir some strange, primeval depths in every man.

A soldier had materialised on the upper stage. Another entered. 'Who's there?' The drum beat ceased; the silence was palpable. 'Nay, answer me; stand and unfold yourself.' 'Long live the king!' 'Bernardo?' 'He.' 'You come most carefully upon your hour.'

Annette Peyre spread her arms on the gallery rail, rested her chin on her hands. She was captured already by the mysterious fascination of the theatre. Two soldiers of the watch, changing guard. A commonplace scene. Yet already Master Shakespeare, by the magic of his language, had lifted it on to another plane; had suggested – ''tis bitter cold, and I am sick at heart' – a menace in the biting air of Elsinore.

Will, in a tiring-room that led on to the upper stage, fingered the hilt of his sword and waited for his cue. If the rest of the theatre was in a volatile emotional state, Will was more exalted than anyone. Tears were behind his eyes. He had just come up from the tiring-room that had led on to the main stage. And there they had been, all gathered for Scene II: Claudius, Gertrude, Polonius, the whole Court of Denmark, magnificent and brilliant as a pride of peacocks; and, already moody, detached, Burbage/Hamlet, in black from head to foot. What a wonderful chance it had been, Will thought, that he had been able to contrast this prince against the rest of the Court, not only by his feelings and intellect, but even by his dress. Othello, it occurred to him for the first time, would have a similar advantage.

He listened to the words he had written being spoken. God, I'm overwrought, he told himself. But he had a part to play. He would play it. 'Friends to this ground,' he muttered.

'Stand ho! Who's there?' came from the stage. A nod, a quick smile to Marcellus, by his side, and they were on.

'Friends to this ground.' 'And liegemen to the Dane.' *Hamlet* was under way...

It was the interval before the fourth act.

The bottled beer was going well. The groundlings were beginning to feel they needed it. Though some were complaining that all this was too clever by half – they'd preferred Kyd's old *Hamlet* – most felt they were at least getting their money's worth. You couldn't really complain about a play that had adultery, incest, murder, accidental killing, a prince talking bawdy to a young girl, blood. Plus, thought the more percipient, poetry, and a wide-ranging commentary on the London stage; plus, thought the absorbed Annette Peyre (one of the most percipient of all) the deepest probing into the mind of modern man that had yet been made. Even the sight of Matthew, beautiful and elegant as a shy lady of the Court, had not distracted her from the sheer, rock-battering power of this tempest of a play. Even the sudden realisation that the grave Horatio was Master Shakespeare, though it quickened her pulse, did not distract her. She was too busy hoping that the Lord Hamlet would survive the last act, though it seemed rather much to expect.

Richard Burbage was sweating profusely. As if that confrontation with Gertrude hadn't been enough to exhaust any man, he'd had to finish the act by lugging the guts into the neighbour room – in other words dragging Harry (Polonius) Condell off stage and into the tiring-room. He mopped his forehead and seized a cup of sack. 'God, Will, you do work a man.'

'I'll work you harder in the last act, boy. How's your swordplay?'

'Phew! No seriously, Will, you ask too much of anyone. Mentally and physically. Especially,' he added, 'mentally.'

'Wait till you try my mad Moor. That'll make the grease paint run. I – ' He fell silent. He was suddenly aware that one man in the tiring-room was not of the Court of Denmark. A stranger. A stranger who seemed to think he might be in Bedlam, so arrogantly did he regard this Court of make-believe; a stranger who said to Will, 'Sir, I am bidden to seek Master Richard Burbage, of the Chamberlain's Men.'

'Who bids you?' said Will. From long experience, the harassed players assumed all men were enemies, until proved otherwise.

The stranger gave him a long, challenging look. 'The King of England and Scotland,' he said, clearly and distinctly. So clearly and distinctly that the room was suddenly silent.

This was it; the summons they had all been expecting: the end of theatres. Lucky if you are not whipped as a rogue and vagabond at a cart's tail. Sell New Place. Turn the gardener out of the Chapel Lane cottage, go there to live – and die; well, it would please Anne, she'd always loved their first little house. And he still hadn't seen the whole of *Hamlet*. Oh, damn, damn damn! Will Shakespeare's occupation's gone. 'That's Burbage,' he said shortly.

The stranger went up to Richard, bowed stiffly. 'Sir, I am to escort you to the Palace of Whitehall.'

Burbage, who had been putting the cup to his lips, checked, stared. 'Whitehall? When?'

'Now.'

'But that's impossible. I have another two acts.'

'You are suggesting the King should await the pleasure of a harlotry player?'

The rest of the company were crowding round now. There were angry murmurs. But Burbage said soothingly, 'I could, of course, go on stage and announce that the play cannot continue, thanks to the interference of a gentleman of the Court.' He looked at the stranger thoughtfully. 'I do not think you would get away with your life; but you would have done your duty, sir.'

The courtier, despite his arrogance, was beginning to look nervous. He said, 'The King is hunting. Perchance he will not return until evening. But my Lord Chamberlain likes always to have matters arranged in good time.'

'I see. He would like me there kicking my heels until after supper.' One of the storms that could blow up so suddenly in the amiable Burbage, blew up now. That magnificent voice fairly pealed forth. 'Tell my Lord Chamberlain, sir, that *his* Company does not break off a performance for anyone except the King. Take him that message, sir.' But already the storm was blowing itself out. 'Or, rather, sit you here, sir, in the tiring-room, since we could not squeeze a marmoset in the house. You shall watch our antics. And as soon as I have been killed, and have washed off the pig's blood and the grease paint, I will come with you to the King.'

The courtier had by now shed his arrogance like a cloak, and was biting his nails in his indecision. Nevertheless, he sat down in the chair Burbage courteously held for him. 'Beat the drum,' commanded Burbage.

The slow, menacing drumbeat began. Claudius, Gertrude, Rosencrantz and Guildenstern crossed the tiring-room and stood near the entrance to the stage. Claudius was biting his lip. Gertrude was already wringing her hands. Will, who had been so carried away by seeing *Hamlet* for the first time, knew that for him the spell had been broken. What did King James want? Whatever it was, it was certain to be bad. For the Chamberlain's Men had been on a pinnacle, equally popular with the better sort and the groundlings, in demand at Whitehall and the Inner Temple and the Inns of Court. No. There was only one direction now for the Chamberlain's Men. Downwards!

The house fell silent. There was not a person in that great wooden building who was not playing his part in the performance: from the absorbed Annette Peyre, leaning forward once more to rest her chin on the gallery rail, to the groundling at the back of the yard, breathing heavily through his mouth, eyes glued to the stage; from the gallant on his three-legged stool, paper in hand, jotting down examples of Master Shakespeare's pretty wit, to Mistress Nell Fox, sitting with today's gentleman up in the twelve-penny seats, a bottle of beer in one chubby hand and a slab of marchpane in the other. She thought the play a right gallimaufry. But she had been excited to see Mistress Mountjoy's lodger in breastplate and helmet, and to recognise sweet Master Burbage, though he shouldn't have worn black, didn't suit him, especially when everyone else was in such pretty clothes, she must tell him. But what excited her most was that her Nicholas was to appear in the last act. He was, he had promised his mother, going to show the Chamberlain's Men what *real* acting was like.

The drum was beating. Nell Fox put the bottle to her lips, drained it, and tossed it into the yard. The man on whose shoulder it fell looked up angrily, shaking his fist. Mistress Fox drew her gentleman's attention to this deplorable exhibition of manners. The gentleman leaned menacingly over the gallery rail, and drew his sword half out of its scabbard. The groundling spat. Mistress Fox's gentleman did the same; and, with the force of gravity on his side, scored a palpable hit. Honour was satisfied. Nell Fox's gentleman returned his sword to its scabbard and sat down. His fair companion gave him a melting smile. 'There is matter in these sighs,' began Claudius, coming on to the stage. They were into Act IV.

Will, despite his anxieties, was soon deep in the play again. It was his part to lead on the mad Ophelia. He was glad that in this scene he had nothing to say. He found those earthy songs on Ophelia's lips almost unbearably moving. He was also thinking: one day Matthew will be playing this part. He will do it well, better than this boy, good though he is.

His thoughts turned to the boys. Matthew looked well as a Court lady, held himself well. Soon they must give him a line or two.

And the other boy? He hoped he had made the right decision there. Burbage, bubbling with indignation: 'Will, that Fox youth wants a part in *Hamlet*. Did you ever hear such cockiness? He'd tear Ophelia in little pieces. And does he really think he could play Gertrude? There are no other women.'

Will, on an impulse: 'Give him a man's part, give him Osric.'

Burbage stared, grumbled, slapped his thigh, roared.

When they reach Act V, Nicholas brought the house down. He pranced, he minced, he fluttered, he twirled his false moustache, he flung his voice this way and that, he did unbelievable things with his hat. In the scene with Hamlet and Horatio he acted both Richard Burbage and William Shakespeare off the stage, no mean feat. The audience roared and clapped and stamped and shouted their laughter. Burbage was livid. So, watching from the tiring-room, was Robert Armin who had sweated blood to get a few dutiful laughs out of that tedious gravedigger part.

But Mistress Fox, up in the gallery, vowed it was the best clowning she had witnessed this side All Fools, and that it was, in fact, the highlight of an otherwise wearisome play.

And now the long afternoon was drawing to its end. So was the play. So was the royal house of Denmark. So was even the young, brilliant Prince, he who was likely, had he been put on, to have proved most royally. But now he would never be put on. For: 'The rest,' he cried, 'is silence.'

And so he died.

It had been more wonderful than anything Will could have imagined. The Court of Elsinore – corrupt, bloody, magnificent – sweeping on and off the stage restless as the sea. Yet no more than a backdrop for that black-clad youth he loved with a curious, hungry adoration. And he, William Shakespeare, his creator, the man who loved him more than a brother or a son, had been, in the traffic of the stage, his friend; the one true, steady person in the whole of Denmark.

And, he remembered, he must still play his part. 'Now cracks a noble heart,' he said. He swallowed. He moistened his lips, swallowed again. His voice came taut, sorrow laden, yet – old actor that he was – controlled. 'Good night, sweet prince' – his eyes were full of tears – 'And flights of angels sing thee to thy rest!'

There were drums, cannon, solemn music; Hamlet borne nobly off stage; a final volley. Applause, cheers, whistles. Even Nicholas Fox was rather grudgingly pushed forward for an ovation. Then, an emotionally exhausted Shakespeare, wandering about the tiring-room like a man who has lost his way. And Richard Burbage briskly cleaning off the blood and grime of Elsinore, ready to go and meet his Sovereign.

After the intense emotional excitement of the afternoon, Will's lodgings were lonely indeed. While taking a modest bow (as Horatio, not as author. The groundlings had been watching mayhem at the Court of Denmark. The question of who was the author, or even of *whether* there was an author, simply did not arise) he had caught sight of Annette Peyre. He thought he had seen a face uplifted by the drama, exhausted by emotion, radiant with enjoyment, yet sad that already this afternoon of make-believe was dissolving before her eyes. On an impulse he had given Matthew the evening to go and keep his mother company. And so he was alone with his thoughts: Othello? Damn Othello. Would *any* man, even a mad blackamoor, be taken in by that creature Iago? And why *was* Iago trying to destroy the Moor? He'd have to find him a reason before the play was put on, or someone would be at his throat. If, as seemed unlikely, it ever *was* put on. No. He was in no mood for Othello. Trees in Stratford gardens would be shedding snow-flakes of pear blossom, buttercups and king cups would be enamelling the meadows, while, from the window of his London lodgings – stench, filth; clouds, like ducks on a pond, sailing in a yard of sky.

But his thought kept coming back to Burbage's summons. Why had he been called to Whitehall?

He wondered what Matthew was doing – and Annette. He missed the boy, the rustle of his books, the way he had of singing softly to himself as he studied, his dog-like adoration. Was the boy happy? He didn't know. Matthew had everything an actor needed except confidence. Oh, he was confident enough alone with Will. But with his fellows – scared, hanging back, fearful. What could you expect, torn suddenly from that beautiful and kindly mother?

He poured himself a cup of wine. Which way would the boy go, he wondered. He, Will, could help a little, but not much. The solution was in the boy's own hands.

But this wouldn't do. He *must* work. He, who never normally wasted a second, had been gazing out of the window, mooning like a love-sick boy. He drew in his head. But as he did so, his eye had caught a movement in the street below. A man, in his prosperous best, striding this way. Will put his head out again so quickly that he caught his forehead on the lattice. It was Richard Burbage; walking like a man who carries tidings.

# CHAPTER 5

## OUTRAGEOUS FORTUNE...

But Will Shakespeare was not the only one who awaited tidings. Master Philip Henslowe sat in his old office at the Rose Theatre, clawing his fur-lined robe irritably about his knees. He had (quite by chance, for he was far too high-principled a man ever to spy on his rivals) walked past the Globe just as the performance ended. And had it not been for what was obviously the personal intervention of his friend God, he would have been knocked down and trodden in the mire by the outpouring crowds. Thousands of them, it seemed. Whereas, at his own Fortune Theatre, there had been more people on stage than off. He picked up his pen, opened his account book. 'Maye 19th,' he wrote. 'In the Yere of owre Lord 1603. From the Admeralles Men playing NABUCHODONOZOR vj$^s$ onlie. My Godde why hast Thow forsayken mee.'

The door opened. Moreton, his servant, entered. After dinner, Henslowe had given him his blessing, the afternoon off, and a penny telling him to enjoy himself where he would. Since Henslowe was freer with his blessings than with his pennies, Moreton, who knew his master, had taken himself off to the Globe.

'Well?' snapped Henslowe.

'Their takings must have been near five pounds. More, with the bottled beer.'

Henslowe groaned.

'And they have two new boys. One, pretty as paint, not allowed to say a word, but holding himself well. The other – showing more promise than any boy I have seen for years.'

Henslowe, who always looked his age, now looked ten years more. 'God blister their souls,' he said piously.

Moreton bowed his head. 'Amen.' He looked at his master. 'His name is Nicholas Fox. Master Alleyn refused him for the Admiral's Men only last month.' Moreton treasured loyalty as much as he did Henslowe; but facts, after all, were facts, and a little discord among one's superiors was worth cultivating. 'His mother is Mistress Nell Fox, of Cripplegate. A lady, I am told, not unsusceptible to the blandishments of a proper gentleman.'

Philip Henslowe looked at his servant more hopefully. 'You mean, if I were to visit the lady?'

Moreton looked at his master. The long, pallid face, the pendulous nose, the crabby eyes, the gown, stiff with mementoes of forgotten meals. 'If you took a well-filled purse,' he said coolly.

'Where can I fill a purse, man? Do you know what we took for *Nebuchadnezzar*? Six shillings! And sold two meat pies and a few kickshaws. *And* there's talk now that James will close the brothels. They say he does not understand a gentleman's occasional needs. They say – he has unnatural affections. You understand me, Moreton?'

'Yes, sir.'

Henslowe groped at the pocket of his robe, found a piece of rag, blew his nose tearfully. The thought of sin always upset him. But for sin that threatened to come between his customers and their simple pleasures, there was only one answer: fervent prayer that the Lord would visit on James the prompt and effective action He had once taken in Sodom.

But this was, at the moment, a diversion. They were discussing Master Nicholas Fox. 'What did he play, this boy?'

'A foolish courtier. In the high manner.'

'I shall visit his mother; point out to her that the Lord would not wish her son to nourish the rivals of Philip Henslowe.'

'Do that, master,' Moreton said, looking duly impressed.

Steps were coming up the stairs, two at a time. Richard Burbage might be plump. He might have had an exhausting day, first rehearsing, then playing, Hamlet; and then visiting the Court. But no one who could not take all that in his stride could hope to be a leading actor. He burst in: 'Will, we live! The King loves the theatre better than figs.'

Will searched on the dresser, found another cup, filled it. 'And will not close the theatres?' Bad news he accepted. Good news he had learnt long ago to question.

'Only if the plague worsens. Oh, I got a fine drubbing for playing *Hamlet* today. The King fears plague as he fears everything else. But that's nothing.' He lifted his cup, touched it against Will's. 'I have news for you' – he grinned – 'you Stratford shopkeeper. King James has appointed you, me, several of us, Grooms of the Chamber.'

Will sat down. It was too sudden. There he had been, on this bright evening, awaiting disaster. And instead – he was a gentleman of the Court!

Flattered, honoured, but appalled. A courtier could not write *Othello, Macbeth*. Much as he loved rank, he could not live without the theatre – and his writing. 'Is it – a command?' he asked bleakly.

Burbage nodded. 'Kings do not request. Not even this strange specimen.'

'But I can't live at Court. The theatre's my world. I – '

'Oh, and I didn't tell you. We are no longer my Lord Chamberlain's Men.'

He'd known it. All day, even in the ecstasy of watching *Hamlet*, he had had this dire sense of foreboding. An end of what was, for him, life: the mystery of turning – with the help of a thimbleful of ink, a yard or two of velvet, and a poor player – a *thought* into a living, strutting, shouting character. It was all very well for Dick to sound so pleased. He –

'We are the King's Men. By letters patent.'

Will stared at him. Burbage said. 'Not only under the protection of the King himself; but with a royal licence to shake in the face of any mayor or university chancellor who bids us begone.' He drained his wine. 'Will, it's been a long road, but from tonight we're no longer rogues and vagabonds. We are the King's Servants.' Suddenly he was crying.

Will took his cup, filled it, and filled his own. William Shakespeare, Gentleman, Groom of the Chamber to his Protestant Majesty James the First, stood with his cup of wine in his hand, staring out of the window; seeing, not the sunset-gilded roofs of London, but the moonlight of long ago on Stratford fields, and the little house in Chapel Lane, and the ineffable joy on the face of Anne when she greeted him, and the frozen sorrow when she kissed him farewell; and himself, young, proud, his wife by his side, his three children before him, walking, like any other Stratford burgher, on summer Sunday evenings by the Avon: simple joys; dead, all dead, killed by the arrows of unbelievable success.

That night, on his way to bed, he took his candle and went into Matthew's room.

The boy was fast asleep, his cheek as soft as the candlelight. His clothes – the purple doublet, the feathered hat – were strewn about the room. A toy – a short stick, surrounded by a jester's head, cap and bells – lay on the pillow beside him. Will gazed fascinated, moved beyond tears by the way, with the coming of sleep, childhood and innocence had once more taken over this anxious, striving boy. Childhood and innocence. If only a man could return, once in a while, and wash himself clean in those crystal waters. Wash away success, and knowledge, and weariness, and the world's stain. Childhood, and innocence! As well search for the winter's snows in June, the summer's rose in December. He turned, and went into his own room, and wept long, bitterly. Perhaps because he had climbed higher than he had ever thought to climb – and from these dangerous heights he saw the valleys dreaming in peace? Or perhaps because tears were the nearest a grown man could ever come to those waters of innocence.

# Chapter 6

### He words me, girls, he words me

There was a knocking at the door. Mistress Helen Fox was surprised. All her regular gentlemen knew that she did not entertain on Thursdays. After all, a lady required *some* time for her devotions.

She went and peered through the window. No. It was certainly *not* one of her regular gentlemen. An old, tall, stooping person, somewhat moth-eaten. She bridled. Still, the kindness of her heart was something she had long ago given up fighting against. 'Send the gentleman up, Rose,' she bellowed down the stairs.

She heard footsteps. The maid showed the gentleman in. 'Master Philip Henslowe,' she announced.

So that was who he was. Nell Fox was intrigued. She wouldn't have expected the owner of Winchester's Geese – Still, perhaps the gentleman liked a bit of quality occasionally. She could respect that. She smiled radiantly. 'Master Henslowe, this is indeed an honour. Rose, a glass of canary for the gentleman. Be seated, sir.'

Henslowe lowered himself on to a chair, plucked his gown about his knees. 'Madam, I come to right a wrong.'

Nell Fox waited, watching him shrewdly. A shy gentleman, she knew, could wander down many a twisting lane before reaching what was uppermost in his mind. But this was a new approach. And she didn't think Master Henslowe *was* a shy gentleman.

Henslowe said, 'A grave mistake has been made, Mistress Fox. I understand Master Alleyn, of the Admiral's Men, informed you that he had no place for a boy actor.'

Nell Fox swallowed. 'That is so,' she said, making rapid mental adjustments, and wriggling her feet back into the shoes she had slipped off when the gentleman was announced.

'Master Alleyn was mistaken. There *is* a place. And that is why I have hastened to see you. I would not like to think of your boy being subjected to the contaminations of some lewd strolling players when he might be with the Admiral's Men. For the Devil, Mistress Fox, goeth about as a roaring lion, seeking who he may devour.'

'Yes, indeed, Master Henslowe. But my son is with Master Burbage's Company.'

Henslowe looked very relieved. Very relieved indeed. 'I am delighted to hear it, madam. He will certainly learn good acting there, even though – ' He fell silent, sipping his wine.

'Even though what, Master Henslowe?'

The poor gentleman looked grievously uncomfortable. Distressed, even. 'May I speak plainly, mistress?'

Mistress Fox looked at him thoughtfully. Then she said, speaking slowly, 'I realise, sir, that there are many things in this sinful world of which a chaste widow like myself can know nothing; and, hearing, could not even understand. Yet I do beseech you, sir, to speak plainly and while doing so, to turn your eyes from the blushes that stain my innocent cheeks.'

Henslowe bowed. 'Even though, madam,' he continued
gently, 'he become morally corrupted in the process.'

Mistress Fox had hidden her face with a fan. 'And you
would be prepared to save him from this corruption by
taking him into the Admiral's Men?'

'For you, madam, yes.' He held his wine up to the light,
studied it. 'Of course, I have no knowledge of your son's
ability as an actor; yet, to save a brand from the burning I
would venture all: even the risk of angering my old friend
Richard Burbage.'

'I thank you, sir.' They were both silent, thoughtful. Then,
with the air of one changing the subject, Nell said, 'There are
rumours that Burbage's Company have been appointed the
King's Men. Have *you* heard this, Master Henslowe?'

It was his turn to look at *her* shrewdly. 'Such is the gossip.
I think it means little.'

She rose, strolled to the window. 'If such a great honour
*were* true, Master Henslowe, it would be worth a little moral
corruption, would it not?'

'*Nothing* is worth moral corruption, madam. Nothing.'
The old man was deeply pained. So much so that it was
some moments before he could bring himself to speak. Then:
'I'll give you five pounds to bring Nicholas to the Admiral's
Men,' he said briskly.

'Ten.'

'You're mad.'

'I'm not. Ten. Take it or leave it.'

'Six.'

'Ten.'

'Make it guineas.'

'Ten.'

Philip Henslowe sighed deeply. He put down his empty
glass. He picked up his hat. He gazed at Nell with eyes that

years of contemplating human sinfulness had filled with sadness. He said, 'Mistress Fox, I will leave you. And' – his voice broke – 'dear sister, I implore you to consider, when I am gone, how hardness of heart such as yours must grieve our gentle Saviour.'

'Rose,' bellowed Nell down the stairs, 'the gentleman's leaving.'

Rose came running. Henslowe walked sorrowfully to the door. 'Six pounds ten shillings,' he muttered. 'My final offer.'

'Ten.'

There was nothing more to be said. But both parties felt quite pleased with the progress that had been made. Dealings between ladies and gentlemen could not be hurried; and tomorrow was another day.

King James had a number of unfortunate habits. One was that of edging ever closer to a man until those round, mournful eyes, and his breath, were within a few inches of his companion's face.

Will Shakespeare sat with his monarch in a narrow window embrasure. The King edged closer. The fastidious Will edged away. But very soon there was nowhere left to edge. The padded royal brocade pressed against his arm, his thigh. The royal breath was hot on his cheek. The royal eyes searched his face as though poring over small print. 'Aye,' said James thoughtfully.

'Your Majesty?' said Will. The excitement of finding himself sitting thus with his Sovereign was already wearing thin. In fact, the whole evening had been a disappointment so far…

There he had been with the rest of the Court, waiting; as once he had awaited the entrance of Elizabeth. The doors had been thrown open. The great officers of the Court had entered, backwards and bowing, followed by –?

Not Gloriana, this time, sailing in, proud and beautiful as a swan – beautiful, and terrible; but a Sir Andrew Ague-cheek of a fellow, shambling, grinning, blinking, and his Queen, tall, elegant, mocking. She would, Will quickly decided, make ten of her husband any day.

The royal couple took their seats. The presentations began. Will was one of the last. He knelt before his Sovereign. The King said, in his thick voice, 'I've long wanted to meet ye, Shakespeare.'

So the King had heard of him, in faraway Scotland! It was a proud moment. Will swallowed. 'Your Majesty is too gracious.'

'I liked fine your *Doctor Faustus*. Aye. I've had a twa-three dealings masel' wi' yon Mephistophilis.'

Will was glad he was still kneeling. It hid the concern in his face. Let it pass, and risk exposure later. Correct a monarch, and risk his immediate displeasure? But honesty usually won, with Will. He said, 'Sire, I would give my right hand to deserve your Majesty's praise. But, alas, I did not write *Doctor Faustus*.'

Silence. He dared to look up. James was staring round the room, biting his knuckles, obviously *very* displeased. He made a curt gesture of dismissal. Impudent fellow! Did he think he knew better than James Stuart?

But now it was the Queen's turn. 'Master Shakespeare, do you know Master Jonson?'

'A little, your Majesty.'

She laughed – a deep, throaty chuckle he found infinitely attractive. 'I vow he is the finest writer ever lived.' She added graciously, 'I will bid him write plays for the King's Men. You will find them well worth the acting, Master Shakespeare.'

'Your Majesty is too kind.' Now he dared look at her. She was smiling. Her smile was open and kindly. 'You are welcome at our Court, sir.'

James went on scowling. Will rose, backed away, bowing. He fetched up beside Burbage. He said, out of the corner of his mouth. 'He congratulated me on my *Faustus*.'

Burbage's eyes glinted. 'What did *you* say?'

'I said it wasn't mine.'

'What did *he* say?'

'I don't think he believed me. And *her* Majesty will intercede with Ben to write us plays.'

'God's blood! Perhaps being the King's Men will not be so easy after all.'

But later, when the presentations were over, and the King and Queen were wandering among their courtiers, Will felt a hand gripping his shoulder. He turned, and found the King's face close to his own. 'Master Shakespeare, I've a wee matter to discuss.' He took Will's arm, steered him to the window embrasure, sat down, patted the seat beside him.

Will, though greatly flattered, sat down nervously.

The King was silent, edging a little closer. At last he gave a long sigh and said, 'Aye.'

It was not a helpful opening. 'Your Majesty?' said Will, as brightly as he could.

The King remained silent. Will was now pressed tight against the stonework of the window. And now the King was drawing something out of his doublet. A book. He gave it to Will. And, still gazing at him solemnly, uttered a cackling guffaw and dug him sharply in the ribs. 'Ye're no the only one who can write, mon. I've penned a twa-three poems masel'.'

Will looked amazed and impressed, though his heart sank. Being given other people's poems to read meant, to a kind and reasonably honest man, agonies of embarrassment, lying and dishonesty. But when the would-be poet was a king, all that was multiplied a thousand times.

The elbow attacked again. 'Go on. Read it, mon. And I want your honest opinion, mind. Nane of your English flattery.'

Will opened the book as though it might contain his death warrant. And read: 'And soe did Cerberus rage with hiddeous beare And all that did Aeneas once befall.'

He tried again: 'To do lyke Erostrat who brunt the faire Ephesian tombes, or him to win a name Who built of brasse the crewell Calfe entire.'

'Ye like it?' asked James. His mournful eyes were fixed on Will's face, from a distance of six inches. He was breathing heavily and expectantly through his mouth. He'd acquired a taste for flattery since coming to England, never having had much in Scotland, poor fellow.

'It is *remarkable*, your Majesty,' said Will, both self-interest and his natural kindness coming to his rescue. 'That a prince – a wise and just ruler, learned in the law, a great theologian, the Lord's Anointed – should also be a magnificent poet: this, surely, is more than his grateful subjects would dare to expect.' And may the Lord have mercy on my soul, he added to himself.

James nodded slowly. 'Aye. I'm no short of gifts, Master Shakespeare.' He thumbed through the book, relishing a few favourite pieces. 'Aye. And ye'll be scribbling a bit piece yourself, maybe?' he asked encouragingly.

'Yes, your Majesty. Naturally, nothing like – ' He waved a modest hand towards James' masterpiece. 'A play. A poor thing, of course. About a Moor. But – ' He would not often sit cheek by jowl with the King. Let him strike while the iron was hot. He said, 'With your Majesty's permission I would like to write a play about your Majesty's noble ancestor Banquo; and about the destruction of his foul murderer, Macbeth.'

The effect on the King was remarkable. He stared at Will, eyes round as saucers. He jerked back into his own corner of the window seat. But only the better to slap a hot hand on to Will's knee. 'My dear Shakespeare, och, but that's masterly.' He nuzzled closer. He lowered his voice. His face was almost touching Will's. 'Mon! We'll write it together!' He backed away again, the better to see the effect of this shattering announcement.

Master Shakespeare was impressed; there was no doubt about that. 'Your Majesty quite overwhelms me,' he gasped.

'Aye.' James put his hands on his knees, stretched himself with satisfaction. 'Aye. I thocht ye'd be pleased. Wi' my poetic gift and your acting experience – mon, it will be the bonniest play ever writ.'

Will bowed his head. Such royal condescension had left him quite speechless.

He escaped at last. But the miseries of that evening were not yet over. 'Henry,' said a clear feminine voice, 'you will not have met Master Shakespeare, one of our actors?'

Will turned. It was the Queen who had spoken. But he was not looking at her; he was staring at her companion. Then he bowed very low, thankful once again to be able to hide his face. 'My lord,' he whispered.

'Master Shakespeare and I *were* once acquainted, madam,' said a voice, in the tone of one admitting that he *had* had the plague, but the Lord had spared him.

Will lifted his eyes, and looked beseechingly at my Lord of Southampton: this man for whom he had felt the warm, almost fatherly, friendship of an older man for a younger;

this noble who had once treated a common player as a friend; before he and his other friend, Essex, borne on a great wave of anger and frustration, had flung themselves against a rock that called itself Elizabeth. Essex had been killed, Southampton broken. Yet here he was, staring with bitter arrogance at the player who had refused to join their hare-brained rebellion.

Unable to turn away, because of the Queen's presence, he said, 'Ah, Shakespeare,' and lifted a pomander to his nose.

Two years in the Tower had aged Henry Wriothesley, third Earl of Southampton; a sentence of death, even when revoked, is not good for a man's health. No, the Earl was still exquisitely dressed, in clothes that would have kept a labourer and his family for a lifetime; those golden locks still fell over his shoulder, but did they not look slightly ridiculous in a man of thirty? The petulant mouth had hardened, the sulky eyes grown crafty. Southampton had nearly met his death through following the wrong man in one reign. Now that, as was the way of princes, the new king had released from the Tower those his predecessor had incarcerated (finding a few outside, such as Raleigh, to put in their place), Southampton was not going to make the same mistake twice. He had gone straight from the Tower to meet King James at Huntingdon, and had carried the Sword of State before him. He had already been given entry to the Privy Chamber. The King was fascinated by him, the Queen hung on his every word. Southampton had no time to waste on a middle-aged poet. Besides, Shakespeare had refused to help him and Essex when they had needed his help. A hot-blooded young noble did not forget a thing like that.

To Will's horror, the Queen smiled and withdrew. Both men bowed. Will kept his head down as long as possible, hoping that Southampton would turn on his heel and walk away. But when he looked up, the earl was staring at him with anger and contempt. 'So. The poor player sits with his king in a window-seat now. You have made good progress while I lay rotting in the Tower, Shakespeare.'

Will said piteously, 'My lord, I did you no harm.' It was weak, feeble; but there was nothing else to say.

'No good, neither. Shall I tell you something, Shakespeare?'

Will waited, silent.

'The Lord Essex cursed you the night before he died.'

Once they had been Will, Henry, Robert. That formal title, 'the Lord Essex', hurt more than the rest. Will said, humbly, 'Perchance, if he had listened to me, he had not died.'

'The Lord Essex was not one to listen to poltroons.'

'Or even to men of sense?' said Will, still humble.

My Lord of Southampton stared. 'Remember, Master Shakespeare,' he said slowly, 'however many shoes you lick, you will always have *one* enemy at Court.' He turned, and walked away. Will bowed to his retreating back, filled with a hurt that was like the cut of a sword. And he was fearful. An enemy at Court was a knife lodged always against one's throat.

So, with the exception of Sir Walter Raleigh, most people were very satisfied with the new reign. King James was certainly a strange fish, but he was not the fire-breathing Calvinist they had feared. He was a man of peace. There was even talk of friendship with Spain.

And his gay Queen, who was a clever enough woman to give an appearance of being completely feather-headed, was immensely popular. So everyone was happy. The King's Men were secure for the first time in their lives. My Lord of

Southampton, raised up in the twinkling of an eye from the dank Tower to the honour of the Privy Chamber, already saw within his grasp, not only the Garter, but also the monopoly of sweet wines that Elizabeth had confiscated from his friend Essex.

Philip Henslowe went down on pious knees and thanked God for a king who had not, after all, closed either the play houses or the brothels. Annette Peyre thanked the Blessed Virgin for a king who seemed prepared to tolerate Catholics, and for a Queen who even favoured them. (She also besought the Blessed Virgin to erase from her thoughts William Shakespeare, for William was a married man, and to think of him was sinful. But this was a prayer that the Virgin, even with Annette's earnest help, seemed unable to answer.)

Her son Matthew fluctuated wretchedly between happiness and misery. Happy in his lodgings with a master who had already, it seemed, slipped into his dead father's clothes. Happy when he was allowed to speak a few lines at rehearsal, and was commended. Happiest of all when Will Shakespeare, grinning, ruffled his hair and sent him off to sup with his mother. But wretched in the morning at waking to another unknown day, wretched entering the rehearsal room, wretched at the rough, cruel, bawdy talk of his fellows.

Nicholas Fox was happy because he had shown Master Burbage and that old fool Shakespeare what an actor who really knew his craft *could* do with a small part.

Only Will Shakespeare did not share England's sense of coming into quiet water from the harsh buffeting of wind and sea. Southampton's bruising had left him sick and hurt; revived the self-loathing that New Place and a Grant of Arms had done so much to cure. What were *they*, compared with Titchfield Abbey and an earldom? And was it true? *Was* he a coward? In his better moments he thought of himself as cautious, sensible. But when he was down in the dumps, he knew that Southampton had used the right word to describe him – poltroon! A man of humble background, of bourgeois pretensions, a harlotry player, a failed poet. (Oh, his *Venus and Adonis* and his *Lucrece* had been pretty enough, but what had he written since then, except a few plays?) And, to come to more immediate matters, what *was* he going to do about Banquo and Macbeth? He would, he decided, have to risk bringing a royal rage about his ears by writing the play first and then showing it James. He *had* worked with others in the past, but never with anyone who could write things like 'And soe did Cerberus rage with hiddeous beare'. No. The sooner he wrote the play the better. He reached for his Holinshed.

It was pleasant while it lasted, this honeymoon between the King and his people; but, like all honeymoons, it was short. The people soon discovered that this James had some very peculiar bees in his Scotch bonnet. For instance, he insisted on ramming what he called the Divine Right of Kings down their throats.

This was no way to treat the English, who show a sheep-like docility when they think they are being led, but will dig in their toes like mules when they decide they are being pushed. James, with all the obstinacy of the weak, went on lecturing his people like a dominie. His class listened, sullen and silent. They were working themselves up into the mood where a few heads would begin to roll, and some wouldn't be surprised if one of those heads was the King's.

He also greatly upset the English by relaxing the penal laws against Catholics and releasing them from fines. On a people who took their children for a treat to watch the disembowelling of traitors, the fires of Smithfield had left a surprisingly strong impression. The lurid light of those fires was still before people's eyes, the screams of the martyrs still in their ears, the smell of burnt flesh in their nostrils. Individual Catholics might be tolerated, but never again must the power be theirs to burn and torture. Yet though many complained, quite a few took advantage of the relaxed laws to return to Catholicism themselves, a fact that caused consternation and even near-panic in Puritan circles.

But God, who was always on the side of the Puritans, very soon showed his disapproval of the King's action. The plague, fitful as distant thunder when James arrived in London, suddenly broke into such a storm as had never before been known. All that year it raged. But the deaths of 30,000 souls did not have the effect that God so obviously desired. James did not take the Almighty's broad hint. He simply, acting entirely in character, fled the plague-stricken city, taking the Court to the tumbledown Woodstock Palace where there was accommodation only, as Sir Robert Cecil sourly remarked, for the King and Queen with the privy chamber ladies and some of the *Scottish* Council. The rest were in tents.

This could not last. James moved on: Loseley Park, Farnham Castle, Thruxton House, Wilton House, Tottenham Park, Basing House; always with the rank breath of the plague on his royal neck. Sir Robert Cecil's poor twisted body longed for its own bed again – and for the ordered days of the good old Queen. 'I am pushed from the shore of comfort,' he mourned, 'and know not where the winds and waves of court will bear me.'

But comfort was at hand for Master Secretary Cecil. During his travels King James had noted the splendour and luxury of Wilton House, the wit and learning of the Dowager

Countess of Pembroke, the absence of any signs of plague even among the common sort. He invited himself and the Court back there. They settled in for the winter.

In London, the plague raged on; obscene, horrible, terrifying.

Matthew Peyre, alone in his master's lodgings, tried to concentrate on his Ovid. But he could not. Bright eyes glazed at the bright candle, while he told himself over and over that his mother *could* die of the plague.

It was unthinkable, but it could happen.

How could he bear it? How did men bear, as they were so often called on to bear, the unbearable? His young mind strove with what was beyond its understanding. But Mother! She had been well when last he saw her, yesterday. But in a day fair flesh could be changed to corruption. He went down on his knees, and prayed to the Virgin, that heavenly simulacrum of his earthly mother.

When he rose, he went and stared again at the candle. He had asked for a sign. Under the bright sword of the flame, there was a shining crater of molten wax. Soon it must be released, run down the candle. If it ran to the right, his mother would live; to the left, she would die.

He watched, scarce breathing.

The tiny walls of the crater were melting away. On the right, a masterly crag of wax, fanned by the hot flame, fell, but did not release the lake of molten gold.

On the left, the low, sturdy ramparts wasted slowly away; but still they held. The dam had not broken yet.

He longed to interfere. He would gladly have plunged his fingers in the flame to have sent wax cascading to the right. But that would prove nothing.

The buttresses and ramparts, the cliffs and peaks changed and rose and fell; and still the glimmering lake held under the flame.

Dazzled by watching the brightness, he glanced round the room. Mist and shadow hung about the high corners, black shapes trod a sinister pavan among the curtainings. The boy's face in the candlelight was fearful. But still he watched the flame. And suddenly the flame darted like a tongue, here, there, everywhere, bringing down a cliff here, a bastion there. And the golden lake was split, left, right, centre, so that there was no knowing whether the gentle mother of God had decreed death or life. And Master Shakespeare had come into the room, scattering the candlelight, weary from a sharers' meeting, and was giving Matthew his cloak and bidding him pull off his shoes and pour a glass of wine, all in a moment. All of which Matthew did happily, cheerfully, lovingly, not holding it against his beloved master that had blown away the Virgin's message by the draught from an open door.

Will rested his chin on his hand. 'Do you know what going on tour means, boy?'

'Yes, sir.'

'Well, we're going. This plague has put the City Fathers in such a canary that they've shut the theatres. So. We can either stay in London and starve or die of plague' – he saw the sudden fear in the boy's eyes, interpreted it correctly, and cursed himself for a clumsy fool – 'or we can go and earn a penny or two in the provinces. The sharers have decided on the latter.'

Matthew's one comfort had been the thought that somehow, he would find out at least once a day how his mother did; for his apprenticeship was not hard, Master Shakespeare was a most understanding master. For a few minutes, every day, he would know a slight easing of the burden of anxiety.

And, more important than the easing of any anxiety, he would know if she were ill. He would be available to fetch the doctor, the priest. Especially, the priest. The possibility of his mother dying without the last rites of his Church was something so abhorrent that he could not even think about it without a kind of physical spasm.

And now they were about to put miles of muddy, rutted roads between themselves and London. Thickets and hills and forests, moorland and bog would separate him, not only from her, but from the knowledge of life and death.

Will, sprawled wearily in his chair, sipping his wine, watching the boy with a kind of detached intensity, said, 'It will be hard for you, Matthew, not knowing how your mother does.'

Hard for her, too, he thought. First husband, now son. And plague howling at the window. Yet, perhaps, he thought, it is the only way to break the cord that binds him to her. He said, 'But it is a good way to learn the player's craft. It is how Master Burbage and I learned. An inn yard, in driving rain, and shouting to drown the din of the nearby market – that teaches a man to make himself heard, Master Apprentice.'

'Yes, sir.'

Will laughed. 'The prospect does not tempt you?'

'I am troubled for my mother, sir. As a widow, and – one who follows the old religion – she is alone.' He said, with all the pathetic courage of his years, 'She needs me to protect her.'

Will shook his head, smiled. 'You are wrong, boy. Your mother is a woman of great quality, great strength. She needs no one to protect her.' The boy was silent. Will rose, put a hand on his shoulder. 'I'm sorry, Matthew; but believe me, your mother will be thankful to have you in the country. Sleep well, boy. Oh, and light me another candle. I have work to do.'

The scratching of a quill. The moth-like flutter of a candle flame. The quiet breathing of a boy. It would be a long time before these sounds were heard again in the rooms above the tire-maker's shop in Cripplegate.

# CHAPTER 7

## A ROMAN THOUGHT HATH STRUCK HIM

God's blood, it was quite like old times. The King's Men were going on tour.

Such a bustle! So much to think about! It was like a military expedition. Horses, waggons, wigs, costumes, swords, armour, manuscripts, bottled beer, play bills, grease paint, hired men, doxies, boys, a thousand and one details!

Once again the London theatres were closed. The City parishes were required to make an official weekly return of plague deaths to the Corporation. And when the grand total reached thirty (fifty, the actors complained, would have been a less unreasonable number) then the theatres were shut by warrant.

But in 1603, thanks to God's displeasure with the King, thirty or fifty would have made little difference. People were dying in their hundreds. Men kept to their houses. The fruits and vegetables, the silks and ribbons, had gone from the drays and carts and barrows that still trundled over the cobbles; now the only merchandise was death.

The streets were almost deserted. Instead of the chatter and shouts and quarrels and laughter, only the heavy tolling of a bell, the endless whining of a dog. Only, in the tunnels of streets under the overhanging houses, the hot, still air quivering at the clash of the passing-bell, at the squeak and rattle of the death carts.

The few people who still ventured out were pale with terror, anguished with bereavement. They watched the players loading their carts with haunted, apathetic eyes (but in their minds' eyes, perhaps, a sweet countryside, a happy bustling town, where to live till Saturday did not seem too vain a hope).

The players were all thoroughly miserable. With their own theatre, and frequent visits to Court, they had become used to their comforts. This upheaval was a monstrous interference with their profitable, ordered lives – something they had all known, and knew how to cope with; but which they had hoped had been put away forever.

For Will Shakespeare it was particularly disturbing. Nowadays he was acting less, writing more. And how could a man write in an inn parlour, in a swaying, lurching waggon? *He* could, of course, with an inkhorn slung at his waist, his left hand clutching a candle and holding down his paper. But he cursed because it took longer to get it all down. And the turmoil in his brain was like the surge of the sea.

Nor would he pay his usual Stratford visit this summer. The King's Men were going further south, Southampton, Bath, Bristol. Here, from the infected streets of London, the memory of the quiet-flowing Avon was like the Peace of God. But he would not walk beside its banks this year. The night before they left he said, 'Matthew, have you said farewell to your mother?'

The boy looked up from his reading. 'Yes, sir.'

'Are you much grieved?'

'Yes, sir.' There was no tremor in the boy's voice when he said, 'I am afeared for her, Master Shakespeare. Her neighbours on the right are dead. Those on the left are sick unto death.'

He looked up from his writing. 'The plague?'

'Yes, master.'

He said nothing, went on writing. But he felt the boy's eyes on him. And at last the boy said, 'Sir?'

'Yes, Matthew?' His pen went on scratching.

'Sir?' A long pause. 'Could my mother travel with us? Away from the plague?'

The pen went on scratching. 'No,' said Will, gruffly for him, not looking up.

'Very well, sir.'

Still he kept his eyes on the manuscript. But he could never leave anyone thinking him churlish. He said, more gently, 'It would not be possible, Matthew. The waggons will be overcrowded as it is.'

'Yes, sir.'

It wasn't true. He knew it wasn't true. As a sharer in the Company he *could* arrange for Annette to go with them. Oh, there would be nudges, innuendos. No one would believe that Will was doing it for the sake of a lonely boy, and to save a woman's life. But he *could* take her. No one would, or could, say him nay.

No. Had she been less beautiful, had she attracted him less, even had she begged to go (which he knew she would never do) he might have taken her. But he was too busy, too involved. He would not risk again the distraction of a pair of dark eyes, the compelling attraction of a lovely woman. Desire, compassion, even kindness he must fling from him; they had been the traitors of his youth. Now he was rising forty; he must behave with the control and self-interest proper to a man. He said, 'You are a Catholic, are you not, Matthew?'

The boy looked up with a sudden fear that passed quickly. 'Yes, master.'

Will said gently, 'Then you must pray to the Virgin, boy, that she will stand between your mother and all harm.' He went on, slowly, 'I am an irreligious knave, but I fully believe such prayers will not go unanswered, Matthew.'

'No, sir.' Matthew looked at him. Will could not interpret the look. Gratitude? Affection? Disillusion? Will did not know.

The boy went back to his Ovid.

There were always a few loiterers to see them off. For some, even the plague could not destroy the magic of the theatre.

Well-known actors, looking just like ordinary human beings at eight o'clock of a grey morning, were throwing bundles on to carts; swords, pikes, crowns were everywhere; some of the hired men, even with this sparse audience, were taking extravagant, mock-tearful farewells. There was Master Burbage, in one of his sudden rages by the look of things. And Master Heminge, in charge of everything, checking long lists, drawn and anxious and absorbed. And Master Shakespeare looking after himself, with a satchel of paper, a wallet of quills, and a couple of inkhorns and a box of sand slung at his belt; also absorbed, but a thousand miles away from the fret and pother of the carts; in Venice, Cyprus, Forres.

But then, looking up, he was suddenly back to a still, airless morning in London. He hurried across, smiling, to a woman in widow's weeds.

He took her hands: 'Mistress Peyre, why have you come?'

She said, smiling, 'A widow's days are not so short I cannot spare an hour, Master Shakespeare.'

He said awkwardly, 'I will look after the boy, mistress. You need not fear.'

'Thank you,' she said.

He could still take her with them. If, when they returned to London, corruption had claimed her (even, oh most foul, while still living) could he ever forgive himself?

Yet he knew that compassion now was the most dangerous of all emotions. He said, 'I trust all will go well with you, Mistress Peyre.'

'And with you, sir.' A secret, formal movement of her right hand. He fancied she was blessing him.

He was, in all probability, condemning her to death. He bowed over her hand, kissed it, and went and leapt angrily into the covered waggon. Angry with whom? With her, with himself, with fate? He did not know.

There were benches down each side of the waggon. In the half-light, under the brown awning, he groped his way to an empty place. Now to write! Never mind the swaying and the lurching. He had things to get out of his soul – callousness, treachery, cowardice again? Weakness? Who but a weakling could condemn a woman to probable death, simply because he dare not risk her promiscuity – in the waggons, sleeping perchance by the wayside, outside adjacent bedroom doors in some distant inn? Who but a dolt would leave a woman in a plague-stricken city, rather than risk spoiling his own image of William Shakespeare, Gent? Who but a fool, he thought as the wheels began to rumble, would not have taken with him a lovely, intelligent woman like Annette Peyre? Well, it's too late now, fool. He looked back angrily through the open end of the waggon. She was still standing there – straight, brave, poised as a statue, in the death-laden street. Yet once again Will Shakespeare looked squarely at Will Shakespeare, and hated what he saw.

Furiously, he wretched open his satchel of paper. 'Why!' cried a pleased voice next to him. 'If it isn't Marie Mountjoy's lodger!'

He was down at the first halt. 'Who told *that* woman she could come?' he demanded.

Burbage looked at his old friend in surprise. It was unusual to see Will in a rage. '*I* did,' he said coolly.

'*Why?*'

'My dear Will, it was you who saddled me with the son. Had we left the mother to die in the plague, I might have found myself in loco parentis.'

The two men stared at each other, Burbage smiling, Shakespeare scowling. Will said, 'And someone to air your bed, belike, in ill-kept inns?'

Burbage nodded. 'The lady is deft with a warming pan, her son tells me.'

Will turned on his heel. Burbage, smiling, watched him go. And what Will saw was this: Mistress Fox descending, like Juno from the clouds, the steps of the covered waggon. And Matthew Peyre looking, in hurt and disbelief, and anguish, first at Mistress Fox; and then at his idol Shakespeare.

'Put out the light,' intoned a black-faced Burbage. 'And then put out the light.'

He hadn't been able to wait to black his face to play Othello. True, this was no many-sided man. Not a quick, nervous, glinting, infinitely faceted creature like Hamlet, but a soldier, a black general, carrying himself noble and assured in a white man's world. Until, one false turn, and he was tearing down a world that had become utterly incomprehensible to him.

But the rain fell remorsely. The bed in which Matthew (Desdemona) lay was becoming sodden and the people of

Guildford were sensibly at home. The inn yard was almost empty. The only spectators were in the inn galleries, and they were blue with cold. The sooner the players got to the jig and warmed everybody up a bit, they were thinking, the better.

But the play dragged on. Matthew Peyre went like a lamb to the slaughter. 'I *told* him,' whispered Will, sheltering under the stage. 'I *told* him not to sound as though he enjoyed being murdered.'

Henry Condell, miserably hunched, knees to chin, next to him, said, 'We must face it, Will. Matthew will make a pretty Rosalind, a pert Viola. But that is all. Letting him play Desdemona to the yokels was wise. It has shown his metal – or lack of it.'

'He's young, Harry. He will learn.'

Condell shook his head.

Will thought: how we hate those who first speak our unspoken fears. On their long summer's wanderings he had thought much about Matthew's future. His betrayal of the boy, as he saw it, by leaving his mother in London; the bewilderment in Matthew's face when he found that Mistress Fox was of the company; the boy's attitude to him ever since that day: courteous as always, helpful, obliging; yet as unresponsive as a broken lute string. These had made him desperately anxious to make up to the boy for his callousness; made him insist on his being given Desdemona when, even he, in his heart, knew the boy would be o'erparted.

But that was only the beginning. He had taken a woman from Holinshed's history of Malcolme Duffe, and made her wife to his Macbeth: a woman of steel and sinew, a part such as he had never before written. And he had written her for

Matthew Peyre! But if the boy was o'erparted as milk and water Desdemona, what would he make of Lady Macbeth?

No, he consoled himself, it was in the writing. Desdemona *was* milk and water. She *didn't* seem to mind being murdered, since it was Othello doing the murdering. Give Matthew a *real* part to play, and he'd be magnificent!

It was not often Will Shakespeare tried deluding himself; he never succeeded.

'Listen!' said Henry Condell.

Will Shakespeare listened, and saw what Condell meant. The play had suddenly sprung to life. Emilia was discovering that Othello had killed his wife, and she was making the heavens ring. People, hearing the commotion, were coming out into the rain to watch. She was screaming, drumming her fists on Burbage's chest. It was magnificent. Will felt shivers running down his spine. *This* was what plays were about: the creation of emotion that shrieked to very heaven.

Oh, if only it were Matthew creating this uproar. But it was of course the insufferable Nicholas Fox. He knew what was going to happen; when it came to Macbeth, the sharers were going to want Nicholas for the lady. And dare he stop them?

There was worse. Recently, in his voracious reading, he had come upon a woman of Egypt: dark, lustful, teasing, as had been that woman who, long years ago, had lifted Will Shakespeare to the stars, and flung him back to muddy earth. But this Egyptian was so much more: royal, noble, magnificent, terrible in rage, unpredictable, a woman to the very core of her being.

Already she was growing in his mind: past her prime, mature, infinitely desirable.

And Antony: the mighty warrior, but scant of breath now, the triple pillar of the world transformed – as he, Will

Shakespeare, had once been transformed, yes, he knew all about that – into a strumpet's fool.

And Egypt: where serpents dart and twist in the baking sand, and lizards flicker over ancient stones where once a princess walked. Oh, there are splendours here! He longed, he yearned, to give life again to these ancient lovers, who had lain so long beside the Nile and had not turned, once, through the dry centuries, to kiss, to touch, to smile.

But who would play Cleopatra? Could the gentle Matthew? Could even the ebullient Nicholas? And the other boys, Ned, Mark, Abraham, were growing old, already being given men's parts, voices cracked and chins stubbled. Oh, boys were an everlasting problem. They left to join the Children's Companies as soon as you got them trained. They got killed or maimed brawling with apprentices. Some couldn't stand the hard life – or their dear mothers thought they couldn't. Worst of all, they deliberately, inexorably, grew up. No. There was no point in writing a part that was beyond any boy. He was a man of the theatre. Plays were to bring in money.

There was something in North's Plutarch about Cleopatra's barge – poop of gold, purple sails, oars of silver – one of the many things at which the tinder of his imagination had flared. 'The poop was beaten gold; purple the sails, and so perfumed that... ' No. Careful he might be, as much of time as of money. Man of the theatre he might be, as fascinated by its still unfolding possibilities as a child by a chest of toys; but he was going to write about his Cleopatra first, and then find someone to play her. He *had* to. Matthew could do it, with Will's training, and a few years of growth. It was wonderful how even one year could change a boy. There, crouched knees to chin, under a dripping stage on which the first performance of Othello was dragging to a longed-for end, he admitted to himself a decision that his creative mind had reached weeks ago.

Yet these thoughts were leading inevitably to a quarrel, and Will dreaded quarrels. To Dick Burbage, even more than most of his contemporaries, they were as much part of life as the itch or the belly ache – and a good deal more enjoyable. But they upset Will for days.

It began pleasantly enough. The rain cleared towards sunset, and shafts of yellow light struck from the west across the glittering countryside. Will Shakespeare walked in a muddy lane; sad, as he was always sad, when sunset flared so hopefully over a weeping day like – a brief candle? Good. He made a mental note.

He heard footsteps. An arm fell about his shoulders. A grave voice said, 'Will. A word.'

Will looked. 'Why, Dick. What now?' He was always pleased to see Burbage.

But Burbage was sounding embarrassed. 'Will, we need a new play.'

Will looked suddenly weary. 'A new play? Listen, Dick. We've been on tour for months. I've given you *Measure for Measure, All's Well, Othello*. I'm doing *Macbeth* to please the King. What more do you want?'

'A new comedy, Will. Another *As You Like It*. Tastes are changing. *Othello* would have been wonderful a few years ago. Now – oh, it's a magnificent part – but people have grown smaller, Will. They cannot tolerate giants.'

And he had been thinking of creating two of the greatest giants of them all! He said, 'Comedy, Dick? Nay, I am too old for comedy.' He smiled wryly. ''Tis a stuff will not endure.'

Burbage was not amused. 'But we *need* comedy.'

'I have given you a dozen comedies.'

'And now we need another,' Dick said coolly. 'Something for these boys to work on. They're good, I admit it; but limited. They need the pert, gay parts only you can write for them. The Rosalinds, the Violas.'

Will was silent. Then he said, 'If you *must* know, Dick, my mind is seized with a new play. And it is *not* a comedy. About a lusting gipsy, a right royal queen, a tempestuous whore; all in the same tawny woman's hide.'

The sun had gone, now. The muddy lane was grey, the sky was grey, the earth was grey and heavy. But no heavier than Burbage's voice. 'And who will play this part?'

'Matthew Peyre.'

'Matthew Peyre! A piping child.'

'He will not long be a piping child. He will be a great actor, Dick.'

'No. Competent, good even, a pert wench in breeches. But that's all.' Yet he could not resist the question that was always uppermost in a leading actor's mind. 'What would be my part?'

'The Roman, Mark Antony. But short of wind, now. Grown foolish. In thrall to the gipsy, Cleopatra, Queen of Egypt.'

'It does not sound inviting.'

'It will be, Dick. The triple pillar of the world. Swaggering, magnificent, rotten. Oh, it could be a tremendous afternoon for groundlings.'

Burbage was silent. Swaggering, magnificent, rotten? It was the sort of thing Will could do passing well. And so could he, Burbage, by God! But an actor manager had to look facts in the face. It was all very well for these playwriters. They were only concerned with one side of the business. (Though here he knew in his heart he was unfair to Will. Will was concerned with *every* aspect of the theatre.

And a man with a keener sense of business you would never find.) But all he said *was* true, he reminded himself. Tastes *were* changing. England was different now from the England of ten years ago as this fearful, foolish James was different from great Elizabeth. All men wanted now was comfort, triviality. (The King hunting, the Queen prancing around in Ben's ridiculous masques, the whole country given over to lewdness and sloth. Only Master Caretaker Cecil crouched, unsleeping, like a spider, at the centre of the tattered web.)

And they *hadn't* any boy capable of a real woman's part. Not the sort of part Will was dreaming of anyway. Nor were they likely to have, with the Children's Companies so popular. Dick Burbage, far from home, in a sodden corner of rural England, felt suddenly very sorry for himself. The commercial theatre, he decided, was doomed. The plague, the Queen's masques, the Children's Companies, a king who never kept awake beyond the first act, playwriters who wrote only to please themselves – all these must eventually make it too difficult to carry on. He said, 'Will, we want comedy. I'm telling you.' His voice was cold. 'We haven't the boys for tragedy.'

'Pert wenches in breeches!' Will's voice was even colder. 'My God, Dick, have you forgotten the voyages of discovery we were to have taken together? That we *did* take together. Have you forgotten *Hamlet, Richard the Second?* You said then that you as an actor, I as playwriter, were treading on shores more strange than the Indies. You said there were even further, mistier realms you felt were in your grasp – if only – I would be your guide. And now all you want is comedy.' Just, he thought bitterly, as Henslowe had wanted comedy all those years ago, as Kempe had wanted comedy. But he'd thought better of Richard Burbage.

'Yes I do want comedy. And I know what I'm talking about. I'm responsible for a Company. And I'm responsible to the King. Do you think *that* jackanapes wants high tragedy after a day's hunting?'

Will said, 'God's teeth, Dick, I don't care what the jackanapes wants. He'll have his *Macbeth*. Then he can have my gipsy.' He saw the anger in Burbage's eye. 'Dick, I've always written what the Company wanted – except *Hamlet*, and *that* paid well – but I *must* write Cleopatra. She's taken possession of my mind. If I *don't* write her, I'll go mad. Do you understand that?'

'No.' He added sulkily, 'It's not like you to be disloyal, Will.'

'Disloyal?' Will walked in silence. No other reproach could have hurt as much. Oh, he had been disloyal in his time; but only when possessed and driven by a demon of lust. For the rest, he had always been the most loyal of companions. He knew it. They knew it. He said quietly, 'I must ask you to take back that word, Dick.'

'I take back nothing.'

Candles burned now in the windows of scattered hovels. Their yellow light made the melancholy evening yet more dreary. But even these tumbledown dwellings were home, places where peace and love could be, havens that the homeless wanderer could never know. Will said, 'In that case, Dick, I shall return to Stratford. God knows my wife, my daughters have need of me.'

The two men stopped, turned and faced each other. Will said gravely, 'I can no longer write to order, Dick. Now I must write what I *must* write. There are things here – ' Lightly he touched his breast.

Dick Burbage was silent. In his heart he sympathised with everything Will was saying. Yet, while this devil anger rode his back, to have admitted it would have choked him.

Will said, 'And the spring of laughter in a man's heart does not bubble for ever, alas.'

Burbage was still silent. Together they began walking once more; but slowly, like men who fear to reach their journey's end before all has been settled between them.

Will said, 'But disloyal I have never been, Dick, except' – and now it was as though he spoke only to Will Shakespeare – 'except to the one who all her life has been loyalty itself.'

'Four shillings and sixpence,' said John Heminge, dumpish. 'And the costumes soaked.'

'And my ruff stained with this damned black,' said Burbage. He still sounded aggrieved, unfriendly. 'It's the last time I play your Moor in an inn yard, Will.'

They were sitting in one of the waggons. It was always wiser not to count the takings in the inn. And it was a foul hostelry, anyway. The fastidious Will, especially, found the sweet straw of the waggon better than the inn parlour, with its stink of ale and sweat and dogs and vomit; even though the day's rain still trickled from the canvas hood, and the autumn night was chill, and the damp seemed to mount into their bones from the sodden grass.

It had been a miserable season. The hot, wet summer in which, in London, the plague had flourished like plants in a hothouse, had come near to ruining the King's Men. Rain had cancelled performances, decimated audiences, ruined costumes, and brought a fine crop of rheums to the players. Roads were mired, often impassable. Shoulders were raw from heaving waggons out of ruts. And now Will's new piece, of which Burbage had thought so highly, had scarce brought in enough for a night's drinking. 'It isn't worth it,' said Heminge. 'We should be better in London, rehearsing new plays, mending costumes.'

'And catching plague,' said Augustine Phillips drily.

Matthew Peyre, sitting at Will's feet, shivered. Will put a hand on his shoulder. 'Do not be fearful, Matthew.'

The boy gave him a troubled look. 'They say the plague – they say the dead outnumber the living in London. They say –' He fell silent, looking scared.

'What do they say, Matthew?' It was better to bring it into the open.

'They say the living are now too few to bury the dead. There are great mountains of corpses in the Fleet ditch. And the rats are grown big as dogs, and run like a grey carpet in the streets.'

The stuff of a nightmare! And she, his mother, was in this grey death-land! He said, 'There are always these tales, boy, in the country. I am certain that by now the plague will have ebbed.'

But he wasn't certain. And even if he had been, who could say that Annette Peyre would still be left on that littered shore?

And if she were not? What then? Would he feel the gentle melancholy one feels for a summer's evening gone, sorrow for a lovely woman he had called a friend, or – anguish for a love who would never, now, lie in his arms? Whichever he felt, he knew he would also know that it was he who had condemned her to death, he who had orphaned Matthew. He knew that for himself, from himself, there would be no forgiveness.

One other thing he knew. He would bring the boy up as his own. There would be holidays at Stratford, showing the boy the splendours of New Place, bowling, archery. Why, he might even give the boy his name. To a man with two daughters and a dead son, a Grant of Arms was but a hollow crown. But – Matthew Shakespeare, Gentleman, living in New Place, the proud Shakespeare motto *Non Sans Droict* over the door; himself begetting sons – why, the name of Shakespeare could well outlive the Lucys and the Cloptons! (But what would Anne say, this stranger sitting where Hamnet should have sat, sleeping in the bed Hamnet had exchanged for a bed of earth? He, who saw so deep into the hearts of princesses, could never be quite sure what his wife would say.)

And the theatre. He would make the boy a great actor, a worthy successor to Richard Burbage. When his voice had cracked, and he had lost the suppleness of youth and put on the stature of a man, then it would be *he* who would cry, 'My kingdom for a horse,' 'It is the cause, my soul,' 'I am dying, Egypt, dying.' Yes, even if Cleopatra *was* beyond the youth, Antony would not be beyond the man.

He put an arm round the boy's shoulders, smiled down at him with deep compassion. 'Sing to us, Matthew.'

The boy fetched his lute. 'What shall I sing, masters?'

'*Come away, death,*' said Heminge lugubriously.

'That is a sad song! I – would not sing a sad song, tonight.'

'Fool!' Will said angrily to Heminge. 'Let us have *Hold thy peace, thou knave.* And *Jolly Robin*, Matthew.'

The boy played, and sang. Rain water still dripped from the awning. Outside, the cattle grazed. Their stampings, and snufflings, and the sickle-like noise of their cropping only added to the melancholy of the country evening. 'Hey, Robin, jolly Robin, Tell me how thy lady does', sang the boy, his voice sweet and young and sad, the notes of the lute plangent on the quiet air. The King's Men listened. Normally they would have been roaring away by now. They loved singing together as they loved working together. But tonight they were too much in the dumps.

And saddest of them all was the sweet singer.

He was suffering desperately from homesickness: that torment of the soul that forces on our view pictures of happy, far-off things, of quiet days of peace and love, of dear havens in an uncaring world. Last night he had dreamed that his mother stood before him, and he had known the ineffable peace that comes only, alas, in dreams. And then she had lifted her widow's veil and he, screaming himself into wakefulness, had seen – a skull. (But what was death, even, compared with the thought that, he being absent, his mother might be flung, *unshriven*, into the common grave, to burn in the Pit through all eternity with adulterers and unconverted Jews?)

And he had played Desdemona ill, he knew it. After the play no one had met his eye, no one had clapped him on the back and said, 'Well done, Matthew!' Not even Master Shakespeare. After that sodden bed he was chilled to the marrow. The only comfort in the whole world was Master Shakespeare's arm about his shoulders, and even that made him sad because this was how he and his father had often sat, and Master Shakespeare was not he and his father, Master Shakespeare had left Mother to die in London, a fact that Matthew had tried very hard to understand and could not.

Oh, but he was tired, what should he sing now? A sleepy tune. Then, if he yawned, they would but think – That new song of his master's: *Take, O take those lips away.* He began to sing. His voice faded, he shook himself. 'That so sweetly... ' His head drooped over his instrument. Shakespeare leaned down, and gently took the lute. Looking up, he found Burbage's eyes on him. And the eyes were friendly. The sudden storm had passed. Burbage said quietly, ' "If thou dost nod, thou break'st thy instrument." ' Will smiled. ' "I'll take it from thee; and, good boy, good night." ' Oh, it was good, on a wet English evening, after the disaster of Othello, to be back with honest Dick Burbage in Brutus' tent, in a camp near Sardis. To have this afternoon's wounds healed by Dick's reminder of that nobler quarrel, playing which (he Cassius; Dick, Brutus) had put an extra dimension to their friendship, almost like the ritual mingling of blood – this was comfort indeed.

# CHAPTER 8

## SOME ACHIEVE GREATNESS...

They gave up. The weather had beaten them. The costumes, always heavy, were like lead now since they were never dry. The men were tired, weakened by colds and chills. An English summer had reduced the King's Men from the world's most successful theatre company to a ragged, dispirited band of strolling players.

Oh, they would recover. Once let them get back to the Globe, dry themselves out, have a few days rest, and they would be their own men again. And the plague must be abating by now. It seldom lasted into the winter.

So they turned for home. Matthew Peyre was delighted – and terrified. What would he find? The house, as he had always known it, with smoke in the chimney, the diamond panes shining, a smiling mother holding open the door? Or the windows grey with dirt, the door barred, no one knowing or caring how death had taken this one woman out of thirty thousand? No one knowing whether the Church had given her that Extreme Unction without which her soul might wander forever, lost, among the byways of eternity. He had to know what awaited him. He was filled with a brittle, nervous, restless, intensity; he could not sit still; he was out on the road beside the waggons, walking, running the long miles to London. In his mood he could have played Emilia with as much intensity as Nicholas Fox. It would have done him good. But there was no acting. They were concentrating all their energies on getting back to the Globe.

But the Globe was thirty miles away. Thirty miles, with winter snapping at the heels of summer, the horses jaded, the waggons in disrepair, the men weary and irritable! Thirty miles! It was as far as Babylon.

It was quiet, friendly Augustine Phillips who (not for the first time) spoke words of comfort in a dire situation. 'Let us make for my house at Mortlake, gentlemen. It is on our way. We can encamp nearby, and use my house to restore ourselves for the journey into London.'

A notable suggestion! They set off in better heart. But when they reached Mortlake, Mistress Phillips came running, and embraced her husband with such tears and fervour as must have greeted Lazarus. 'Gus, I thought you dead. There have been men here, asking, demanding, almost every day. Asking news, for *they* had none. They thought, *I* thought in the end, you had all died of plague, or cut throats.'

Gently, smiling, he unwound her arms, kissed her nose, her eyes, her hair. 'What men, my love?'

The others crowded round, anxious. They might be the King's Men now. But they had all been rogues and vagabonds long enough to fear this sort of news. And now Mistress Phillips was groping in the pocket of her kirtle, pulling out a letter that bore a great red seal. 'One of the men left this. Some days since.' Phillips took it, read the address, handed it to Burbage.

Burbage broke the seal, read. And, reading, looked even more tired and dishevelled. 'Gentlemen, we are commanded to Wilton House. The Court lodges there. King James has a whim to see Master Shakespeare's *As You Like It*. His eyes rested on Will. They said, plainly: 'What did I tell you, my friend?'

No storm-tossed mariner had longed for harbour more than they had longed for the Globe. For days it had been in their thoughts, their conversations, their dreams. It had shone like a beacon. And now, when they were within a day's journey of it, they were suddenly jerked back – to Wilton. 'Where in God's name *is* Wilton House?' grumbled Condell.

'Near Salisbury,' said Will shortly.

Salisbury! They had spent a month travelling from there. 'God's teeth,' said Condell. 'I had as lief take my hat round the villages with a dancing bear as be a King's Man.'

But they were not the King's Men for nothing. Already astute minds were turning to deal with work they knew best. 'John, have we the plot of *As You Like It?*' 'Yes.' 'Thank God for that. We'll rehearse this evening, when we've cleaned up. Will, you'll be guider? Now what about Celia? Abraham, I think, and pray God he do not croak. And Nicholas Fox for Rosalind. Mark for Audrey. Will – forgive me, old friend – but I do not think your Matthew is ripe yet to play before the King.'

'As you wish,' said Will, sounding sulky. (Sweet Will, sulky! It was unheard of.) But Will knew Burbage was right. Something had happened to Matthew. Before this tour, and the long anxiety about his mother, he would have played elegantly before the whole Court. But now – nervous, stretched, feverish – he was incalculable. He was not, both men knew instinctively, to be trusted.

Burbage shot his friend a quick look. But there wasn't time to waste on Will's precious feelings. He swung round to

Condell. 'Harry, send one of the hired men to the smith with that lead horse. Tom, see what you can do with that axle.' And then, with remembered courtesy, and a deep bow, 'Mistress Phillips, you shall have your husband this evening. I would not keep so good a friend from such delights.'

She laughed, the pretty creature. 'Sirs, you are all welcome. Master Burbage, sir. Master Shakespeare. Come with me. The maids shall prepare baths for you.'

Two steaming baths stood side by side in the stone-flagged kitchen. Beside each stood a ewer of hot, a ewer of cold, water. On the former were folded hot towels. The maids had withdrawn, giggling. All around were homely things they had not seen since their travels began: rolling pins, jars of spice, bundles of herbs, a fire in the great range, strings of onions, kettles, pans; all that paraphernalia of living from which the soldier, the scholar, the strolling player is cut off; woman's timeless, unchanging domain in which, more than in the boudoir, she casts her spells and mixes her potions. Will thought wistfully of Anne's great kitchen in New Place, Dick of his wife, eight children at her skirts (pray God the plague had not touched the pretty knaves) in Halliwell Street.

But Will did not think of Anne for long. He had seen nothing as inviting as that bath since, a boy, he had gazed into summer-drowsy Avon, knowing that in a moment he would plunge from the friendliness of sunlight to the rough embrace of this sparkling, fishy element, he would become fish, diving, twisting, gasping, rejoicing.

He was off with his doublet, out of his shoes, hose, breeches, in! It was wonderful. A great splash as Burbage flopped into the other bath. They splashed, they sang, they poured in more water, now hot, now cold; water running down hair and nose and beard, down arms and chest. Thank

God for water when it is not rain, seeping through the canvas of a covered waggon.

For ten minutes in that kitchen in Mortlake, London's greatest actor, and a well known playwriter, were boys again. Fears, quarrels, weariness, overwhelming success all washed away by two tubs of bath water. Then Burbage said, 'Who lives at Wilton House?'

'My Lord of Pembroke. And his mother, the Dowager Countess. A most illustrious and learned lady, Dick. A generous patron, it is said.' He grinned. 'Had we not the King's patronage, we might have turned for Wilton more eagerly.'

'Aye.' But Dick's mind was on another tack. 'The Earl of Pembroke? He that was friend to Southampton?'

'He that was friend to Southampton,' Will said in a flat voice. And still is, he thought. And suddenly all the fears were back. For Southampton would be at Court.

Throughout that dying summer, they had set off with the morning sun in their faces, its Judas kiss on their cheeks before its heat called up the thunder that drenched each afternoon.

But today Matthew suddenly noticed that they were travelling with the sun behind them. And his happiness changed to alarm.

Happiness, because they were at Mortlake, nearly home. Alarm, because they were travelling west when they should have been going east.

There had been much talk last night of being summoned to Court. But he had not paid too much attention. Court was London, so what did it matter?

But now – every plod of the horses, every turn of the wheels was taking him away from the place where he would be.

He groped and floundered over piles of legs and water casks and pikes, dropped down from his waggon, ran and pulled himself up into the waggon where the sharers travelled in the greater luxury of wooden benches and a cask of canary and a lantern for Master Shakespeare's writing. 'Master Shakespeare, sir. Where are we going?' Fear gave his voice an impertinent edge.

Will looked up. The irritations and frustrations that this hot summer travel had engendered, had affected even the gentle Shakespeare. Interruptions, discomfort, the endless chattering of Mistress Fox... How, he had begun to ask himself, did they expect him to write anything useful when he *never* had more than ten minutes' uninterrupted writing. Ten minutes! You couldn't get into the skin of a medieval Scottish thane's lady, in ten minutes! 'I heard the owl scream and the crickets cry.' And now: 'Master Shakespeare, sir. Where are we going?'

'There's one did laugh in 's sleep, and one – ' Damn! Had no one told the boy? Did they have to leave everything to him, leaving him to write *Macbeth* in ten minute snatches? He was too good-natured, that was his trouble. If he snapped at all who came near, like an ill-tempered cur, they would soon leave him alone, and the King's Men would have more plays, and better plays, plays with some depth to them, whether they wanted them or not; not things botched up in brief intervals when no one wanted him for anything else.

'Master Shakespeare, sir, where are we going?'

The boy's peremptory tone added to his annoyance. He said, shortly, 'We are summoned to Court.'

Matthew said sharply, 'I know that. But Court is London, sir.'

'It is *not*. It is where the King is. And the King is at Wilton House, near Salisbury.'

It was the first time Will had ever snapped at the boy. Almost the first time he had snapped at anybody. They both looked angry: two people who, liking and respecting each other, yet know that they are both being swept away, against their wills, by a single wave of irritation.

Will made a great effort. He said gently, 'We shall play before the King. It is a great honour.'

'I do not *want* to play before the King. I want to be at home.' He stamped his foot, wept. Desdemona, the grave young actor, the composed young gentleman, all forgotten in the April storms of childhood. It was the first time Will had seen the child that still lingered in the boy. He was irritated, yet above all pitying. 'Patience, boy. Think, what you will have to tell your mother. That you met my Lord of Pembroke, perhaps the King himself.'

'I do not *want* to meet the King. I *hate* him.'

Will said tartly, 'The world, Master Peyre, does not care a green fig what you want, and never will. And the sooner you learn that the easier it will be for you.'

The hot, angry eyes glared at him through the tears. So now he hated Will as much as he hated the King. Will smiled at him. 'Anyway,' Matthew said sulkily, 'my mother is dead.'

It was Will's turn to be angry. 'You must not say that. You must not even think it.'

Matthew stared at him. And it was as though the hate and anger had dried the tears. 'My mother is dead.' Still that level gaze. 'And you left her to die.'

'Oh God,' said Will hopelessly. 'So that's what you think.'

The boy lowered his gaze. He sat for a long time staring at his finger running up and down, up and down, the edge of the wooden form. Then he sighed. Will was surprised that so small a body could produce so great a sigh. He looked up, still truculent. 'I am sorry, Master Shakespeare. I should not have spoken thus.'

'You should, if it is what you believe, Matthew.'

His finger began again its tracing. 'I was discourteous, sir.'

'Good.' He felt a great surge of warmth. 'Then it is forgotten. And draw me a cup of canary.' He wanted to relive this incident. Matthew had come out of it well, he thought. And he? Could he have helped the boy more, could he have had more care for the brittleness of youth? But there was no time for the luxury of thought. He sighed. Where had he been? 'There's one laughed – did laugh – in 's sleep, and another – and one – ' Damn! Now his quill was blunted. He groped for his pen knife, trimmed the point, got ink on his fingers, something that always hurt his fastidious nature. Now. 'And one cried "Murder".' He read it through. Yes, it would serve. 'Really,' cried Mistress Fox solicitously, 'I vow you will wear your brains out, Master Shakespeare, all this writing.'

The Court had been at Wilton for months now.

And it seemed like years.

Things were not so bad when the King could go hunting. It kept him happy all day, and he came back too tired to do anything but eat and drink himself into an early bed.

But now the weather was closing in. More and more did mist, fogs, east winds drive the royal huntsman back to the comfort of Wilton. And then things were desperate indeed. Wilton House seemed like an ant heap. In addition to the Pembroke family and their many retainers there were now courtiers, Members of the Privy Council, Gentlemen of the Table, the Privy Chamber, the Bedchamber, and the Bath, secretaries, greater servants, lesser servants, cooks, scullions, grooms, bear wardens, mastiff wardens, falconers, musicians, jesters – all with one duty in life: to save the King from the tediousness of it.

There was Master Inigo Jones to design the Queen's masques, and Master Ben Jonson to write them. There was a small army of stage hands to carry out Master Jones' ideas. There were leeches, barbers, apothecaries. And now, God ha' mercy, here came the players, drawing their great baggage train wearily through the park like a defeated army.

The privies were overflowing. Behind the house, the piles of bones and grease and rotting fruit grew daily higher. Flies swarmed, too busy to waste time on hibernation. Wasps, drunk with rotted plums, half-paralysed with cold, dozed balefully on chairs, in beds, in clothing.

The noble and gracious house stayed noble and gracious. But, to the more fastidious, there was already a whiff of corruption. One day even the King was going to notice it – and depart in dudgeon. And for Mary, Dowager Countess of Pembroke, that day could not come a moment too soon.

She was a huge, ebullient woman, considerably larger than life. Her features were rough hewn. When she laughed, it was like a gale tearing through a forest. With her, laughter was not a flicker of eyes and mouth. It took over her whole being. When she stormed, lightning and thunder came together; terrible, devastating, but over in a moment. Her generosity and hospitality were like herself, ample and vast. A woman, one would have said, to spend her days in hunting, her nights in dicing and cards. And one would have been wrong. Mary Herbert, Countess of Pembroke, was a scholar and a great lady, who delighted above all things in witty and ingeniose persons. She even, alone among women, wrote herself.

What she thought of this Scotsman and his followers no one would ever know. She would only have confided in one of her peers. And in this Court, tinctured already with decay, she had no peer. Her brother, Sir Philip Sidney, had been one of the proudest jewels in Gloriana's crown. The sister of such a one did not open her heart to the new men.

But, she knew, one of the old Queen's men was already toiling up to the back entrance of Wilton. Another of Gloriana's bright jewels. He was the one person in all this glittering, frenetic throng she was interested in. She called one of her ladies. 'Send to the players. Say that I would speak with Master Shakespeare as soon as he has eaten and prepared himself.'

She had seen many of the plays at Court, even at the public theatres. And she believed that this common play-writer understood more of what it meant to be a human being than any man who had ever lived; that his words awakened feelings that had lain deep in men's hearts from the beginning.

She remembered what had been told her about him. A countryman, not even – though this sounded quite unbelievable – not even a University man. A genial fellow, a good companion.

The door of her privy chamber opened. Her steward came in. 'The man Shakespeare, my lady.'

She was furious. 'Show *Master* Shakespeare in,' she said. 'And next time announce him properly, Master Steward, or by Heaven – '

The steward bowed himself out, trembling. Gentle though she was, one crossed the Countess at one's peril.

Yes, off the stage, Master Shakespeare looked like a countryman. Sturdy, his colouring warm, fresh complexioned. Clothes sober and good, beard neatly trimmed. (One did not find Will Shakespeare looking as though he had been on tour for six months.) A gentle mouth. Eyes and lips that looked as though they laughed often, though at the moment a little wary, what did a Countess want with a strolling player, even one who was also Groom of the Chamber to his most Christian Majesty?

And how he was bowing. She smiled. He was no fool, this man. Not the courtier's bow, mincing, waving, posturing, such as she had seen him perform so exquisitely on the stage, but an honest, respectful, countryman's bow. Her smile deepened. She held out her hand to be kissed. 'Master Shakespeare, you are most welcome to Wilton House.'

Her voice was liquid, lilting, somewhat deep for a woman's. It held a great warmth. He, to whom the speaking of words was part of the world's music, was entranced. He kissed her hand. 'I will convey your ladyship's gracious message to my fellows.'

'I did not mean your fellows; though they are of course most welcome, they were bidden here by the King. I meant you, Master Shakespeare.' Her smile was as warm and welcoming as her voice.

He bowed again, silent. She said, sadly now, 'How my brother would have welcomed the creator of *Hamlet* to his house.'

He was still silent. ' "The glass of fashion, and the mould of form. The courtier's, soldier's, scholar's, eye, tongue, sword – " ' she said softly. 'Do not tell me you had not my brother in mind when you wrote that, sir.'

It was a strange thing, he thought, how everyone knew just whom he had in mind when he created Hamlet.

Southampton, Essex, Sidney? Could no one give him the credit for creating Hamlet out of his own imagination, out of his own suffering soul, out of a misty tale of the Lord Amleth, who feigned madness in the morning of the world?

But he knew well how to play the courtier. Besides, there was already a great bond of affection and respect between this illustrious woman and himself. Like had already called to like, above the addled heads of England's Court. He said gravely, 'Your brother was flesh and blood, my lady. A true man. Mine – a creature of shadows.'

'Who will live, sir, when the stone that bears the name of Philip Sidney has fallen into dust.'

He was outraged. 'Madam! These are but trifles for an afternoon.'

She sat looking at him thoughtfully. '*Are* they, Master Shakespeare? *I* do not think so.' She smiled again, that smile that was like autumn sunlight. 'But now you must rest, sir. I hear you are to give us *As You Like It*. We will talk again, when you are refreshed.' She inclined her head. At a signal he had not seen the steward had reappeared, and bowed him out with an almost Oriental obsequiousness. Her ladyship watched her servant with a tight, thin smile.

Will did not see the bones in the yard, the buzzing clouds of flies. He saw only the beauty of great chambers, of tapestries, of noble staircases. One day, a strolling player, whose home was a lurching waggon; the next, Master Shakespeare once more, in a room high in a tower, with a warm bed, with a desk, ink, sand, books, with flowers scenting the room from a mullioned window embrasure. Master Shakespeare, under the same roof as his king. Master Shakespeare surrounded by the beauty and order that he loved, strolling with his friend the Countess in the dusk of a winter's afternoon.

They walked in a formal garden; they walked, as it were, in a forest whose trees were mellow stone, whose leaves were the traceries of windows, whose rides were of stone and gravel, whose undergrowth was the tangle of last summer's flowers. She wore a furred cloak and hood, he a furred gown of rich quality. Windows glowed softly with candlelight. From far away drifted the sound of a lute, and viols. The house waited: warm, filled with yellow light, ready for another evening of music and dancing.

The Will Shakespeare of only a few years ago would have been thinking: this woman beside me is a countess; I have come a long way from the shop in Henley Street, the cottage in Chapel Lane.

Not any more. Although he still had a high respect for rank, it had not taken him long to learn that earls could be at least as foolish and dangerous as the next man; that what was important about this woman was not her title but her character and the quality of her mind; and the fact that she, a woman, had overcome both convention and the limitations of the female intellect in order to become a writer herself.

She said, 'And how far have you travelled to give this king his *As You Like It?*'

'From Mortlake, my lady. About six days' journey.'

'And he will be asleep and snoring in the first act. Still, kings must be served.'

'Yes, my lady.'

They walked in silence. Then she said, 'What thought you of Elizabeth Tudor?'

'She terrified me.'

Her laughter rang out among the echoing stones. Rooks, just settling for the night, scattered in angry protest. 'She terrified us all, Master Shakespeare. Yet, she was kind. When

I was but fourteen she sent for me to Court, promising to have a special care of me – *and* kept her promise.' She was silent for a long time. Then she said: 'But this new man, he frights nobody – except it be a poor hare or a witch or two. Yet' – she turned and looked at him – 'he is a learned fellow, and his Queen a clever woman, who only *pretends* to think of nothing but posturing in one of Ben's masques.'

'Is Master Jonson at Wilton, my lady?'

'He is. *And* Master Inigo Jones. Lord, how those two jar together!'

And now, the question he *had* to ask: 'And the Earl of Southampton?'

'Yes. Oh, of course, your patron. Yes, he and his wife are here. But I warn you, he's in an ill humour. Did you know he had been visiting at the Tower again?'

'No?' This was news indeed.

'Sent there to mend his manners. He quarrelled with Lord Grey – in the Queen's private drawing-room, before the Queen.' She peered at him round the hood of her cloak. 'It is a pity, Master Shakespeare, that more young men are not given such a sharp lesson in manners. It would do them all the good in the world.'

Yes, he thought. One would expect the sister of Philip Sidney to champion good manners. But now she was saying, 'Sir, you must forgive my forwardness in asking, but – when are you going to write another *Hamlet*?'

He said, 'You mean – tragedy?'

'Yes. Oh, your comedies are exquisite. But – if you will forgive me – the man who wrote *Hamlet* could open windows on to our very souls. I feel, sir, that – again forgive me – you can see *deeper* than any mortal man has seen before.'

He laughed, really amused. 'Madam, I am Will Shakespeare, a Warwickshire poet. I devise entertainments to fill an afternoon for the groundlings. "Pleasant trifles", the old Queen rightly called them. I am no sage, no philosopher. And yet' – and now, suddenly, the laughter had gone. He was intensely serious – 'and yet, recently, I have felt – '

He was silent. They had stopped walking. Now they turned and faced each other in the darkening day. 'Yes, Master Shakespeare?' she said gently.

He did not finish. Instead: 'Lady Pembroke, I have had unbelievable success. Because I have written what was needed. What the Company needed. What the audience liked. But *I* wanted to be a poet. And what poetry did I write? Two poems, a few sonnets. And for the rest, greed, good nature, love of the theatre, kept me writing plays. And now – next year, Lady Pembroke, I shall be forty; and nothing achieved.'

'I would not agree,' she said drily, 'that you have achieved nothing.'

He did not seem to hear her. He was too busy with his own thoughts. 'They want only comedy,' he said. 'They say it will please the King, the people. But I am beginning to feel, Lady Pembroke, that the time has come for me to please myself. When a man reaches forty, there is but little time.'

She was smiling. How young he seemed, this poet who saw so deep into the heart of things. Yet he was only a few years younger than herself. She said, 'And what would you write?'

'Earth-shaking tragedy,' he said simply. And was astonished to hear himself say the words. It was as though they came from somewhere outside him.

She nodded, with deep satisfaction. 'This is what you must do.'

Oh, how wonderful it was to think aloud before this understanding woman, to find that Sir Philip Sidney's illustrious sister agreed with him as to what he should do. But he said, doubtfully, 'And yet, my fellows; I must serve them. And the taste is all for comedy.'

'*You* can form taste, sir.'

'I?' He looked at her in amazement. And yet it seemed that she was speaking things he had already known in his soul. Perhaps this growing sense of power, of greatness even, was not the illusion his modest nature had assumed it to be. Perhaps, given better conditions, his Othello would prove to have some of the cataract-like force he imagined. Perhaps he *had* been right to let himself be carried away by the evil Macbeth, in what was to have been a tale of Banquo. Perhaps he *was* right to prefer his tawny-fronted gipsy to another Rosalind. But it wasn't going to please the others. Even Burbage was no longer on his side.

He looked at the Countess, standing there smiling at him in the gloom. Very reverently he kissed her hand. Perhaps, he thought, the true patron is the one who encourages an author to write what he knows in his heart he should write, who supplies strength of will and courage.

His gesture seemed to move her deeply. She began to speak again. 'If you write what others want you to write, you will – have greatness thrust upon you. If you write to please yourself, you will achieve greatness.'

The words had a familiar ring. Marry, she was quoting his Malvolio. He was flattered. She said, 'And generations unborn will pay you homage.'

How could this be, with ephemera like plays? You took good care *not* to publish plays; otherwise every company in

England would be acting them. Still, it was pleasant to be told these things.

She said, eagerly, 'Tell me what you will write.'

'There is a tale in Plutarch, of Mark Antony, and his meeting with Cleopatra, of Egypt, and his jars with Octavius. A tale of ageing lovers, against the background of a world in flames.'

'And is already written, Master Shakespeare,' she said gaily.

'By whom?' He had heard of no play about Cleopatra. And few plays were put on in London without the knowledge of the King's Men.

'By myself.' Her laughter rang out in the winter's dusk. 'Come, I will show you.' Swiftly, for such a heavy woman, she was across the garden, in at a side door, the cold, empty night air suddenly changed for the fetid air of the house. Along a corridor she led him, to a great double door guarded by two servants. At sight of the Countess the doors were flung open. She swept through, turned impatiently to lay her fingers on Will's arm. Then, together, watched by all eyes, they crossed the great chamber, and gathering an escort of the Countess' ladies as they went, entered her private drawing-room.

The door was closed behind them.

For a moment there was silence in the great chamber. It did not last long. Too many in that room knew the prominent actor who had just been so honoured by the Dowager Countess. The Earls of Southampton and Pembroke, poised in elegant conversation, looked at each other with delicate raised eyebrows. 'Was that not Shakespeare, the actor, with my mother?' said Pembroke.

'Indeed, yes. You should chide her for the company she keeps, William,' drawled Southampton.

'Perchance the little man seeks a new patron,' Pembroke suggested, smiling.

'Well, he has lost his first, by God,' said Southampton peevishly.

They were not the only ones staring at that closed door. 'God's blood,' cried a man with a face of red sandstone. 'There goes my Lord Player, worming his way in as usual. Dedications to the Lord Southampton, a family motto, "Not Without Mustard" or some such nonsense, and now – escorting my lady into her chamber as to the manner born. That man, Inigo, writes sprawling, undisciplined plays – and the world falls down at his feet. While I – a craftsman, Inigo, a creator of *form* – go unremarked.'

'Peace, Ben, you will bring on an apoplexy.' But Master Inigo Jones also looked at the closed door with interest. So that had been William Shakespeare: the man who used *words* to paint a scene withal, rather than Master Inigo's inventive devices and contrivances. He rather hoped Shakespeare was not staying long at Wilton.

Yet even he, Ben, and Southampton between them could not have devised for him the misfortunes that actually befell.

# CHAPTER 9

## NOW O'ER THE ONE HALF-WORLD NATURE
### SEEMS DEAD

Wilton House slept.

Under that wide roof scullions lay in their grease, curled up in the warmth of the kitchen. Courtiers lay in smocked linen, in lavender-scented sheets. Mastiffs twitched by the fire, as they dreamed of tearing a bear's entrails. Bears snuffled in their cages, dreaming of far Caucasian forests. Fleas and rats danced, scurried, gorged, too busy for sleep. In the grounds, the King's Men (all except William Shakespeare, Gent.) stirred and moaned and snored as they sought comfort in their cold waggons.

Not everyone slept. My Lords Pembroke and Grey were still at dice. And if even one of my lords was awake, then a dozen servants must be awake also, lest my lord should demand a glass of wine, another log on the fire, fresh candles, music, a maid to sleep withal; and, finally, to fill the warming pan, escort him with candles, search the bed for poisoned daggers and intruders, undress him, tuck him in, and beseech the Almighty to keep his sleeping lordship from all perils and dangers of what remained of this night.

117

Yes, in the great hall the lights still burned. And, high in a tower, a single window glowed in the darkness. Will Shakespeare, wrapped in his furred gown, was reading, enthralled, what Mary of Pembroke had made of his tawny-fronted gipsy.

Not very much, he decided (with respect, of course). *Antonius* was her translation from the French of Robert Garnier; stiff, formal, lifeless. But what could you expect, translating a French classicist? And it would probably have appealed to Ben. He thought Will a dreadful fellow for treating Seneca's classic principles with such disrespect.

Yet, in some strange way, this dead play was striking sparks from Will's imagination. *His* Cleopatra would not speak in these milk and water accents. *His* Antony – braggart, besotted, swaggering, would tear the world down with his dying. *His* lovers would die to a great, soaring paean of poetry such as had never been heard before. Already phrases were taking fire in his mind: 'O! wither'd is the garland of war.' He could not wait. And yet he must wait. *Macbeth* was not yet finished. *Othello* was in disrepair. They all, even Dick, wanted comedy. There was, he knew in his heart, no boy capable of Cleopatra. Everything – common sense, loyalty to his fellows, his highly developed money sense – everything told him to forget this tormenting gipsy.

He could not forget her. Anymore than he could ever forget that dark whore who had once led him, like a dancing bear on a chain, to a high, forgotten room in Essex House…

He was not the only one engaged in literary activities. The foolish face of James peered out of a veritable ocean of pillows and bedding, in a bed the size of a haywain. The firelight danced on dark wainscot, on heavy silks and damasks. The candle flickered on nostrums and draughts and salves and purges (he was a great one for medicaments, was James).

What caused the furrows in that unsleeping royal brow tonight? Not cares of state. Not his unrelenting fight with the Devil. Not some theologian's quibble. Not even plans for tomorrow's hunting. No. He had learnt that Shakespeare was in the house. And he vowed that, the very next day of weather too vile for hunting, he and Shakespeare would write this play about his noble ancestor Banquo. And, to prepare himself for the task, he was busy devising a plot. He rang a bell. The door was immediately flung open and two soldiers with pikes flung themselves into the room. Finding that their Sovereign was not, in fact, being murdered, they sprang to attention, flanking the entrance of the Gentleman of the Chamber, my Lord of Southampton.

Southampton bowed very low. God, what a time of night! Did princes never sleep? 'Your Majesty?'

'Paper, my dear Henry. Ink. Pens.'

'Very good, your Majesty.' Another low bow. He reached the door. 'Oh, and Henry?'

'Majesty?'

'I'm gey hungry, mon.'

Another bow. 'I will see to it, your Majesty.'

'Aye. Nothing elaborate. Just a leg of mutton, maybe.'

Southampton backed to the door, bowing. 'Henry?'

Bow. 'Majesty?'

'Mark ye. With gallandine sauce, Henry.'

'Majesty.' He went off to rouse the kitchens, the secretaries, the Gentleman Usher, and the other Gentlemen of the Chamber. Within half an hour James had been got out of bed, draped in a gown of furs, seated at a desk, sprinkled with rose water, paper set before him, a quill dipped in ink and placed in his hand, a blessing pronounced. 'Act I Scene I,' wrote James. 'A desert place.' He sucked his pen.

There was a further commotion. The soldiers entered once more, clanking to attention, followed by the Gentleman Usher, the Yeoman Usher, and the Yeomen of the Ewry, the Pantry and the Cellar. A table was laid. The leg of mutton was borne in by menials, flanked by gentlemen-in-waiting to ensure that no one of the common sort gazed on majesty in his night-clothes. Master Carver carved. The pen was taken out of the King's hand. He was helped to rise, escorted to the table, eased into a chair. A hastily-summoned chaplain uttered a sleepy grace. 'Act I Scene I,' thought James as he greedily watched the gallandine sauce being poured. He looked forward to showing his masterpiece to Shakespeare. He didn't think the actor, despite his admittedly greater experience of theatre, would have much to add by the time James had finished.

It was cold in the waggons. The clouds that shrouded the damp evening had thinned with the coming of darkness. The stars drifted into sight, a fleet of lanterned boats glimpsed on a misty sea. But, towards dawn, the clouds crept away, the stars glinted evilly, like the eyes of predators, each tiny grass stiffened to a grey knife blade, the moisture that coated every branch and twig froze into droplets that would sparkle like a queen's jewels in the morning sunlight.

But the sun was not yet. Only cold, that walks hand in hand with fear! Only darkness, that bedfellow of despair!

Cold, fear, despair, darkness. Matthew Peyre was wrapped, smothered in a shroud woven of all four, so that he strove hard to breathe.

Again his mother had appeared to him in his dreams, bringing a peace such as he had never known in waking.

Again she had lifted her veil. This time, not even a whitened skull; but a death's head to which still clung foul gouts and clots of corruption, in whose eye sockets heaved an everlasting worm. He screamed, over and over, sucking in air and forcing it out of his lungs with all his strength, as though to rid his body of these horrors.

There were curses, mutterings from the boys and hired men in his waggon. Nicholas Fox dug an elbow into his ribs. 'Peace, for God's sake.'

He lay, silent, scarce breathing. Quickly the snoring, the heavy breathing in the waggon settled back into its rhythm. Matthew lay staring into the darkness, shivering in the cold. Fearful. Fearful because his father was dead; and, it seemed almost certain, his mother also; dead and buried without the healing grace of Mother Church. Fearful of this great house where he had seen men strutting like peacocks in silks and satins, men who would strike a boy player from their path with a cut of their jewelled canes, with no more thought than they would slash a nettle.

Fearful because, for all he knew, he might have to play before these haughty, mocking creatures: he who had played Desdemona so ill before yokels might now play before the highest in the land. Fearful, most of all, because Master Shakespeare had deserted him to go and live in the great house. He was alone, miles from London, alone among the players, alone in a world which, as Master Shakespeare had cruelly said, did not care a green fig about him.

Despairing, because he would never make an actor, because when he went home he would find the door barred, the windows broken, Annette Peyre no more than a name scrawled in corruption.

He felt the tears running down his cheeks. Holy Mary, Mother of God, help me not to cry. He groped down among the blankets, found the one personal possession that had gone with him on all his travels – the child's toy, the grinning jester's head on its stick of a body, with a crossed stick for arms.

Gently, he pulled at the jester's clothes, tugging them away from their frame. Then off came the head. Now there was only the frame. Something glinted in the grey dawnlight. Matthew held it close to his face, staring at the body, writhed in agony, on its silver cross. He touched the crucifix to his lips. So had God Himself suffered. What pains of mere man could approach the pains of God, weighed down moreover in His agony by the black weight of the world's sin?

Beside him, Nicholas Fox stirred. Hastily, Matthew fumbled to disguise again the crucifix. Too late. Nicholas, Fox by name and Fox by nature, was wide awake immediately. He snatched, stared at his prize with incredulous glee. 'God's blood, you're a Papist,' he whispered. 'Hey, men,' and he was shouting now, 'Matt Peyre's a snivelling Papist.' He held the crucifix aloft, moving it in a sign of the cross. '*In nomine Patri*,' he intoned nasally, '*et Filii et –* '

'Give me that,' said Matthew, hurt almost to tears by this blasphemy.

The men were awake now, stirring, sorting their minds and bodies in the growing light. Young Peyre a Catholic? They were aggrieved. They should have been told. Sleeping in the same waggon as a Papist – well, one didn't know. There were stories – witchcraft, poisonings, sudden unexplained deaths.

Matthew's soft, boy's face had changed. It was taut, stretched, eyes brilliant as fever. 'Give me that,' he said again.

Nicholas tossed the crucifix out of the waggon. And then, suddenly, looked afraid.

Matthew was on to him.

It seemed to Matthew that all the humiliations and failures and anxieties of the past summer were concentrated in that tormenting face. He wanted to beat it into a pulp, to smash the teeth, nose, the chin, to destroy forever its ability to hurt. He screamed, on a high sustained note. He pounded, he beat, he smashed.

Not very successfully. Nicholas Fox knew how to look after himself. He parried most of the blows. And then, suddenly, he grabbed Matthew round the waist, hugged him to the end of the waggon, and tried to throw him out.

But Matthew had the strength of ten. In fact, most of the watching men assumed that the Devil, known to favour Papists, had entered into him.

The two boys, viciously locked, swayed on the edge of the waggon. Leg curled round leg, seeking to trip. Hand forced back chin, fingers tugged at hair. The men watched, sleepy, cold, uninvolved. They were against the little Papist but unsympathetic to Nicholas Fox. If Fox was hurt, no one would shed a tear. And as for Peyre – he had behaved shamefully, sharing their waggon without declaring his Catholicism.

Then, suddenly, the fight was over. Nicholas, with his own back to the inside of the waggon, had Matthew bent back over – nothing. He had Matthew's leg gripped firmly by his own. His fingers, knotted in Matthew's hair, were slowly dragging back the boy's head. All he had to do now was wait until Matthew's weight was concentrated outside the waggon, and then – a swift disengagement, finish, Matthew falling four feet backwards on to the sodden earth.

Now! The moment had come. He was actually supporting the other boy's weight. He let go of Matthew's hair, in order to wrench the boy's arms from about his own waist and push him away.

Matthew fell. But, strengthened no doubt by the Devil, went on clinging to Master Fox, so that both boys fell to the ground. And when Matthew, panting and dishevelled, struggled to his feet, Nicholas Fox still lay writhing on the ground, his kneecap smashed by landing on a boulder which, everyone swore, had not been there last night when they went to bed. There was no doubt, they were to reiterate as they told the story over many a cup of ale in many a tavern, there was no doubt that the Devil looks after his own.

Matthew went and picked up his crucifix from the wet grass. Very carefully he wiped it with his fingers, slipped it into his doublet. Then he turned and looked unemotionally down at the jerking, groaning, twitching Master Fox.

And suddenly he was on top of him again, pounding, punching, battering; screaming and shrieking with anger.

Fox joined in the uproar, howling with pain and terror. The noise was appalling. Some of the hired men, fearing that the hubbub would disturb the gentry in the house (in which case no one's hide would be safe) bravely dragged Matthew and the Devil off, afterwards quietly crossing themselves, for one could not be too careful when dealing with the Devil, and there was always a chance the Catholics were right after all about their grievous superstitions.

But if the uproar had not pierced the sound walls of Wilton, it had aroused the sharers in their waggon. Burbage came running, pulling on his doublet, his great roar of 'What in God's name is this?' adding to the general commotion.

He was a man who concentrated on essentials. And the essential thing here was that, by the look of things, the only way of getting Rosalind on stage tomorrow night was going to be on crutches.

He bent down, ran gentle fingers down Fox's leg. Then he felt the knee. He did not need the boy's yell of pain to tell him that here was where the trouble lay. A mingle-mangle of shattered bone moved under his fingers. So much for Rosalind. He straightened up. He looked at Matthew, still held by four men. 'You, I suppose,' he said sourly.

'He blasphemed,' Matthew explained.

Burbage looked at him curiously. This was not the Matthew Peyre he had known in London, gentleman Will's gentlemanly apprentice. It only bore out what he always said. One could never rule out any action, for any human being, however much it seemed out of character. It also bore out what he'd said about Peyre not being ripe to act before the Court. God, this wild creature might do anything.

And yet? God preserve us, who else *was* there to take over Rosalind? Damn all boys! They were the curse of the theatre. He said, curtly, 'Two of you take Fox to the house. Have him attended. The rest – listen to me.'

They clustered round, in the grey dawn. In shirts, hose hanging about their calves, unshaven, tousled, scratching, fidgeting. He looked at them. The King's Men? A rabble of tinkers, rather. And yet, he knew, tomorrow night these unkempt rogues would be mincing it on the stage, gentlemen all, trim of hair and beard, upright of bearing, richly apparelled, a Company of whom he could be justly proud. That was what discipline did for you.

He lifted up his voice. He said: 'We are the King's Men. The best, most regarded, most able Company in the land.'

They gave a half-hearted cheer. Dawn was not the best time for rhetoric, even from old Dick.

'We are the King's Men *because* we are the best Company in the land. And we're the best Company because we're what Will once called a band of brothers. We've had our troubles, God knows. Weather, plague, illness. But we've always fought them, and fought together.'

'Aye.' That was true. Old Dick could be a bastard, but somehow you always backed him up.

'But' – and suddenly his eyes were boring into Matthew Peyre – 'one young gentleman has not yet realised this. One young gentleman thinks that, because he is virtuous, he can disrupt the entire Company the day before we are due to play before the King.' He walked up to Matthew. He jabbed a fleshy finger into his chest. 'Let me give you this choice, Master Peyre. You become one of our band of brothers, or you go – with a heavy boot in the back of your breeches. Now. Which is it to be?'

To his surprise, Matthew stared at him, arrogant, contemptuous, silent. At last he said, in a level voice, 'You have been grievously unfair, Master Burbage.'

'Silence!' roared Burbage. Of course he'd been unfair. This was no time for careful weighing of fair and unfair. This was a time to crush.

He would have no brawling in his Company. An example had to be made. He called Condell. He said in a voice of cold fury, 'This – creature – will have to play Rosalind. Make sure he knows the part, keep him up all night if needs be. See that he attends every rehearsal.' God, it was a risk. Not only would the boy be o'erparted; but he knew boys. When they were walking this tightrope between boyhood and manhood they were as volatile as women. This boy especially. Taut as a fiddle-string. He could wreck the performance. Before the King, the entire Court! He could make them the laughing stock of London. Yet there was no one else to play Rosalind.

'Treat him like an unbroken horse, Harry,' he said brutally. He turned away. But suddenly he swung round. 'And you men,' he cried with contempt. 'Any *one* of you could have prevented this. But no. You stand by and watch it happen. And leave me to pick up the pieces.' He turned, and stumped away, a short, sturdy figure, as compact with power and dignity as an old bull in a meadow. Not for nothing was Master Richard Burbage leader of the world's most famous company of players.

Slowly, languorously, deliciously, Will Shakespeare drifted into wakefulness.

He was in a small, square room whose floor was of pillows and sheets, whose walls were of crimson brocade, whose ceiling was a tent of white silk.

Except when they were on tour, he was used to waking in such surroundings. The only difference was that here there were sounds of hushed activity in the greater room that encompassed his small room: the crackle of sticks, the hiss of flame, the sound of jugs being set down, of water sluicing into a bowl; the swish, delectable sound of women's skirts. Finally, a sweet, respectful, feminine voice crying softly, 'Master Shakespeare, sir, Master Shakespeare. Seven of the clock, and all prepared.'

He drew back one of the bed curtains, peered out.

A pleasant sight! Two pretty maids, smiling and curtsying shyly. A fire of logs, already burning bravely, candles, jugs of hot water covered with warm towels, the smell of lavender soap.

'Thank you,' he said, smiling. They curtsied again, and withdrew. He heard their muted giggles in the corridor.

He lay back in the great bed, hands clasped behind his head, picking up the threads he had abandoned when he slept. He was at Wilton House, he had to act as guider at a rehearsal this morning, the Dowager Countess had been very gracious. And, more important than all, was the warm, comfortable feeling that a new play was opening in his mind like a flower to the sunlight, that even while he had slept those tremendous lovers were chanting in his mind their dying antiphon.

He rose. He, who never normally wasted a moment, wandered round the room, savouring the luxury: the comfort of the fire on this chill, grey morning; the hot towels, the balls of perfumed soap, the unguents for hair and beard, the tooth soap and cloth, the Spirits of Salt for cleansing the teeth of stains, the combs and brushes, the paste of almonds, egg yolk, and raisins for the hands. He thought of his lodgings, with bustling Marie Mountjoy banging the hot water jug down on the chest; of his own New Place which he had, until now, thought so grand. How he would like to spend a leisurely hour, trying the various soaps and unguents, dressing slowly before the fire. No! He could, and very often did, waste time on others when they needed him. Never on himself. If he dressed and washed hurriedly, and snatched a little breakfast, he could manage a whole hour's writing before the rehearsal.

There was a knock at the door. A servant entered, looking embarrassed. 'Sir, there is a person would speak with you.'

Will pulled on his gown, went and lolled elegantly in an X chair. He felt grand, but uneasy. Who could want him at this hour of the morning? 'Bid him enter,' he said. Already he had mastered another new part. He might have been giving his audience in his chamber at Wilton from his youth up.

A man, dishevelled, his doublet unfastened, marched into the room. 'Will.' Then he stopped and looked about him in wonder. 'God's wounds, man, you are lodged well.'

'And you, Dick?' Will thought he detected a note of sourness.

'Oh, a very comfortable waggon. Cold o' nights, and the roof leaks, but good enough for a common player.'

Will tried not to look amused. 'Oh, Dick, I did not ask for this. But come. While you are here, try this soap. And this hot water.'

'No, the pump in the yard is good enough for me! 'Twill not be the first time.' He wandered round the room, making scornful noises over the unguents, the lotions, the soaps. Then, suddenly, he seemed to pull himself together. He flung himself into a chair, stared hard at his old friend. 'Disaster, Will.'

If Burbage said disaster, he meant disaster. What had happened? What could they least afford to lose? Two things, as he a sharer well knew. Costumes, and boy players. Costumes, because they represented most of the Company's capital. Boy players because by the time you'd taught the little devils anything they were croaking and sprouting beards. Youth, as he himself had pointed out, was a stuff did not endure. So. A waggon of costumes up in flames? Or plague in the boys' waggon? He could think of nothing else to merit the word 'disaster'. 'Tell me,' he said, sounding judicial and detached, but with a strange sinking in his stomach. Since he was a sharer, the Company's disasters were his disasters.

'Young Fox, tomorrow night's Rosalind, has smashed his knee joint.' Will shuddered. 'And you know the boy position.'

'But – he'll be lame for life.'

'I imagine so. He'll certainly be lame for tomorrow night.'

The lithe, swift youth, doomed suddenly to drag a limb through life, like a hurt crow! 'How did it happen?'

'He and young Peyre. Brawling.'

'*Peyre?*'

Dick nodded, not without satisfaction. 'He's like a wild creature. I know boys are kittle cattle, but I've never known one change like that little lordship.'

Will said, 'He's anxious about his mother, Dick. The plague in London – '

'God's agony, Will. *I'm* anxious. About my wife, children. But *I* don't try to kill Harry Condell.'

'Did *he* try to kill Nicholas?'

'Yes.'

'I'll talk to him.' Goodbye, he thought, my hour's writing. Goodbye for today, my tawny gipsy. And next year I shall be forty. Oh, how mere everyday living gnawed away at the fabric of life! A man's life worn away by the simple living of it. Marry and amen, a poet should be able to order things better.

'I'll send him,' Dick said grimly. He rose. He planted himself foursquare before his friend. 'Will, things are grave. Our first play before our new king, and a new Court. A tired, dispirited Company. Jaded costumes. And now, God save the mark, Rosalind played by a green youth I won't trust not to fly off stage and strike the King if he do but cry "Hem!" '

'I'll talk to him, Dick.'

'Aye. Terrify the little devil.' He sighed. He looked gloomily around the room. 'No lutenist to greet the morn for you? No wench, to comb your beard?' He went off, tut-tutting; rumbling, despite all his troubles, with inward laughter.

Will went on sitting in his chair; weary, as he was always weary when his pen was not allowed to relieve the turmoil of his brain.

There was a knock at the door. Not Matthew's courteous tap, but a defiant, aggressive knocking.

'Come in,' he called.

The door opened briskly. Matthew came in.

Could this really be the quiet, amenable youth who had set out on this tour? Could months of anxiety and hard living really have wrought this change? He had shot up, pale and lanky, like a shade-grown plant. His eyes and cheeks were feverish. But it was his manner – quick, impatient, arrogant – that had changed most. Will, looking at him, thought: he really believes I left his mother to die. He hates us all. Me most of all. He said, 'Nicholas is a boy. And he may never run or dance or swim again.' He sighed, with a great sadness. 'You have robbed him of his youth, Matthew.'

'I am sorry for that, Master Shakespeare.'

'Sorry? You should be down on your knees, weeping, begging God for His forgiveness. Why did you do it?'

'He stole.'

'What?'

'My crucifix.'

'*Crucifix?*' O gentle Galilean, he thought. You have caused more strife than all the mighty Tamburlaines. But blaming, punishing would not help Nicholas walk again. He said, 'Master Burbage tells me you are to play Rosalind before the King?'

'Yes.'

'Are you afeared?'

'Not any more.'

'Why?'

The boy shrugged arrogantly. 'I have outstripped fear,' he said.

Will looked at him thoughtfully. There was something wrong here, something dangerous. There were few mortals, he thought, who could outrun fear. And he didn't think this boy was one of them. But all he said was, 'We have thirty-six hours. It is absurd. But you can do it, with my help. Now. Have you your part? Good. We have to work, Master Peyre.' *Oh, farewell, my tawny-fronted gipsy. You must wait in the tiring-room for another day.*

# CHAPTER 10

## SOME COME TO TAKE THEIR EASE
## AND SLEEP AN ACT OR TWO

There were parts to learn, costumes to clean and press, beards and hair to trim, swords and ducal crowns to furbish, the great hall to inspect, tiring-rooms to be arranged and emptied, ceremonial to be considered (were the players to enter and bow to the King before the play began? Or at the end? Was there anything in the play to offend Majesty? Any lewdness to offend the Queen? Men had lost ears or tongues for such oversights). Greatest task of all, Master Peyre to be groomed, instructed, eased into a part for which thirty-six days would not have been too much, let alone thirty-six hours.

And now, to add to Will's troubles, my Lady Countess, tart for once, a little less enamoured of Master Shakespeare, it seemed. 'Sir, one of your band is grievously hurt. I would have thought that perhaps one of you – perhaps you yourself – might have found time to enquire after his wellbeing. Even, perhaps, would have visited him.'

Oh, damn! To be accused of callousness, by a woman he so admired! And she was right. And yet thirty-six hours, to prepare a play for the King! Not a moment could be spared;

no one outside the theatre would understand that. He said humbly, sadly, 'How does the boy?'

'Well, thanks to me and his foolish mother. No thanks to his companions.'

He said, hesitantly, 'It will be difficult, perhaps impossible, for you to understand, my lady. But for us the play is the thing. If we do not concentrate all our thoughts on that, then – there would be few plays, Lady Pembroke.' Then he asked, because he really wanted to know: 'Will he walk again?'

'I think so. I have some skill in medicine. I have bound his leg, and put him in my maid's bed. Without the maid. He would be in no mood – ' Suddenly her laughter rang out. The storm, it seemed, had passed. 'You must proceed with preparations for your play, Master Shakespeare.'

Plague might rage up and down the land. The common sort might rise up and have to be quelled. There might be wars, and rumours of wars. All these things came, and passed, and came again. But for King James' Court there was one enemy that neither slumbered nor slept; that had to be fought, day after day, evening after evening, year after year; one enemy that not all their inventiveness and ingenuity could hold at bay: tediousness.

They had many potent weapons: gossip, hunting, love-making, cards, dice, music, dancing, plotting, masques. But there would come a time when even all these would pall. And then my lords would sprawl in their chairs, scowling, kicking their heels petulantly against the floor, ready for any viciousness. To fill a seventeen hour day, seven days a week, with trivialities, called for more application than most of them were capable of.

It was difficult, even in London, with its brothels and theatres and gaming houses and hangings. But in Wiltshire, in

December! The search for novelty and sensation became almost frantic.

So the courtiers were in a brittle mood. They had been starved of entertainment. Now these player fellows had come to entertain them with Shakespeare's pretty conceits, and gratitude was the last emotion they felt. Amuse me, make me laugh, tickle my jaded palate, or by God I'll tear your stage to pieces.

At least they were to have comedy. They'd have made short work if Master Burbage had tried to give them one of those interminable histories. But *As You Like It*! Most of them had seen it divers times performed. It was that one with *All the world's a stage*, was it not? Tedious stuff. It might do no harm to enliven the play a little, thought the younger sort.

The great hall was prepared. A dais, with adjoining chambers arranged for tiring-rooms. Facing the dais, the two lesser thrones that always travelled with their Majesties. On the King's right, a great chair for my Lady the Dowager Countess. On the Queen's left a chair for my Lord Earl. On both sides, and behind, the chairs for the nobility, stools for the royal servants, benches for the common sort.

The hall was beginning to fill. Southampton was sitting on the front row, talking vivaciously and, to judge from his expression, spitefully. On the row behind, delicately poised between gentry and servants, were Master Ben Jonson and Master Inigo Jones; Ben snarling and critical because it wasn't one of his masques; the gentle Inigo looking sadly at the bare, unadorned stage. You really would have thought that, in this year of grace 1603, the King's Men would have learnt something of stagecraft, he told himself.

Will Shakespeare, perched on the book-holder's, or prompter's, stool, just inside the tiring-room, and infinitely susceptible to mood as always, was aware of two highly charged atmospheres: from the tiring-room a tense nervousness, taut as the strings of a viol; from the hall, a mocking, brittle impatience.

He was uneasy. One such mood, on the side of the house, augured ill. Two such moods in the same house were like tinder and spark. He peered round into the hall. It was full now – except for the King and Queen and their attendants. And there, on the front row, were the thin, bitter features of his old friend and new enemy, Southampton. And there his rival and savage critic, Ben Jonson. No. The King's Men could expect no mercy if this performance went ill.

He turned, peered into the tiring-room. Burbage, at thirty-five a plump and ageing Orlando. Heminge, on whom so much of the burden of the tour had fallen, looking old and weary as Oliver. Robert Armin, almost voiceless from a rheum, a dejected Touchstone. And the greatest question mark of all, Matthew Peyre, still poring over the great scroll that contained his part and cues, too bright of eye, too flushed of cheek, too quick and restless of limb.

The audience were fidgeting, growing noisier. Laughter rang out; not the laughter of an eager, expectant audience, but a cruel, scarce-controlled laughter. In the tiring-room the actors were like hounds on the leash, pacing up and down, gesturing, muttering, glancing appealingly at Will for the signal to start.

No signal came. The great doors through which their Majesties would enter, remained closed. The thrones remained empty, the Earl's and his mother's seats remained empty. If James and his Annie didn't arrive soon, thought Will, something, somewhere, was going to snap.

Burbage hurried over to him. 'Will, I've been watching Peyre.'

'So have I, by heaven.'

'I think he's near breaking point. He may be all right if we can start, but – Where *is* this fool of a king?'

But at this fraught moment, the great double doors opened. The audience rose. My Lord Chamberlain advanced into the room, turned to face the doors. The Queen's ladies in waiting floated in like swans, turned to face the doors. The Queen entered on Pembroke's arm. She was scowling. As a notable actress herself – and *everyone* said that Master Jonson's masques would be *nothing* without her – she didn't relish having to sit still for two hours while some tedious boy got all the applause. She went and flounced on to her throne.

Flanked by his gentlemen, the King entered. And on his arm, God save the mark, not my Lady of Pembroke, but the aged Bishop of Bath and Wells, the only man on the Bench who had not read assiduously the King's little treatise on Daemonologie, and who had therefore known no better than to assert, over supper, that the Devil was able to contract a large, solid body into the space of an atomy, a belief which the King had firmly and specifically rejected in his little treatise, and was now at great pains to enlighten the aged cleric about. So much so, and since the Bishop was almost wholly deaf, that the sound of the argument could be heard in the tiring-room.

The King reached his throne. The Queen rose and curtsied. Courteously, James bowed Bath and Wells into the Countess' chair. He sat down himself. There was a great sighing and stirring as the audience re-seated itself, and a great flurry of bowing and protesting as several courtiers offered their chairs to the unseated Countess.

Silence began to fall.

It fell. Will raised his hand. Burbage and Condell walked towards the stage. Burbage was licking his lips. Will suddenly waved them back. For the King's voice had cut into the silence like a saw into timber. 'But, mon, it would be impossible. 'Tis quite contrary to the nature of a physical body.'

The Bishop thought this over. And while he was doing so Will gave the signal. 'As I remember, Adam – ' Burbage began loudly, strolling on with his arm round old Adam's shoulders.

The play had begun. The King cast an irritated glance at the stage. He was used to complete silence while he conducted an argument – except of course for the odd deferential remark from his opponent. What, he tried to remember, was toward. Oh, yes. Some play by Shakespeare. Which reminded him. He must see the fellow about his Banquo. Writing a play had been more difficult than he expected. Obviously there was some kind of trick or conceit in it. He must ask Shakespeare to explain it to him.

The playhouse was as far outside the Bishop's experience as the brothel; nevertheless he was a courteous old gentleman, and preferred to remain silent while others were speaking. So it was not until the slight pause for a change of scene that he spoke. Then he said, 'But there have been so many accredited instances, your Majesty. In Taunton, Richard Furmidge – he was invoking the Evil One, the foolish fellow – o'erstepped the magic circle – but by the knuckle of his big toe, mark you – and was changed immediately into a crumb of bread. And William Stroud, of Frome – '

'On you go, boy. And good luck,' whispered Burbage.

Matthew Peyre swallowed, and went on stage like one mounting the scaffold. Will smiled, patted his back as he went past. Abraham went with him, both pretty and girlish in their farthingales, even though Abraham did not know whether when he spoke his voice would come out falsetto or bass.

Abraham said, 'I pray thee, Rosalind – ' Bass as a drum. He swallowed hurriedly, tried again. 'I pray thee, Rosalind, sweet my coz, be merry.' High and shrill as a robin in the spring time.

There was a single titter from the audience. It was enough. Others joined in. There were guffaws. People saw that the Queen was laughing spitefully (yes, let them see how boys, squeaking one minute, groaning the next, could spoil a play, not that it needed much spoiling) so *they* laughed spitefully. Will, poised between his two worlds, glanced into the tiring-room, caught Burbage's eye, and grimaced.

Matthew Peyre said in a flat voice, 'Dear Celia, I show more mirth than I am mistress of – '

And got no further. For the King's voice, angry now, grated through the room. 'Have a care, Master Bishop. What ye speak of has a whiff of the little transubstantiate God in the Papists' Mass.' He glared at the unfortunate prelate.

Will looked at Matthew with alarm. He would not have found it easy himself to ignore this royal interruption. But for a fledgling actor, already in a highly emotional state… He did not wait to find out whether Matthew had forgotten his lines. ' "And would you yet I were merrier?" ' He prompted quietly but clearly.

But Matthew did not hear him. Matthew felt as though he were supported a foot or two above the ground, in a world of kings and dukes and courtiers and players and woodlanders, some of whom were real, some make-believe. But which were real, he no longer knew. Ahead of him lay thickets and tangles of words, stretching to the world's end; words he knew, but which seemed like an ants' nest in his brain. But at the moment none of this mattered. He had been most discourteously interrupted, by – God save the mark – a sneer at his religion. He stepped forward to the edge of the stage, glared at the King.

' "And would you yet I were merrier?" ' Will said, more loudly this time.

In the tiring-room they were already, with the foresight that made the King's Men what they were, working Peter Graves into a farthingale. He had played the part often enough as a lad, and a gruff-voiced Rosalind was better than no Rosalind at all.

The rest of the cast were crowding round the tiring-room door. Never, perhaps, had the King's Men felt so helpless. Except for Abraham, none of them was within yards of Matthew. And Matthew, unless they were very much mistaken, was about to insult the King.

It would be the end of the King's Men. There was no doubt about that. Worse. If they didn't all find themselves in the Marshalsea they'd be lucky. They watched, paralysed with foreboding.

They saw Matthew open his mouth to speak. They saw the King look up and, apparently, see Matthew for the first time. They saw fear, annoyance, anger on the royal features. ' "And would you yet I were merrier?" ' Will said desperately.

Matthew did not hear him. Matthew no longer knew where or who he was. His world was a whirling mass of hated and hating faces, of words swarming like bees. All he knew was that he had to speak some of the words with which his mind was so crammed. Words of plays, of songs, of everyday life: 'My mother had a maid call'd Barbara.' 'And would you yet I were merrier?' 'Jolly Robin, Tell me how thy lady does.' 'Hold thy peace, thou knave.'

Which was he supposed to say? He racked his brains. Mother's dead, I played Desdemona ill, Master Shakespeare is angry, poor Nicholas, I have hurt him sore, someone spoke ill of the holy Mass; and I am alone, gazing down into a sea of mocking faces, with the unspeakable loneliness of a man on the scaffold.

The audience, most of whom had often watched without a thought of pity the slow, long-drawn-out slaughtering of a man, the tearing to pieces of an ape, were not likely to waste pity on a youthful player who had forgot his lines. Their eyes were interested, hard; ready for mockery, laughter, hate.

But one face held Matthew's gaze: a red, peevish face, the face of the man who had spoken scornfully of the Mass. He stared angrily at that face. And words, appropriate, yet no more than the words of a popular song, came ready-made to his lips. 'Hold thy peace, thou knave,' he shouted.

For a long moment nothing happened. Only a hiss of appalled breath in a hundred throats, like the sound of the undertow dragging at a shingle beach.

Then a sharper, angrier hiss as a sword was whipped from its scabbard. If anyone had taken to heart Will Shakespeare's words about that tide in the affairs of men, it was Henry Wriothesley, Earl of Southampton. Here was yet one more chance to demonstrate to his Sovereign his loyalty, devotion, and courage. 'Treason, by God,' he roared, and reaching the stage from his chair in one leap, he prepared to spit this twelve-year-old before his insolent tongue could utter more treason; much to the distress of James, who couldn't stand the sight of blood, and would much have preferred the well-deserved execution carried out off-stage.

Matthew looked at the point approaching his breast, and the furious face of Wriothesley, without interest. Was this part of the play? He couldn't remember. He didn't much care. But now there was suddenly a very solid body between himself and that darting sword-point. And a voice – Master Shakespeare's voice – was saying urgently, 'Back to the tiring-room, Matthew.'

The boy stood where he was, dazed.

Henry Wriothesley looked at the poet who, in another reign (and in another life, it seemed) had dedicated two popular poems to him. The poet looked at the man who had, on a whim, made him; and who now, in a burst of anger, looked like unmaking him.

That bright point advanced. Now it was pressing rather uncomfortably against Will's doublet. 'Out of my way, Shakespeare,' Southampton said with a contempt as sharp as the sword-point.

Will did not move.

Nobody moved. The general feeling in the audience was that this beat cockfighting, and certainly beat *As You Like It*. And though everybody in that sophisticated crowd knew exactly what Wriothesley was about, many of the younger courtiers were kicking themselves that they had not thought of it first.

Wriothesley said, loudly and clearly. 'Come, Shakespeare, you have played the poltroon too often for this to impress anyone.'

Will did not move. He was sweating. He did not *think* Henry would be allowed to kill him in cold blood before the King and Queen. But when only an inch or two of one's own flesh lie between one's heart and the sword of one's enemy one prefers a little more reassurance than that.

Nevertheless, he did not move. He had drawn the sword away from Matthew and was prepared to keep it there, even if his heart had to be its scabbard. Why? Love for a son who was no son, compassion for a soul lost in the byways between boyhood and manhood? He did not know. All he knew was that for the first time in his life Will Shakespeare had outfaced danger. And he exulted, even with the knife at his breast.

Behind him he heard a scuffle. Burbage and Heminge had dragged Matthew into the temporary safety of the tiring-room.

He watched, fascinated, Southampton's face: the scornful lips, the hard, arrogant eyes. He searched, in vain, for any traces of humour, or mercy, of the friendship they had once shared. A flick of that steely wrist, he knew, would be enough to kill him; and any attempt to escape, to seize the blade, would mean a quick end.

So he waited.

Silence. The audience were intrigued to see whether this player would live or die.

The whole drama had lasted a few seconds. To Will it had been like an evening. And, suddenly, from the silent audience, a deep, rich, feminine voice, used to command: 'Henry, you fool, come and sit down.'

Mary Herbert, Dowager Countess of Pembroke, had broken the spell. Wriothesley turned a furious face in her direction, swung back at Will.

'My lord' – now the Countess' voice was like the whip of a rapier – 'I will be obeyed in my own house. Back to your seat, sir.'

Wriothesley slammed his sword back into its scabbard, and went back to his seat. Will, left in the middle of the stage, with an impossible exit, returned sheepishly to his prompt stool, where he examined the cut in the breast of his doublet and wondered how long it would be before he could take it to Anne for repair. My Lord Bishop, who had been unable to make head or tail of the play so far, clapped politely. Burbage, faced with two courses – the entire Company to abase itself before Majesty and beg forgiveness, or carry on with the play as though nothing had happened – chose the latter. Celia and Rosalind strolled on. 'Rosalind, sweet my coz, be merry,' piped Celia. 'Dear Celia, I show more mirth than I am mistress of,' boomed Rosalind. The King's Men, for the time being at least, had surmounted one more crisis.

# CHAPTER 11

## SOME SAY THE EARTH
## WAS FERVOROUS AND DID SHAKE...

Wilton House, well equipped in so many ways, lacked dungeons. But they found a reasonably noisome cellar, put Matthew inside, locked the door with a great padlock, and set a couple of men armed with halberds to guard him. There was an air vent, high in the wall, and a stone slab to lie on. Everyone agreed that, for someone who had called the King of England a knave, and for a Papist to boot, it was luxury indeed.

Dick Burbage bustled into Will's room while he was dressing. 'Will, the King last night was so full of wine and theology I think he will not remember what happened.'

'No?'

'We must slip away before he awakes. It can be done. I had the waggons loaded last night.'

Will looked puzzled. 'But we cannot. He has a hostage. The boy.'

'Whom we disown. Naturally.'

Could he have heard aright? 'But Dick, he's – he's one of the King's Men. We can't – '

Dick was tired, irritable, and suddenly very angry. But, for once, coldly angry. 'Listen to me, Will. Are you suggesting I should keep the Company here, reminding the King of our presence, while they decide when to hang this boy?'

'I certainly am.'

'Then I must tell you that I am not prepared to risk the Company I have built up over the years for the sake of a young Papist. It was he, and he alone – '

'We pushed him too hard, Dick.'

'God's teeth! He's crippled another boy, brought us all in danger of the Marshalsea; and he'd never make an actor even if they didn't hang him.'

'He *will* make an actor. I shall intercede with the King for him.'

Burbage looked at him in amazement. 'But I've always known you for a man of sense.'

Will gave him a long, cold look. 'I've always known you for a man of honour.'

Dick's hand moved, of its own volition, to his sword. Then he shrugged wearily. 'And now I am not? Because I am prepared to sacrifice a troublesome boy to try to save the Company? A boy who is doomed anyway?'

'I shall intercede with the King. Peyre is my apprentice. I am responsible for him.'

'Much good it will do you. Get yourself hanged as well, as like as not.'

'If it has to be.'

Dick Burbage looked at his old friend in alarm. And some of the old friendship came back into his voice. 'But Will – you were always such a cautious fellow. And now – '

'Once I failed the boy sorely. I will not fail him again. Besides' – he actually smiled – 'perhaps I've grown up, Dick.'

'Well, do as you please.' The friendship had gone again. 'But we leave within the hour.'

'Then I shall follow, when I have done what must be done.'

Dick Burbage stood up, began to pace up and down. 'I don't like to say this,' he said harshly, 'but this Company made you, Will. When I took you in you were a green youth. And now you no longer want to write the plays we need. You no longer even want to travel with us.' He looked scornfully round the bedroom. 'A few more days in the comfort of Wilton, I suppose, and then fast horses to London. And high-minded conversation with the Dowager Countess is doubtless more to your taste than the company of unwashed players.' He was pacing swiftly, furiously now. It was as though the room had become a cage.

Will watched him. How often had he seen his old friend in this sort of rage, and loved him the more for these hot-blooded outbursts. And if today was different – if today Dick's unfairness hurt and stung – he would not show it. He went on rubbing a scented unguent into his beard, watching himself carefully in the looking-glass. And said quietly, 'You are thinking perhaps, that the time has come to dispose of me as well as the boy, Richard?'

'No, by God.'

Will, now combing his beard, smiled at himself in the mirror. 'Very well, Dick, I will give you my terms for staying. I no longer wish to act. That wearisome Sejanus was *my* swan song. *I* will decide what I will write, and if the Company does not like it they can go to Ben Jonson or the devil.'

'And you too may go to the devil.'

Will went on unperturbed, still concentrating on the lie of his beard. 'That apart, Dick, I will serve the Company with the loyalty and devotion and – yes, ability – I have always shown.'

Dick was standing still now, staring. What had become of the humble, amenable Will of yesterday. But Will was speaking again; slowly, for his scissors were delicately trimming off an unnecessary growth. 'For a year or two, that is, before I return to Stratford, and my long-suffering wife, and neglected daughters.' He turned to his friend, and laughed. 'Don't be so troubled, Dick. Last night, when that young fool's point was at my breast, I knew, *really* knew, for the first time that I was mortal.' He smiled wistfully. 'I knew that I still owed God a life, many lives: Anne's, my daughters', Cleopatra's' – he moistened his lips – 'my own.'

Still smiling, he pulled on his doublet. It was sober, as always, but suddenly Dick noticed the richness of the brocade. He noticed the carefully-kept hands, the clear complexion, the serene lift of the chin, the steady, amused eyes. And knew, suddenly, that the green country lad he had taken in, almost out of pity, had outstripped them all; that they could all *act* the courtier, both on and off stage, Will *was* the courtier. Or the honest countryman. Or the landed gentleman, leading that unlikely other life of his among the Stratford burghers. Or the writer, wandering off alone into those strange countries of the mind where none could follow. He had noticed a change in Will after his two years in Stratford: a confidence, a maturity that before had been lacking. But now, at Wilton House, another change: an access of authority, of stature. Will, thought Richard Burbage, had not only created Hamlet and Falstaff and Richard III. He had used (no doubt quite unconsciously) every ounce of his percipience and sensibility and cleverness and observation and amiability to create that most attractive of men, known to his friends as Sweet Will, Gentle Shakespeare; William

Shakespeare, of New Place, Stratford-upon-Avon, Warwickshire: Gentleman.

And now this poet, this man of property, turned from the mirror and came and clapped both hands on Dick's shoulders, and smiling said, 'Is it agreed, old friend?'

Dick was still sulky; trying perhaps to hide the fact that he had been so suddenly overawed. 'I suppose so. But I still say we need comedy. And no one can write it like you.'

Will let his hands fall. He smiled gravely at Burbage. He spoke almost pleadingly. 'Dick, my friend, don't let success spoil you.'

'Me?' It was almost a squeak. '*I* don't have a room scented like a harlot's. *I* don't chatter all evening with the Dowager Countess. I – '

'Do you remember those voyages of discovery we were going to make, Dick, you and I? Do you remember what you said when I gave you Richard II? Hamlet? Here were many-sided men such as had never trod a stage before, you said. Lead me further, you begged, into the labyrinths of men's minds.' He paused, looked at his friend sadly. 'But now – comedy, you cry, to amuse a foolish king.'

'And if I hadn't chosen wisely? Do you think we should be at Wilton House today? No. Deciding to disband, more like, in some drear provincial town.'

Will laughed. 'Oh, go and lead off your victorious army, you mighty Tamburlaine. I will go see the King. And we will meet at the Globe.'

'Or Philippi,' muttered Burbage glumly. 'I doubt you may put your head in a noose, you too noble Brutus.' But then he grinned, and went. Will Shakespeare and Dick Burbage had far too much respect for each other to quarrel for long.

The Earl of Southampton, very point-device, bowed himself into the bedchamber. God, James does look ghastly this morning, he thought. Aloud he said, 'Majesty, the man Shakespeare has desired an audience. But I would humbly suggest, Majesty – '

'Och, show him in, Henry,' cried James. 'The very man I want to see.'

James drooped on the edge of the bed. He did indeed look ghastly. Enormous slippers, thin white shanks, a tousled gown pulled anyhow over the padded, dagger-proof vest he wore even in bed, sagging eyes, a raffish night cap. But at sight of Shakespeare he cheered up, much to Southampton's quiet fury. 'Shakespeare, come and sit ye down. A chair for Master Shakespeare, Henry.'

It was too much. Commoners did not sit in the royal presence. And Gentlemen of the Bedchamber did *not* pull up chairs. God, this Scotsman tried one hard. Southampton banged down a stool, smiled thinly, bowed deeply, and stood.

James waved him out with a much-ringed hand.

Southampton went, seething. This – this royal ape just didn't know Court behaviour. Gentlemen of the Bedchamber *always* attended audiences. And here he was, dismissed like a lackey. And for Shakespeare, of all men! If it hadn't been for the sweet wines monopoly, he vowed he'd have asked leave to go and quell the Irish. Court life under this – this barbarian was impossible.

Will bowed very deeply. He didn't know which was going to cause more trouble – his pleas for Matthew Peyre or the King's discovery that he'd finished *Macbeth* without even consulting him.

Before he could decide which subject to bring up first, the King surprised him by saying, 'Mon, I need your help.'

Will recovered quickly. 'Sire, if a humble subject of your Majesty *could* help your Majesty in any way – '

'Aye. Save your breath to cool your pottage.' Clearly the King was not pleased that he had to ask a subject for help. ''Tis the play about my noble ancestor Banquo. There's a twa-three difficulties – nothing serious, ye'll understand.'

'As a matter of fact, your Majesty – ' Will pulled the almost completed *Macbeth* out of his doublet. 'I have done some preliminary work on this myself. If your Majesty would care to glance… '

Will waited. He waited a long time while Majesty leafed through the play. And he saw the King's face changing from concentration to irritation to incredulity. And at last those round moon-eyes looked up and stared at him with anger and bewilderment. 'But – ye've killed my noble ancestor Banquo in the third act.'

'He – does come in again later. As a ghost, your Majesty.'

'I'll ghost you, Master Shakespeare.' He gave a curt gesture of dismissal. 'Och, never mind. I'll write my own play.' He tapped *Macbeth* with his finger. 'This is a sair disappointment, Master Shakespeare.'

'I am sorry, your Majesty. But it does deal at length with the downfall of your noble ancestor's murderer.'

'Aye.' And now the pedant had begun to get the upper hand of the angry monarch. 'But ye see, when writing plays, ye need to maintain a balance.'

'Yes, your Majesty.'

"Now that's verra important, Master Shakespeare. Balance. When ye've learnt a bit more about playwriting, ye'll not go killing the hero halfway through and devoting the rest of the play to the man who killed him.'

'No, your Majesty.'

'Here.' He handed the manuscript back to William. And his voice was kindly now – the schoolmaster helping the pupil who, though promising, has yet much to learn. 'See what ye can do with it. And if ye're in any difficulties, come and see me.' He smiled archly. 'I may be a king, but I'm also a man learned in the art of writing. And I'm not one to refuse help to a fellow author.'

'Your Majesty's kindness is matched only by the breadth of his learning, sire.'

'Aye.' The King looked smug. His hand reached for a bell. Will said hurriedly, 'Your Majesty. I crave your Majesty's pardon most humbly. But there is another matter I would fain – '

'What is it, Shakespeare?' He was still the kindly schoolmaster.

'Sire, last evening one of our Company, being grievously troubled in his mind, almost to madness, spoke words which your Majesty must find it hard to forgive.'

The eyes, which before had been like twin moons seen through cloud haze, had changed. Suddenly they were crafty and cunning, watching him with a frightening intensity. And when he spoke the voice had changed too. No longer the harsh but comfortable Scottish burr. King James, it appeared, could speak a steely English with the best when it suited him. 'What of it, Master Shakespeare?'

'The boy is my apprentice, sire, and has served me well. A sober, industrious youth. But last night some fever of the blood, which has been growing for days – I beg you to be merciful, sire.'

The King was silent for a long time. His eyes never left Will's face. At last he said, 'You are a brave man, William Shakespeare.'

Will's lips were becoming dry. He licked them. 'I, your Majesty?'

'Openly allying himself with a Papist and a traitor,' the King said smoothly.

'No traitor, sire. One of your Majesty's most loyal subjects.'

'Who calls his anointed Prince, knave. And who, with the help of that friend of Papists, the Devil, grievously hurt one Nicholas Fox, a player.'

'That was done in fair fight. Fox tormented him.'

'How?'

'By stealing one of his belongings.'

'To wit?'

Will was silent. Then he said, quietly, 'A crucifix.'

It was the King's turn to be silent. At last: 'As I said before, sir, you are a brave man. But do not press my kingly forbearance too far. Go, and leave this utterer of treason to the mercies of the Council – and the hangman.'

He had rung the bell. Southampton entered. 'Ah, Henry, Master Shakespeare's audience is at an end.'

Southampton waited, all impatience. Will bowed deeply, and backed slowly out of the chamber. He who only this morning had been so serene, so assured, was now trembling and shaken. Not only had he failed utterly to free Matthew. He had been given a terrifying glimpse of the wolf that lurked within that fearful, foolish Scottish sheep.

It bore out what he had always really known: that anyone who sat upon a throne of England must have a tiger's claws and a tiger's teeth; and the will, when necessary, to use them like a tiger.

There had been a time, he thought with shame, when that audience would have sent him skulking back to London, chastened and afraid. Well, he was afraid now. And by heaven there was plenty to be afraid of. Monarchs did not deal gently with those who tried to bring solace to their enemies. But he wasn't running off with his tail between his legs this time. He was responsible for his apprentice. Besides, how could he ever face Annette if he abandoned her son? Annette, he knew in his heart, would abandon no one she had once taken under *her* wing.

But what to do? He was no man of action. Rescuing a prisoner from the King's guards was not for poets. (He could, he realised, become very bookish when danger threatened.) No. There was only one possible way of helping Matthew: to enlist the aid of the great and powerful.

King James was dressed when it came to his second audience of the morning, and was eating a rather messy breakfast of succory pottage, capons' wings, and pomegranates.

He greeted her jovially, for he was always a little ill at ease with this noble English lady; suspecting, quite correctly, that she had not the wholehearted admiration for his qualities that he would have expected. Also, he and his Court were guests in her house. He was very comfortable there; and in London the plague was still raging. He wanted to stay; yet there had been reports of some unseemliness on the part of some of his courtiers – chambermaids raped, an old manservant run through by his dear friend Robert, gentlemen relieving themselves in corridors – of which this patrician lady might not approve.

So Jamie put himself out to be pleasant. He even rose, and extended greasy fingers to be kissed. 'Ma bonny hostess! Will ye not try one of these capons' wings? They're grand, woman.'

'No, I thank your Majesty.' She took the seat to which he gestured. 'I broke my fast early.'

'Aye.' She would, he thought. She'd be up with the servants and the maids, seeing they were at their work, keeping an eye on everything.

She spread her skirts comfortably, with jewelled hands. 'I trust your Majesty has every comfort.'

'Aye.' He was watching her warily, the whole of the time it took to claw a pomegranate seed from where it had taken refuge in a hollow tooth. What had she come about, he wondered uneasily. That last chambermaid? A pert wench, who'd asked for everything she'd got. If Lady Pembroke thought that he, James, would favour a little doxy like that against one of his own Privy Council, she must have some very strange ideas about the Monarchy.

But ravished chambermaids seemed to be the last thing on Lady Pembroke's mind. For she gave the King that warm and mellow smile, and said, 'Your Majesty is more than welcome. It is my earnest hope that your Majesty will stay with us until the plague abates. After all' – again that wonderful smile – 'it seems to me there would be little point in returning to, say, Woodstock, when we have laid all the pleasures and comforts of Wilton House so gladly at your Majesty's feet.'

James felt very pleased with himself. He knew, of course, just how the Countess' mind was working. What, she was asking herself, were a few deflowered maids, an old man gone a few years early to the grave, what were these compared to the honour of entertaining the King. A small price, indeed! And, having heard the reports, she had come to reassure him, in this oblique way, that he must not trouble his royal head about such trifles.

'There is, however, one point I would crave to bring to your Majesty's attention.'

155

The wind had shifted. Easterly. There was now a wintry edge to the Countess' voice. Well, what did that matter to the King of England and Scotland?

But it did matter. Even a king does not forget the cuffs and humiliations and degradations of childhood. And of these James had had his fill, so that he was still very capable of being made to feel an untidy, clumsy, slow-witted small boy. And that was the effect Lady Pembroke had on him exactly.

He watched her slyly over the capon wing he was gnawing. Now he had thrown away joviality as a defence, and taken up truculence. 'What point is that, my Lady Countess?'

She said: 'Wilton House is my home, Majesty. And yours, so long as you choose to honour us.'

He nodded; waited.

'But I will not have it turned into a prison, sire.' It was like a ring of trumpets.

The round, foolish eyes had drawn closer together. They seemed to have tightened. '*Will* not, Madam Countess?'

'*Will* not, sire.'

Those eyes, contracted with anger, went on watching her. 'And if your Sovereign *does* will it, my lady?'

'The keys of Wilton are mine, to have and to hold. It is not meet that even the King of England should hold one of those keys.'

'You go too far, madam.'

'No, sire. It is you, with humble respect, who go too far. Your Captain of the Guard has taken one of my keys and used it without authority.' She laughed, with some of her friendliness. 'Imagine, sire. He has taken bolts and bars, and two soldiers with halberds, to hold prisoner a crazed boy of twelve.'

'Who cried treason.'

'Treason! He but cried a song that swam into his addled brain.'

James was furious. He leapt to his feet. 'He called me – knave. *Me* – the anointed of God!'

She stayed serene. 'Might I suggest, your Majesty – humbly – let the poor fool go, and use his prison to house your Gentleman of the Chamber who killed my poor old servant Piers.'

The King was silent. She went on. 'Then I would hold the key. And I warrant you he should not escape, your Majesty.'

So she *did* know. The whole, wretched story. God, she could make trouble. Not only for his dear, hot-headed Robert whom he loved so tenderly, but for himself! There were plenty of people only too eager with their criticisms nowadays...

The King had sat down again. Petulantly he picked up a handful of capon bones and flung them across the floor; but when he looked at the Countess, she was calmly reading a sheet of paper. She looked up. 'There is also the case of Judith Mears, with child by one of your Majesty's Privy Councillors. Simon, a scullion, blinded by one of your gentlemen flinging a bowl of scalding soup in his face.'

The King moistened his lips. ''Twas a jest.'

My lady looked at him in silence. Then returned to her paper. 'Rebecca Woods, raped by four of your Majesty's courtiers. Doubtless another jest.'

The King said nothing.

The Countess said, 'This is a long, wearisome tally, your Majesty.' She sighed heavily. 'And will, I doubt not, grow longer and more wearisome as the weeks go by; but I am a loyal subject of your Majesty, and honoured that you should be my guest.'

She waited for him to reply. He said nothing. 'But I will not have my house a prison,' she added quietly.

The King had at last stopped looking at his hostess. He stared down at his plate. And suddenly he banged the table furiously and roared, 'Talbot!'

The door was flung open. The Captain of the Guard and two soldiers rushed into the room.

The King transferred his furious gaze to his Captain. 'Escort the Lady Pembroke to the boy player's cell. Give him into her hands. Unharmed, mind.'

Talbot could not believe his ears. 'An avowed traitor, your Majesty?'

'Do as I say,' the King said wearily.

'But surely – at least he should be whipped for insolence?'

'No.' It was a whisper.

Talbot bowed stiffly to the Countess, disapproval in every inch of leather and steel. She rose and acknowledged his bow, with grace and kindness. Then she swept his Majesty a low and respectful curtsy. 'I thank your Majesty.'

He sat sprawled, staring at the table. He let her get to the door. Then the mottled, angry face came up to stare once more. 'I shall not forget this audience, my lady,' he said coldly.

She curtsied once more; graceful, despite her bulk, as a young girl.

And was gone.

It was dark. It was cold and dank as a charnel vault. Somewhere, near at hand, water dripped endlessly. There was no other sound in the whole world.

Was it day, or night? Day, for a little of the grey December light filtered in at the high grating.

Was he alive, or dead? Alive, for his head and shoulder throbbed and pulsed, hurt no doubt when they flung him into the cellar. Sad, to recognise life by the pain of it!

Was he sane, or mad? Sane, for he knew who he was:

> Matthew Peyre is my name
> Humble is my station.
> Heaven is my hoped abode,
> And Christ is my salvation.

But why was he here? All night there had been dreams: at home, with mother and father, attending Mass in the kitchen of a great house; the grey-haired priest; the people loving and united in their peril; the watchers at doors and windows; the peace, and happiness, of that far-off Sunday morning: strange flowers to flourish in such danger.

A stage. Himself, alone, shouting treason at a king!

Master Shakespeare's lodgings. Himself at his Ovid, his master at his playwriting, not a word spoken, yet friendship, love, respect, filling the room like a blessing.

A bed. Himself lying in the rain. Master Burbage holding a pillow over his face until he was dead. Lying there, wanting to shiver but he must not shiver because he was dead. 'And further say that, in Aleppo once – '

Which were dreams, which reality? He did not know. The only reality he knew was the pain in head and shoulder, the lock outside the door, the cold, the fear.

Fear! He was a prisoner. He was at the mercy of men who perhaps did not know mercy. And as alone and friendless as he had been on that stage, as the man on the scaffold.

His forehead burnt. He could not stop his teeth chattering. Fear? Cold? Fever? He suspected all three. Fear most of all. Sometime, sooner or later, he would hear footsteps in the corridor, the key turning in the lock, his name called in a rough voice.

And at that moment, he knew, his heart would stop for fear.

Far away, in the great house, a door slammed.

He strained his ears, biting his knuckles until the flesh was raw. Footsteps *were* there, coming nearer. The dread, marching step of armed man. Now he could hear the clank of breastplates, the thud of halberds.

Near, now. Outside the door. Yellow light, running in like water under the door. A shouted order. The boots, stamping to silence. The harsh, resentful grating of the key turning the lock. The creak of the door. The trickle of light changing to a sudden flood, dazzling, revealing, so that he felt naked before his tormentors. He lay face downward on the stone slab, trying hopelessly to bury his face in the cold stone.

A woman's voice said, 'Boy, you are free. I have come to take you to your master.'

He shuddered uncontrollably, as with an ague.

'Come,' said the gentle voice. 'No one will harm you.' Then, a little impatiently, 'Look at me, boy.'

In his fever he had a strange fancy – and buried his face deeper in his arm. 'Holy Mary, Mother of God, I am not worthy,' he cried.

'You flatter me,' said the Countess coolly. '*My* rank is purely temporal.' And she pulled him round so that he must look at her.

She saw a pale, fevered, terrified boy – a boy who needed caring for and tending just as much as the other one with the broken knee – and who tore much more keenly at her woman's heart. So, in addition to King James and his Court, she had two boys to nurse. It looked as though she would have a busy Christmas.

'Horses! Fast horses for Master Shakespeare's coach!'

'A room! The best room for Master Shakespeare! And good lying for his young gentleman.'

There was no doubt about it. Will Shakespeare was travelling back to London in a better state than he had travelled from it. It seemed as though Christmas at Wilton, as the personal guest of the Dowager Countess, had given him a reputation in the south-west. Will Shakespeare. Yes, a great friend of the Dowager Countess. 'Tis said she do help him write those plays of his.

And, in some strange way, this was true. Long, ranging conversations, her *Antonius*, her views, her ideas, all strangely focused his mind on *his* Antony, *his* Egyptian woman. So that, by the time he left Wilton, he had built the whole ancient world around them – Rome, Alexandria, Athens, Actium. All that remained was for these ancient lovers to take on life, and passion, and a noble dying.

At his parting from the Countess: 'My lady, how can I thank you for your warm hospitality – and for saving Matthew?'

That smile, sweet as an autumn day. 'Sir, the greatest in the land are lodged at Wilton House, yet none honours it like yourself.'

He bowed his head, to hide the tears that sprang to his eyes. And said anxiously, 'Yet I fear, madam, you have displeased the King. And for my sake.'

'It could not have been long,' she said serenely, 'before I displeased him. He and I are not of a feather, Master Shakespeare.'

They had smiled, he still anxious, she reassuring. He had kissed her hand, plump and scented and heavy with noble rings, and had come away.

And now:

'Send Ralph on to Stockbridge, to bid the Greyhound prepare for Master Shakespeare's coming.' Oh, how often had he ridden the Stratford–London road on a tired nag, no best rooms for Master Shakespeare then. A bundle of hay in a barn in the early days, and thankful for it. But it was good to have known poverty and hardship; it made one appreciate the new fangled coach, these inns with individual bedrooms for the gentry.

He had gained new stature for this part of honoured guest, important traveller. His cheeks were fuller, his beard a little fiercer, what was undoubtedly a paunch had acquired a certain majesty. The amiable, friendly Warwickshire lad had changed, by imperceptible degrees, into one of the most important commoners in England: a landowner, a sharer in London's leading theatrical company, a royal servant, a court official, a writer of popular plays, a friend of England's greatest patroness of the arts. (He had almost lived down the deplorable fact that he wrote, not like a gentleman, but for *money*.) And at last he had, with astonishment, recognized and accepted his position; he had grown accordingly.

Yet he remained the same sweet Will – kind, thoughtful, friendly, but with this difference. He knew now where he was going, and what was to be done. He owed God a life, several lives.

Master Shakespeare's young gentleman was also enjoying travelling in style. The Countess had done wonders for both of her patients, Nicholas Fox's knee supported him soundly if painfully. (But Will had insisted the boy was not yet fit to travel. *He* wasn't travelling halfway across southern England with Mistress Fox. And Mistress Fox, torn between a further sojourn at Wilton House, where there were *so* many pleasant gentlemen, and travelling with Master Shakespeare who had no time for *anything* but writing, mercifully agreed to stay at Wilton.)

Matthew Peyre had been brought back, gently, from nightmare to reality. The Countess had soothed and relieved his fever, Will had soothed his tormented mind. He seemed once more the quiet, courteous boy Will had made his apprentice.

But he still did not know whether his mother was alive or dead. He was tortured by the slowness of the journey, through the snow and sleet, the rain and mud, the rare, bland days of sun and warmth that bejewel an English January. At last, however, they were in the outskirts of London, and there were people, crowds even. *Some* had survived. And if some, why not she?

Will said courteously 'I have enjoyed your company, Matthew. You have made the journey pleasant.'

It had indeed been pleasant to look up from his interminable writing and see that young face across the coach, staring out with all the wonder of boyhood at passing towns, or gazing inward at his own anxieties, or smiling shyly at his master; or Will would gaze at the sleeping boy with that compassion he always felt for a fellow human being saved by sleep from the fret and cares of waking.

Matthew said, 'I have been but poor company, sir. Master Shakespeare, sir, do you think I could visit my mother as soon as we reach your lodgings? I have been troubled for her.'

'Of course, boy.'

But when, at last, the boy was ready to set off, Will thought: if she's dead he's too young to face the truth alone. He said, 'I will walk with you, Matthew.'

The boy looked uncomfortable and said bravely, 'Sir, forgive me. But I would rather go alone.'

So. He had still not been forgiven for abandoning Annette Peyre. Despite all his efforts he still stood, rejected, outside the boy's heart. 'I understand, Matthew,' he said. He smiled. 'And I am sure all will be well.'

Matthew did not answer. He set off. The young mouth was drawn in a tight line. He stared straight before him. He walked as a man walks towards a line of bowmen who stand, arrows poised, bows at the stretch, awaiting the order.


Mistress Mountjoy was lighting fires that smoked, putting warming pans in beds that steamed, and questioning, not for the first time, the wisdom of taking in theatrical folk.

You never knew where you were with them. Off at a moment's notice, away for months, and then back in the middle of January without a word of warning, and expecting a warm room and a warm bed and a pickled herring for supper as though they'd never been away.

Not that she could complain about Master Shakespeare. A proper gentleman, no trouble, always treated you like a lady. *And* the boy, untidy of course, but he took some of the work off her hands, the way he ran about after his precious master.

And here *was* Master Shakespeare, smiling, rubbing his hands, looking round the gaunt room as though he were pleased to be back. 'Well, mistress? They tell me the plague is much abated.' But not really listening to her reply; over to his books, picking up one here, one there, opening, reading, snapping them shut so that the dust flew. Not that Master Shakespeare was one to notice dust; give him peace and quiet, feed him now and again, and Master Shakespeare was as easy as anyone could wish for.

# Chapter 12

## All my pretty ones?

He was running now, taut as a fiddle-string, breathing heavily. A hundred paces down this street, then left, and he would see the house.

The house of the living? Or the house of the dead?

He came round the corner. It was facing him.

No light in any window, this January dusk. His home looked cold, empty; unwelcoming as a tomb.

With the coming of night, a mist was beginning to crawl about the empty streets, the cobbles glistened with the clamminess of toads. Death, it seemed, still crouched among these crouching homes.

He dared not go on. He dared not knock upon that door, to hear the sound within go echoing about the empty house. He dared not push the door, lest it open and let him in to the dark, waiting silence of those empty rooms.

He was being foolish, he knew it. There could be a dozen reasons why no light burned in his mother's house this winter afternoon. Yet he could think of only one.

Biting his lip, walking slow and fearful, watching the house as a wrestler watches his adversary, he reached the

'Aye. What a strength we lost in your husband, Mistress Peyre.'

And now, once again, bolts were being drawn. Matthew, staring into the darkness from the kitchen, saw the door open, a man pass stealthily through, the door close, then open again to release another man then in turn close behind him. It took a long time. But at last he heard the final bolting, his mother's footsteps. 'Matthew, where are you? Come into the parlour.'

He hurried in. She was lighting a taper from the fire, lighting the cluster of candles. With his mother, everything had to be done methodically and in order.

Then, this done, she turned, smiling, holding out her arms, the candlelight caressing that smooth, lovely face and brow. 'Oh my dearest, you've come home, but what a welcome, forgive me, pretty sweeting.'

He ran into her arms, held her close, smothering her with kisses. *This my mother was dead and is alive again.* 'Mother! Oh, you did not catch the plague.'

'No, boy, not I. But Mistress Paget is dead, and the Williams baby, and old Johnson at the shop.'

He tried to care, could not. Mother was alive. No one else mattered. He broke away, looked at her. 'I vow you are more beautiful than ever.'

She laughed, delightedly. 'Nay! You speak more like a flattering courtier than a son. But now! Some food for you. And while I prepare it, tell me about your travels. How is Master Shakespeare?' she asked, turning her face away from the candlelight.

'Well. He is most kind. I love him a little as I – loved Father. Mother, what did that gentleman mean tonight when he said what a strength they had lost in Father?'

'He meant – come into the kitchen, Matthew. There is bread and cheese and kickshaws. And milk. That will serve? – he meant Father was a great support for our religion.'

'But  – ' It had not sounded quite like that. And Father – gentle, kindly. But strength? No, he did not think so. But already, he knew, he was beginning to confuse in his mind Father and Master Shakespeare: their understanding and their thoughtfulness; and in the case of both, it suddenly occurred to him, a sense that they walked at times in another world than this, a withdrawing, a detachment, in Shakespeare's case of course his plays, but in his Father's – what?

It was all too much for his young mind, too dimly apprehended. Yet it left him troubled, as though he had discovered in his dead father some secret, some shame even. 'Who were those gentlemen?' he asked, nibbling cheese, gulping milk, a milk mustachio already about his lips.

'Friends of your father's.' She was savouring a pleasure that only mothers know – of watching her son enjoy the food she has prepared for him. Yet she, too, was troubled, troubled and afraid.

'And they came to hear Mass?'

'Yes. And then they talked.'

'In the dark?'

'Yes.' She was silent, making a decision. Then she said, 'Things are not well with us, Matthew. The new King has made a proclamation, banishing our priests. We fear very much for the future.'

He said again, 'But in the dark?' He did not know why he was so troubled.

She said, throwing a log on to the fire, 'It is the King's proclamation, banishing the priests. If Father Grainger were caught, it would' – she shuddered – 'it would be death for him. And it would go ill for all who were found with him.'

It did not sound like his calm, controlled mother. Something was wrong. And his supper? Cheese and kickshaws! He would have expected her to provide something a *little* more like a fatted calf. No. His mother didn't *really* seem to have noticed his homecoming. Her mind, it seemed, was too troubled by her own fears. He rose from that table, went and put his arms round her. 'Mother, why are you afraid?'

She said, sharply for her: 'I told you. The new King is being turned against us.'

'There is more than that,' he said.

'Nothing.' And, with a great effort seemingly, a hug, a smile: 'Come! You have told me nothing yet of your travels.' And for the first time, it seemed to him, she looked at him. 'How you have grown! But you are so pale, Matthew, and thin. Is not Master Shakespeare caring for you?'

He was home. *This my mother was dead, and is alive again.* Surely, surely that was all that mattered, this answer to his months of prayer! But – a black priest, hooded. Men; muffled, whispering, secret men. What were those names he had heard? Already he had forgotten, for they meant nothing to him.

But he feared for his mother.

Once again, in the rooms above the tire-maker's shop in Cripplegate, a candle burned late, a quill squeaked and spluttered in desperate haste.

Will's ranging mind had been in the silversmith's house. What would the boy have found? Dare even death ravish that serene and lovely creature? Yes. He who had taken Cressid and Helen and Cleopatra, would go to it greedily.

But the boy had not returned seeking comfort where there was no comfort, as Will had dreaded. So presumably she lived. He was thankful – for the boy's sake, he told himself. Yet he felt a strange excitement that he would meet her again, that he could still pursue that sweet, forbidden relationship that they both yearned for and shrank from.

Then he sat down at his desk, and in a moment his mind was in ancient Scotland. He heard the storm wind tearing at trees and battlements, he saw clouds scudding low across the wild heath, he smelt the blood. He began to write.

Yet, even as he wrote, a part of his mind, the part where compassion lurked, was on the boy: living among men, expected to have the same intelligence and understanding and strength as a man, working from dawn to midnight, learning, rehearsing, dancing, tumbling. And, through it all, the aches of loneliness and homesickness and anxiety. Never for him the drowsy summer afternoons of country boyhood, thought Will, remembering his own child life before lust and folly trampled it underfoot: the swimming, running, helping round up the sheep, bringing home the hay; the long, long daydreams among the swaying meadow grasses.

But quickly the boy was forgotten. Now he was with two of Macbeth's enemies; and, so well had he created them, it seemed as though they spoke and he but wrote down what they had to say.

But then he remembered that King James wasn't going to like any of this. King James wanted Banquo.

Well, Banquo was dead. He *could* bring him in as a ghost again, but the King hadn't been impressed by his first ghostly appearance. So, remembering that this scene was taking place in England before the King's palace, he had a doctor walk out of the palace, give the two grief-stricken Scots a quick dissertation on the English monarch's ability to cure the King's Evil, and go inside again. He then let Malcolm give a brief summary of the blessings the King of England had brought to his throne, hoped King James would take it personally and that the audience wouldn't object to this slight irrelevance, and brought in Ross to get the pot boiling again with his terrible news of the slaughter of Macduff's wife and children.

Very soon Will had forgotten all about King James. Ross was telling his tale with tormenting slowness. But at last he spoke plainly the words for which he had been preparing Macduff, the words Macduff already expected: 'Your wife and babes savagely slaughtered.'

Will waited for Macduff, for a cry of horror and revenge that would shake the Globe to its foundations.

Macduff was silent. In the end it was Malcolm who spoke, begging him to give sorrow words, lest his heart break.

And at last Macduff spoke. But nothing to shake the Globe. Almost a whisper: 'My children too?' And then: 'My wife kill'd too?' And then: 'All my pretty ones?' And only then, rising from a whisper to a great roar, like a sudden wind in the season of thunder, the cry for revenge.

Will sat back in his chair, read through what he had written. 'My children too?' Marry, that was good. Everyone waiting for the explosion of rage and horror. And, instead, the short, stricken questions, like the introductory tapping of a kettledrum before the great clash of drums and trumpets.

Yet he hadn't written it. Or had he? The passage about the King's Evil, yes, he'd written that, consciously, every word. But these others, where it seemed his characters spoke out of their own mouths (and spoke well, i' faith), where did *they* come from? Where, in fact, *was* fancy bred? Heart, head, a divine prompting, or – as Burbage had once feared about *Hamlet* – the work of the Devil? Sometime, when his brain no longer teemed with men and women and the clash of arms, sometime he would sit down and examine this phenomenon. Surely he, who was supposed to know so much about the labyrinths of the mind, could solve this mystery of his own.

Yet, in his heart, he knew that when his brain *did* cease to teem it would be an end. It would be time for the trip to Stratford churchyard, and the sad bell, and the long rest under the violets.

The boy came in.

It was late. So all should be well. He looked at his face, expecting the ineffable joy that shines in the eyes of young girls dancing.

It wasn't there. The boy looked unhappy; yet not, surely, grief-stricken? Will put down his pen, smiled. 'Now Matthew, what is your news?'

'Good, I thank you, Master Shakespeare. Mother escaped the plague, by the mercy of God.'

A tremendous relief. Had she died, who but he would have been responsible for leaving her in London? Yet there was something wrong. 'I am so thankful, boy. And she is well?'

'Excellent well, sir.'

Will waited, giving the boy time to unburden himself. But Matthew said, 'Thank you, Master Shakespeare.' And then, moving to the door of his own room. 'Give you good night, sir.'

'Goodnight, Matthew.' Yet he could not help feeling a little hurt. 'It is good to be back in London? Your mother safe and well, everything unchanged.'

'Yes, master.'

He went into his room. Will could have shaken him. He had expected the boy to return either radiantly happy or dumb with misery. But this grey in-between, this holding at arms' length of a man he had once loved and respected – it was baffling and hurtful. He picked up his pen once more. 'Dunsinane. A Room in the Castle… ' he began.

# CHAPTER 13

## PRAY YOU, LOVE, REMEMBER

'Here's the smell of blood still,' Matthew said for the sixth time. 'All the perfumes of Arabia will not sweeten this little hand. Oh! oh! oh!'

'No, no, *no*,' cried Will. 'Despair, boy, despair! Cry out, moan your despair. You're talking about murder, not cosmetic.'

Matthew looked at him sulkily. Well, that was better than the bravely choked-back tears they once had. It hurt Will less anyway.

But now a voice at Will's shoulder said, with supercilious courtesy, 'Master Shakespeare, sir?'

He turned, still irritable. 'Well, Nicholas?'

"Might I try this scene, sir?"

'Yes,' Will said shortly. A limping Lady Macbeth wasn't what he'd imagined. But a limping Lady Macbeth was better than a limping Viola, anyway. 'Matthew,' he called. The boy jumped down from the stage.

All Will's irritation had suddenly vanished. Now he had to twist a knife in a wound, something that usually hurt him far more than the victim. He said, 'Give your part to Nicholas, boy. Let us see what he makes of it.'

'Yes, sir.' Matthew handed over the paper with a smile. Something like a smile also flickered in Master Fox's close-set eyes. Strangely, that disastrous fight seemed to have taken the enmity out of their relationship without putting friendship in its place.

Nicholas glanced at the paper, climbed with gritted teeth on to the stage, shook off helping hands, gained the upright, and stood sweating but composed.

'Back to "Look, how she rubs her hands",' said Will.

Nicholas walked forward, staring, chillingly – at nothing. And when at last he spoke, his voice had the unmistakable ring of high tragedy. 'Hell is murky! Fie, my Lord, fie! A soldier, and afeard?' Will felt the shiver in his spine, the trembling inside his cheeks, the pricking behind the eyes that meant he was listening to true drama or true poetry.

The rehearsal continued. Burbage said in Will's ear, 'If his leg but mend properly, he'll be the best boy we ever had.'

Will nodded glumly. 'I suppose you're thinking he's the man for my royal gipsy?'

Burbage shot him a quick glance. 'Still on with that?'

'Yes.' Will was short. 'And I still think Matthew can do it.'

But where was Matthew? He looked round. The boy was standing next to him. Will hoped he hadn't heard the conversation.

But Matthew had. And when Burbage, without looking at him, said, 'Fetch me a cup of ale, boy', he pretended not to hear, and slipped away to a dark cupboard under the stage where, when life became unbearable, he would sit, knees to chin, and hug his misery to himself in solitude.

And in this black hole he thought of his little room at home, of his bed under the sloping ceiling, of summer bedtimes blessed by evening sunlight and his mother's prayers. Most of all, in this uncaring world of men, he thought of his mother's soft femininity, her gentleness and friendliness. He did not, he decided, care for men. Everything about them was rough – clothes, hands, faces, speech, manners. He did not want this player's life. Even the company of his tarnished idol Shakespeare did not make up for all his miseries.

*This my mother was dead, and is alive again. I will rise and go to her…*

He would never make an actor. They had all made that quite clear, even Master Shakespeare. He slipped out of the cupboard, groped his way under the creaking, thumping stage, out, away from the shouts, the raucous cries of men, back to a world of peace and love; yet knowing in his heart this was cowardice, a running away, something of which his father would not have approved, nor Mother, nor Master Shakespeare; though he felt that, strangely, of the three Master Shakespeare would understand it best. He understood everything.

He looked back at the Globe. There it stood, towering like a castle, a galleon, above the neighbouring houses. His prison, his place of torment! And he had walked out of it into the afternoon sunshine; he had simply walked out, it had been as easy as that. He began to run, filled with exultation – and guilt.

He knocked cheerfully, yet a little defiantly, at his mother's door.

It did not open. No light, brisk footsteps coming up the hall.

He knocked again. Silence.

So. She had gone to the market, or to visit a friend.

Then, out of the corner of his eye, he caught a movement, the stirring of a curtain. He ran and peered through the window.

A man, half hidden by the curtain. A tall man, with a full, curly beard and long moustaches. A man who looked grave, but unafraid.

Matthew, furious, went and hammered the wrought-iron door knocker.

The door was opened by the man. 'What are you doing in my mother's house?' demanded Matthew. His voice was taut with anger and a fear of something unknown.

'So you are Matthew,' said the man.

'*What are you doing in my mother's house?*'

'I had the honour to be your father's friend. And, while I am in London, your mother lets me use her house for my – business purposes.' For the first time Matthew noticed that he had a quill in his hand. 'I – have been writing letters, Master Peyre.'

A likely tale! 'Where is my mother?'

'Out. I do not work here when she is at home. It would be unseemly.'

The man did not smile. He seemed a man who saw little cause for smiling. And yet a fine, soldierly man.

But Matthew, who had come home yearning for femininity, hated him. He had had enough of men. He drew himself up to his full height. 'Sir, I must ask you to leave this house. Until I have my mother's confirmation of your unlikely story, I –'

'I was about to leave,' said the man. 'If you will permit me – a few papers –' Matthew followed him into the parlour.

On his mother's desk was a jumble of papers. The man scooped them up hurriedly, checked carefully to see that nothing was left, and turned to the door.

Matthew, still seething, went to see him off the premises. But the stranger was not ready yet. He clamped a high-crowned hat on his head, pulled it well down over his eyes, stuffed his papers carefully into a leather wallet, went to the front window, peered out, left, right, then went and opened the door. More hasty glances left and right, and he was gone with a murmured, 'Commend me to your mother, boy.'

Matthew wandered round the empty house, troubled and angry. He had fled from a world he hated to a nest of tenderness and peace. And had found the nest – what? Defiled? No. He would never believe that, even if he understood quite what it meant. But strange, alien. The other night, those secret men, furtive in the darkness. Today, this handsome, soldierly man making himself at home in his mother's house. Matthew knew something of the world, but not enough. Not enough to see clearly. But enough for his young mind to be tormented by half-formed, half-understood suspicions.

And suddenly his mother's running footsteps, his mother's clear voice. Alarmed. 'Who's there? Who's there?'

He came into the hall. 'Matthew! Dearest! I found the door wide open. I wondered – what – '

She seemed more afraid than an open front door warranted. She said, 'But why are you at home in the afternoon? Is –?'

He said, 'You didn't expect me, did you, Mother.'

'No, of course not. You never – '

He was looking at her closely, with narrow eyelids. Really, it would have been comic, if only –

'Who was that man?' he said.

So they *had* met. She could not stop a hand lifting to her breast, as though to steady her heart. She said, 'An old friend of your father's – and of mine. A – ' she seemed to come to a decision. 'A Master Catesby. But – but why are you home, sweeting?'

Catesby! He remembered now: one of those names he had heard and forgotten that other night.

He said, swept on by a great wave of anger and jealousy: 'Is he your' – he wasn't quite sure of the word – 'paramour?'

For a moment she looked at him in shocked silence. Then her laughter pealed out and went ringing gaily round the quiet house, as it had not done since her husband died. 'Oh, you ridiculous little creature,' she cried. 'Of *course* he isn't. Why, I don't believe you even know what the word means.'

'I do,' he said sulkily, flushing crimson.

'Then you should be the more ashamed of yourself.' She was no longer laughing. 'Robert Catesby honours your father's memory. And is of our faith. And I' – her voice cut now – '*I* am a virtuous woman. And you will remember that always, Master Matthew.'

'I am sorry, Mother.' Oh, that young face, the soft cheeks so flushed, the expression so chastened yet trying so desperately to retain some dignity, some worldliness!

'And so you should be,' she said sternly. 'But now – come, tell me why you are at home.' She sat down, smiling, held out her arms.

He came into them, turning his face away from her, like the child he could still be. But he said, stubbornly, 'Why was he here?'

She sighed, with mock exasperation. She said, 'Because when he is in London he lodges at Puddle Wharf. And who could do business at Puddle Wharf?'

'What business?'

'How should I know what business? Your father loved him. That is enough for me.'

He was filled, nevertheless, with foreboding. A sudden memory, one, in fact, that was never buried deep: coming home from school, being drawn to a crowd, a mocking, jeering crowd; the man on the scaffold, alone, friendless, deserted by man and God; the hiss of a knife, the hangman's hands, bloody and steaming, clawing obscenely in the man's belly: the howls of execration, 'So perish all Papists!' Himself, vomiting in the corner, bitterly ashamed of his womanliness, why, this was one of the entertainments on which London prided itself.

He said, still burying his face in her breast, 'Mother, I beg you be careful. It could be – for our religion, against the State.'

'Nonsense, boy.' Thank God he could not see her face!

'Was he not one of those who attended Mass?'

She said, sharply, 'I told you he was one of our faith. But so am I. So is Father Grainger. I hope you do not suspect *us* of plotting against the State?'

'Of course not, Mother.' He looked up at her now, smiled anxiously. 'Only – I once saw – I never told you, it was so horrible – a Jesuit Father – hanged – may light perpetual shine upon him.'

'And now,' she said hurriedly, 'tell me why you are here.'

'I do not wish to be a player. 'Tis a hateful life.'

She hid her consternation. 'But – oh, Master Shakespeare thought so highly of you.'

'He does so no longer. 'Tis all Master Fox.'

'Matthew! You're not *jealous*!'

'No. But I cannot act, Mother. My Desdemona, my Lady Macbeth – '

'But you are still a child. Obviously you will need training.'

'I tell you, Mother. I will not go back to the King's Men.'

It was a bitter disappointment! To have apprenticed the boy to Master Shakespeare, of all people! And now – Besides, she had always believed that no happiness ever came from running away; that no one worth his salt ever *did* run away. She said firmly, 'Matthew, you are prenticed to Master Shakespeare. You cannot break your articles like this.'

'I remember no articles.'

He was right. That excellent man of business, William Shakespeare, had signed no articles; for the good reason that he was not entitled by law to have an apprentice, having no wife and family in London with whom the boy could lodge.

She said, 'You will go back in the morning, and apologise to Master Shakespeare.'

'I shall not, Mother.'

She looked at her own son with interest. It seemed that he had grown up since he went on tour. It wasn't surprising. But it was certainly going to make life more difficult. She said quietly, 'Surely you know by now that I will not be defied, Matthew?'

'But, Mother?'

'When we have supped, you will go to Master Shakespeare's lodging. I shall come with you, to hear your apology.'

'Mother!' He was almost in tears now. 'I *can't*. I hate it. I hate them all. I shall never be a player.'

She looked at him thoughtfully. It was more serious than she had imagined. She would not wish him a lifetime of fear and misery, doing work he hated. Yet Master Shakespeare had spoken so highly of him. It would be wicked to throw away this golden opportunity when, by gritting one's teeth for a few more weeks – Besides, she did *not* like running away. It was contrary to her whole way of thought. She said, 'When does Master Shakespeare normally return to his lodgings?'

'Six, seven.'

'Then I shall visit him before it grows to late to be seemly.' She put her hand on his. 'I would not be hard on you, Matthew. But I would not have you throw your life away at twelve years old.'

'Where the devil's that boy?' demanded Burbage. 'I sent him for ale half an hour ago.'

Will looked round anxiously. Where *was* Matthew? Hurt, probably licking his wounds in silence. Will was beginning to know his apprentice's habit of retiring within himself.

But even he could not waste time on a boy's emotions. Before his eyes, in his ears, was the surge and fret of blood-soaked Dunsinane; shouts, screams, the clash of swords, drum and trumpet, death, murder, revenge, all moving in a tremendous sweep of horror to its inevitable end. This might not please Jamie, but by God it would please the groundlings. It was going to sweep them off their feet. Why, even Burbage/Macbeth, slain now, was looking more cheerful that he had done for a long time. He mopped his brow, squeezed Will's arm. 'It's good, Will. Now write a comedy as good, and I'll call you friend.'

They grinned, yet knowing this thing was still unresolved between them.

And then, suddenly, the rehearsal was over, and everyone was off, pulling on cloaks, laughing, calling farewells. Macduff, Banquo, Ross, Macbeth himself became commonplace Londoners, hurrying off for a quiet evening with their wives, or a night's drinking in the tavern. And Moreton, Philip Henslowe's servant, who had managed to see something of the rehearsal through an unguarded door, hurried to his master and said, 'They're doing a new play about a Scotsman, trust them to butter the King, and young Fox limps but is still the best boy actor I've seen.'

'So he still acts?' Master Henslowe looked thoughtful.

Only Will was left in the silent Globe. The stage was no longer Dunsinane (or Elsinore, or the Boar's Head Tavern, or the Forest of Arden). It was a platform of bare boards, its value a shilling or two. It possessed neither beauty nor form nor colour. Yet a handful of men could come together and, by their wit and imagination, transform it in the minds of other men into the Capitol, or moon-drenched Belmont, or the field of Agincourt. Great Caesar could die there, poor Richard Plantagenet could be deposed there, it could be laced with Duncan's golden blood.

Will Shakespeare, looking at that bare and empty and silent stage, trembled and wept at the revelation that flooded into his mind: that the creatures who had stormed and cursed and wept and laughed on that stage had all sprung from *his* brain. He had given them life, these shadows of an afternoon; shadows that would fade and be forgotten as other men wrote other plays.

But, while they still lived their shadow lives, they were his, he thought with a sudden pride, yet with a deep humility that was the cause of his tears. And there would be others. He gazed, fascinated, at the stage. And already it was taking on life – snakes, writhing in the hot sand; Antony, Octavius Caesar, Lepidus, the clash of Roman arms; and – beautiful, terrible, magnificent, dominating the stage, the groundlings, the furthest galleries – his royal whore!

No one could play that part. His brain had conceived a creature beyond the reach of any boy.

Yet he knew that conception, whether in the womb or the brain, cannot be reversed. He would, in the fullness of time, bring forth his Cleopatra. So it was important to begin preparing Matthew for the part. The boy *could* do it, if any boy could. He had the acting ability. He needed the fire, confidence. Well, that would come. And, as he had discovered at Wilton, there was, banked down under that polite and conventional exterior, a feverish intensity. Once release *that*, and let him grow an inch or two, and give him the presence he could not fail to acquire with a few years' acting, and he'd be better than that posturing Fox any day.

But how release the fire? And where was the young devil, anyway?

'Why!' cried Mistress Fox cordially. ''Tis Master Henslowe. Rosie,' she bellowed, 'a glass of canary for the gentleman.'

Philip Henslowe bowed courteously, and lowered himself on to a chair. He was getting an old man, too old for all this traipsing about on behalf of the Admiral's (or, as they were now known, Prince Henry's) Men. But you could never trust anyone to do anything nowadays. Besides, he reminded himself, this errand was surely the Lord's work, commiserating with a stricken mother. And when it came to the Lord's work, Philip Henslowe was indefatigable.

He held his wine up to the light. He sipped. He looked at Nell Fox, a deep sorrow and compassion in his sagging eyes. 'Mistress Fox, the Lord has dealt hardly with you.'

In what way, wondered Nell Fox, had the Lord dealt hardly with her. Then she remembered. She lowered her eyes to her lap. 'Alas, yes, Master Henslowe.'

'He chasteneth those whom He loveth.'

Mistress Fox waited. Henslowe sighed. 'So young. And crippled for life.' He looked at her sadly. Perhaps I should not say this, mistress, but I cannot help feeling that the Admiral's Men would never have let this happen.'

Nell Fox said tartly, 'Crippled for life? Nonsense. A slight limp which will not last a twelvemonth.'

Henslowe shook his head, sighed even more deeply.
'Perhaps, if he were to come to Prince Henry's Men, we
could find him some small employment, some – '

'It's still nine pounds,' said Mistress Fox firmly.

'But' – the old gentleman could not believe his ears. 'I was
offering you a kindness, Mistress Fox, a charity.'

'Nine pounds.'

'Five. A crippled youth, fit only to sell quinces – '

'Nine.'

Philip Henslowe rose, and went his way. It was a sad and
disappointing world for a God-fearing gentleman to have to
live in.

He came from the high, romantic clamour of the Globe, to
his lodgings: the heavy table, draped with the carpet that had
once stood beside the Mountjoys' bed, till it became too
worn; the stools, the great high chair, battered but still well
tapestried; the modest shelf of books – North's Plutarch,
Holinshed, Seneca, Plautus, Cinzio (books which, through
the alchemy of his mind, had been transmitted into pleasant
trifles for an afternoon); his desk on to which he now tossed
his completed Macbeth, and on which lay – oh, excitement!
– some notes for his Cleopatra; the great ugly sideboard; the
lath and plaster walls, criss-crossed by beams that warped
and wandered like a map of country lanes. No. They were
not quite the lodgings one would have expected for
London's leading playwriter, for the owner of New Place, for
a Groom of the Chamber; but they served. He could eat,
sleep and write here. That was all he needed. This was his
place of work, where he carried on his far from respectable
trade of writing. The man of property lived at New Place,
Stratford-upon-Avon; but carried on his despised trade here,
above the tire-maker's shop in Silver Street, Cripplegate.

He threw off his cloak. Where *was* that boy? No one to hang his cloak in the closet. He took it himself, hung it carefully. With a wife usually ninety miles away, and having a fastidious nature, he had long ago learnt to tidy up as he went along.

Usually, when a boy disappeared like this, they found he'd been seduced away by one of the Children's Companies. He knew instinctively that this would not be the case with young Matthew. But he would have to speak firmly to him. A boy couldn't go and hide himself away just because he'd been found o'erparted at a rehearsal. Besides, as soon as he'd finished supper, he wanted to settle down with this new play. He didn't want to have to break off for an emotional scene with a twelve-year-old.

His supper was on the table, covered with a linen cloth. He removed the cloth. A herring in vinegar, a little blurred round the edges, bread, cheese, wine. Well, 'twould serve. For a Frenchwoman, Marie Mountjoy showed little culinary imagination. But 'twould serve. It was his evening's writing that mattered.

He sat down at table, propped his notes against the wine bottle, and ate his herring with knife and fingers, too absorbed to use the newfangled fork he usually insisted on.

There was a knock at the door. Marie Mountjoy held it open. Annette Peyre entered.

He rose hurriedly, bowed with grave courtesy, yet all the while conscious of the herring and vinegar on his fingers; conscious, too, for the first time in his life, of the drabness of this room; fearful, too, that something ailed Matthew, that he would no longer enjoy the boy's quiet, sunny presence in his lonely room.

She said, 'Sir, I disturb you at your meal.'

He shook his head. 'I was not hungered. Pray, Mistress Peyre.' He beckoned her to the great chair, hoping she would not notice the tear in the tapestry.

She sat down with her accustomed grace, grasped the chair arms with her small hands.

They looked at each other. It must, he thought, be nearly a year since they met. And she hadn't changed. Living through a plague summer had left no mark on those calm and lovely features.

And he? She had come fearful, lest he should not be the man she remembered. But he was. Courteous, handsome, a depth of kindness and compassion in those dark, wonderful eyes. He had aged a little, she thought, but it suited him, gave him authority. And somewhere, she thought irrelevantly, there is a woman married to this man who will not budge from Warwickshire to live with him. If I were such a one – 'I come about Matthew,' she said. 'You have shown him every kindness, Master Shakespeare. But he is not happy. He says he will never make an actor.'

'He does?' But she could read nothing in Will's expression.

'I came to ask you what *you* thought.'

He said sternly, 'First I want to know where he is. He is my apprentice. I want to know why he is not here.'

She bridled. 'He is at home.'

'Then he will never make an actor. It is a life for men, not for those who run home when they are found to be o'erparted.'

'He is only twelve, Master Shakespeare,' she said reproachfully.

'We have had many boys younger than that who have not found the life unbearable.'

He wondered why he was being so hard on the boy. Disappointment, he thought. He loved Matthew, almost as much as he had loved his own son. And he would have expected the boy's fondness for him to have outweighed any dislike of the player's life. What hurt, too, was the fact that the boy had not come to him with his troubles. He had thought of himself (foolishly, perhaps) as a father. Too clearly, the boy did not see it that way. He said, 'Tell him that if he is not back in this room by seven o'clock tomorrow morning, I shall regard his apprenticeship as terminated.'

She rose, angry, beautiful in her anger. 'Apparently my son lacks the *character* to be a player. Has he the *ability*?'

'Yes, if he would only abandon himself to a part. But he acts as though – he were bound in gravecloths.'

She said coldly, 'I will give him your message. But I do not think he will return.'

He inclined his head.

They walked to the door. He put his hand on the door-knob. She stood waiting for him to open the door for her. He thought: Will Shakespeare, being vindictive to a silly boy of twelve! She thought: he is a harder man than I imagined.

He tugged at the door. It opened. 'Goodnight, Master Shakespeare,' she said.

But for a lonely (and frightened?) woman, and a man suffering a ridiculous hurt, they were standing too near. Suddenly they were clinging to each other with a lonely desperation. She hung her head, her eyes closed. Her fingers gripped his arms. He pressed his lips against her hair, smelling her sweetness, and knew himself drowning in a sea of longing. 'No, no no,' she moaned, pulling away, looking up at him now, a hand brushing away her tears. 'Sir, we forget ourselves grievously.'

He had to clear his voice before he could speak. Then he heard it – he heard Will Shakespeare speaking with the cheap, oily, insincerity of the lecher: 'Madam, will you not stay a little? My poor lodging – ' He heard yet again the mind of Will Shakespeare saying: wife? honour? integrity? What are they, compared with the knowledge that could be mine of this dear woman's flesh? What are they, compared with the possessing of so costly a jewel? My life is two-thirds gone, and how little have I known of the loveliness and the wonder of women? Yet knowing in his heart that this was but the mood of the moment speaking. He wanted no involvement. He had work, he had a wife. The scent of a woman's hair, the love in a woman's eye, the comfort of a woman's arms were the traitors in his brain.

He was almost relieved when she pushed him gently away. 'Goodbye, sir. I should not have come alone. It was unseemly – and foolish. I beg you forgive me, sir.' And she was gone, down the steep, dark stairs. He heard the street door shut behind her.

For a moment he made to go after her. Then he came back into the room. A herring in vinegar, a glass of wine, a guttering candle, a play to write. A lonely room. Such was the life Will Shakespeare had made for himself. God what a fool he was! He could have found women in London to ease his loneliness, if he hadn't always been too busy, or too righteous. And why wasn't he in Stratford, with his wife and two fair daughters, in the fine house he had given them to live in? Why did he choose London, and loneliness? Because of this demon in his brain, that spawning house of characters. Furiously he flung himself down at his desk, knowing of old that for him the only cure for the pains of life lay in his writing. He seized his quill, dipped it in the inkhorn. 'Alexandria. A Room in Cleopatra's Palace.'

But for this evening at least, he could not forget the ecstasy and despair of finding Annette Peyre in his arms, or the smell of her hair, or the knowledge that, for one desperate moment of forgetting, she had clung to him as a woman clings to her lover.

The boy did not return. Will was curiously hurt. Under his quiet manner Matthew was highly-strung and unpredictable, he knew that. But he'd seemed so happy, sitting here in the evenings with his Ovid, or waiting on Master Shakespeare's supper. Will had even been fool enough to imagine that Matthew had taken Hamnet's place, and he the boy's father's. And he'd been kind to the boy, spent on him his most precious commodity, time. How ingratitude in others distressed his own generous nature! Still, he was only a boy. And everyone said it was no use expecting courtesy from the young. The world was changing. Manners, it seemed, were a thing of the past.

But he remained hurt. Even if the *boy* saw nothing wrong in leaving, without a word, someone who had befriended him, surely his mother would have sent him to apologise. Or come again herself, he thought with a tormenting mixture of fear and excitement.

But no. That would never happen. Annette Peyre, he knew, had found herself of a sudden on a brink. And had recoiled, horror-stricken. She would not again go near enough to peer down into those unknown depths. And he felt a certain relief in this knowledge. Perhaps he was getting old; but he wanted no more adventures, stealing his time, consuming his thoughts. Yet he knew that, alone in the same room with Mistress Peyre, his resolution would melt like wax before the flame. Still a coward, he thought wryly. Grasping at a woman's resolution to save him from his weakness.

A letter arrived. A neat, strong handwriting. He unfolded it.

Sir. My son has behaved ill. I would have him come to you with an apology. Yet will I not force him, because I feel that what is ended should stay ended, for all our sakes.

I pray that God may have you always in his keeping.
Remember me!
Annette Peyre.

'Remember me.' It had certainly been inserted above the signature. An afterthought. She had tried to make the letter impersonal, and then had not been able to resist this small appeal that she should not die altogether to him. A sad letter. He felt the tears in his eyes. He put it to his lips, hoping to catch from it some of her fragrance. But there was nothing.

'Mistress,' he wrote back. 'Do not force the boy. I am not one of those who busy themselves about apologies.'

He paused, re-read her letter, took up his pen once more. He wrote: 'I shall remember you, madam, all my days. And pray *you*, love, remember! Will Shakespeare.'

Would she recognise the quotation from his *Hamlet*? He thought not. But it allowed him a little tenderness he could not otherwise have used.

He sanded the letter, sealed it with his ring, with the 'speare hedded argent' that he had won for his family. And sealing the letter, pressing down the hardening wax, it was as though he sealed a chapter in his life; as though he caught and fastened back in their Pandora's box emotions that might have torn apart his life, Annette's life, Matthew's life, those three gentle lives in Stratford.

Finish, good lady. He gave the boy a penny to take the letter. And now work. He sent for Nicholas Fox.

'Master Fox, I am writing a play about Cleopatra, Queen of Egypt: a tempestuous, fiery, clever woman. A woman in every way regal. Could you play such a part?'

'Of course, Master Shakespeare.'

Will looked at the youth. Marry, he'd grown since they took him into the Company. And he held himself straight and well, and his limp was scarce noticeable, especially under a farthingale. His eyes still crowded that long nose of his, but he was handsome enough. Darken his face, give him a black wig, dress him in a gored skirt and a long-waisted, pointed bodice, and he'd be Cleopatra to the life. Will wished he could like him better. He said, tartly, 'What makes you so sure you could play the part?'

A scornful twitch of those arrogant nostrils. 'Did not my Lady Macbeth please you mightily?'

'I never said so.'

'I have noticed you are not fulsome with your praise where I am concerned, Master Shakespeare. But it liked you well. Come now, admit it.'

Will said, 'You will please remember, Master Fox, that I am a sharer in this Company. And that you are a boy actor.'

Fox looked at him coolly, and was silent.

Will suddenly grinned. 'Nicholas, I don't think I like you very much. And I'm quite sure you don't like me. But you're very young. And if we're going to work together, we may come to tolerate each other.'

He waited. He was no longer smiling. Just the relaxed, established employer waiting for one of his junior staff to sort out his feelings.

At last the youth, almost unsmiling, said, 'I should like to play the part, sir.'

'That will depend on your progress in it.'

'I am not given to failing in anything I undertake, Master Shakespeare.'

'I have observed that. So. I have a few scenes already written. I shall of course guide you myself. I would like you in the rehearsal room at seven o'clock tomorrow morning.'

Nicholas Fox rose, bowed stiffly, and went.

Will sighed. And it might have been young Matthew, eager and friendly. It would have been like guiding his own son. It would have taken longer, of course. One, two years. But Matthew could have done it, once he'd broken down his fears and his reserve.

# CHAPTER 14

I HAVE DONE THE STATE SOME SERVICE...

The sharers' meeting was getting noisy. 'But he can't just walk out like that,' stormed Burbage.

'He has done,' said Will.

'Good riddance, if you ask me,' muttered Sly. 'Looked as though butter wouldn't melt in his mouth, yet he's brought us nothing but trouble.'

Heminge was staring unbelievingly at Will. 'But his articles, man.'

'There were none.'

'No articles?' cried Heminge. Really, it was impossible being a business manager. You couldn't trust anyone else to do anything properly.

Burbage said bitterly. 'There were no articles because Will knew he'd no legal right to take the boy, with his family hidden away in Warwickshire.'

'That is true,' Will said blandly.

Condell said sternly, 'This is no shrugging matter, Will. We shall soon have no boys left, the way they're growing up. Mark's beard looks like coal dust. And – when I heard Abraham was Ophelia, t'other day – I vow I thought it was a sheep coughing.'

Augustine Phillips said gently, 'We must get more boys.'

'More boys!' Burbage turned on him furiously. 'There isn't a boy left in London outside the Children's Companies. Children of the Chapel, Children of Windsor, Children of Paul's, Children at Blackfriars, Children's Companies everywhere! It's bad enough when they take our audiences; but when they don't leave a single boy in London without a squint or a hare-lip – '

They were laughing, now. Dick's rages often spilled over into anti-climax. Even he grinned, pleased in spite of himself to have reduced the tension.

'We shall have to play *Caesar, Henry IV,*' said Phillips. 'Fox can play Mistress Quickly and Calpurnia. It will not matter if Lady Percy booms like a cow in calf.'

'We need more than two plays,' grumbled Heminge.

'Perchance,' said Burbage scowling at Will, 'Master Shakespeare will write us a new comedy, with a pert wench for Master Fox and all other parts men.'

The others looked at Will hopefully.

Will was silent.

Burbage said, 'No, gentlemen, you need not look to Will. Will has his own plans.'

Will said heavily: 'I am writing a tragedy. It will have several women, one of them a part that perhaps *no* boy can play.'

'Then why write it, for God's sake?' demanded Heminge.

'Because I must.'

God's teeth, thought Heminge disgustedly. How was a business manager supposed to maintain profits when nobody troubled to tie their precious boys in properly, and authors wrote to amuse themselves?

And he was not the only one thinking thus. Will, always so sensitive to atmosphere, felt a chill emanating from his usually friendly colleagues. The small room at the Globe where they had held so many sharers' meetings – cheerful, depressed, quarrelsome, anxious, fateful meetings – had seldom worn this air of disapproval for anyone. And never for Will, the most helpful, the most popular of them all.

He hated it. He, who so enjoyed being liked, who was so soon in the dumps at a breath of criticism, wanted to cry out, 'Men, I will write you the best comedy ever was.' But he stayed silent. For once he would not budge. He owed God – and Will Shakespeare – a life.

And when the sharers broke up, there was for once no friendly arm about his shoulders, no cheerful, 'Come to the tavern, Will,' not even a comforting meeting of eyes. Only the swarthy Heminge, gathering up with concentrated care his account books, and lean Condell poring over his notes as he strolled to the door, even the melancholy amused face of Robert Armin was turned away from him. Burbage gave him a long, thoughtful look, a curt nod. What was wrong? Could it be that they thought Will was becoming too grand for them? His own room in Wilton House, while they slept in waggons? Staying over Christmas, because of that wretched boy (or that was the excuse)? Or just that for the first time he was not their tame playwright, prepared to dance any jig they called for?

They all crowded out. None waited for him. None turned in the doorway to call goodnight.

He went on sitting at the long table. His lodgings would be lonely this evening, thinking of the players in the tavern; the boy with his mother; the mother whom he had once held, for so brief a moment, in his arms, and whom, he now knew, he so desperately wanted to hold again; Anne, the wife whose love would have sheltered him from all despite, had he but let her; his daughters, whom he had so shamefully neglected; Hamnet, dead child. He would think of them all tonight, while the shadows danced and jigged in the high corners, and the watchman cried the long hours in the streets.

He rose wearily, and went out of the door, expecting no one.

And there, waiting, smiling a little shamefacedly, was Augustine Phillips who said, 'Will, old friend. You will miss the boy. You will be lonely.'

'Yes,' said Will.

'I had hoped,' said Augustine, 'that he might have taken the place of your lost son.'

'I had hoped,' said Will, 'that *I* might have taken the place of his lost father.' He smiled wryly at the gentle Augustine.

Slowly they walked out together in the quiet evening. Phillips said, 'You have served us well, no man better, Will. And the sharers know it. If you were to join us at the tavern?'

Will shook his head, smiling gratefully. 'No, thank you, Gus.'

'Then I will walk with you as far as your lodgings. A man should not be alone when he is dumpish.'

And walk together they did, saying little; while the sun turned the river to cloth of gold, and gilded the boats like gondolas of Venice, and set Paul's aflame. And so did Augustine's friendship warm the cold heart of William Shakespeare.

# CHAPTER 15

## SIR, YOU AND I MUST PART...

And so, yet once again, the old earth tilted England back into the sunlight. This time, to see what 1604 would bring.

It didn't bring much, except a growing disillusion. Elizabeth had been in her grave a twelvemonth, and to many it already seemed a lifetime. James, that very odd Scotsman, had been on the throne of England a year. But the English would have understood him no better if he'd been there a thousand. And it was obvious that James wasn't even going to try to understand the complexities, the contradictions, the infinite subtleties that go to make up the simple, honest-to-God Englishman.

But there were compensations. It soon became clear that James' banishing of the Popish priests had mollified God considerably. The plague was abating. The Court returned to London. And London, that flower of Cities all, once again began to pick up the threads, to teem and steam and sweat and jostle with the glorious business of living, such a happy change after so many months devoted to the tiresome business of dying.

The King hunted with yet more zest, the Queen frolicked ever more gaily, Ben Jonson and Inigo Jones produced ever costlier and more splendid masques with even greater acrimony; the French ambassador, whose invitations to the masques always seemed to go astray, grew more and more livid, and the Spanish ambassador, who always seemed to be on the front row, more and more smug. James had actually taken time off from his hunting and from his personal feud with the Devil, quietly to make peace with the old enemy. Everything signed and sealed. It was the most creditable performance.

And was anybody grateful? Not a bit of it. The continental countries were hostile and suspicious. The English Puritans were furious, the English Catholics dismayed. With Spain a friendly power, what was going to happen to those cosy, hare-brained little plots that all depended, in the long run, on help from abroad? It was, the Catholics felt, a very underhand move on James' part.

And Will Shakespeare was not so much livid as affronted. *Antony and Cleopatra* was going well. Master Fox was taking a patronising interest in the part, and showed promise. It was time, at last, thought Will, for a holiday in Stratford. He could hardly wait. Sweet Anne, the girls, his mother whose astringent wit he so loved yet slightly feared. Avon, the splendour of New Place. Oh to wake in New Place, with the river mist white and lucent against the window, and the sparrows quarrelling in the eaves, and a long idle day before him! He wrote to Anne, saying he would spend August at home. And, having sent the letter, he imagined her breaking the seal, reading it slowly, for reading did not come easily to Anne. Then: 'Susanna! Judith! Mother-in-law! Oh, girls, your father is coming! Will is coming, Mother!' The shy delight on her pleasant, homely face.

And then – all the sharers of the Company were commanded, as Grooms of the Chamber, to wait upon the

Spanish Ambassador at Somerset House, where he was lodged for the peace negotiations from 9 August to 27 August.

It was monstrous. Will was a poet, a playwriter, not a lackey. He'd been angry enough in March, when Burbage had tossed him a bundle of red cloth and told him it was to make himself a livery to wear in James' coronation procession. He, Will Shakespeare, dressing up to strut through London without a line to speak, or worse, to write! But this! He wrote again to Anne, more curtly in his anger than he need have done. He would not, after all, be coming to Stratford this year. He was, he added (not importantly, but because he knew it would please Susanna), about the King's business. Poor Anne! It would be yet one more disappointment to add to her store.

So the year passed, in disillusion and disappointments. Parliament harangued the King. The King harangued Parliament. The King lectured the Puritans, who lectured back.

But that was not all the picture…

A foolish King, a pleasure-loving Queen. A fractious Parliament. A people, living their ill-nourished, disease- and superstition-ridden lives with surprising cheerfulness. This was England; a reasonably harmless concept, one would say.

But there was another concept: the State.

The State was watchful, unsleeping, clever, and merciless.

The State's duty, as it saw it, was to keep the King on his throne. And, to this end, to dig out the King's enemies wherever they could be found. (And not only the King's enemies, but all who gave them succour, all who sheltered them, even innocent people who knew them; for most people, given a little encouragement, could be persuaded to betray a friend or two.)

The State's weapons were spying, the rack, and the hangman's knife.

The State was never afraid, when open treason threatened, to use a sledgehammer to crack a walnut.

The State was Robert Cecil, and the dedicated shadows who flitted, day and night, in and out of his ante-rooms and about his desk.

And who were the King's enemies? Not starving countrymen, men wrongly condemned, men whose lives were so wretched that they had nothing to risk by rebellion. No. This being a Protestant country, they were Papists and Jesuits. The King was not threatened by men whose bellies were empty. He was threatened by men who sought the same Heaven as himself, but by a different path.

It was all very simple and straightforward. To the Church of Rome the thought of an entire nation doomed to perdition was truly unbearable. And it was selflessly prepared to use every persuasion of fire and steel to save these wilful heretics from the flames of everlasting Hell.

But before it could do this it had to regain a foothold on the tight little island. And the Protestant English were determined to fight to the death for their right to go to Hell in any way they chose.

The greatest fleet ever known, packed to the gunwales with grandees, soldiers, priests and monks, with statues of the Virgin clamped to every mast, had unaccountably failed to make a landing.

That had been sixteen years ago. Since then, the only thing left had seemed to be infiltration: Jesuit priests smuggled into the country to give comfort to the English Catholics, and to convert by degrees the rest of the population.

It looked like being a slow process. And there were always some who maintained that anyone who killed the bastard Elizabeth or the Calvinist James would be doing God a service.

So there were plots. And when James, angered by rumours that he himself was turning Catholic, intensified and increased the fines for recusancy, the plots flourished like mushrooms in a cellar. All over England men crouched over tables, the curtains drawn, their hats pulled over their eyes, and whispered together. Usually at least one member of the party was a spy, but they were not to know that. So they hatched, and plotted, and sent messages which were promptly intercepted, and trusted men who would have sold their grandmothers for a handful of crowns; their one glorious object: to win the approbation of the Trinity by killing the Lord's Anointed; for only thus could they gain a free hand to save the heretic English from damnation.

And Robert Cecil watched, and waited. And every now and then a plot would be uncovered, a priest would be smoked out of some hole behind a great house's plaster; and the rackmaster and the judges would begin their game of catch-as-catch can, until the guilty, with a few of the innocent thrown in for good measure, had felt the hangman's knife. And all in the name of the Pope, or of the jealous God of the Puritans, with the loving, compassionate, sorrowing face of the Galilean curiously forgotten.

But in 1604, the most absurd, the most outrageous plot of them all was still locked safely in one man's brain. Master Robert Catesby had not yet mentioned his Grand Design to a soul.

Not surprisingly, 1605's crop of portents was horrendous in the extreme. It made other years' portents look quite humdrum. The year was but two days old when a headless bear came shambling down the aisle of a small country church, mounted the pulpit, and squeezed the life out of the Vicar before the eyes of his distressed congregation. All through January a great ball of fire hovered nightly over St Paul's, so bright that a man might read a book thereby. Rivers ran blood almost as a matter of course. Dogs howled, ravens croaked, owls shrieked, a cat at Ottery St Mary devoured its own tail, at Winchester starlings invaded the Cathedral and perched on the choir stalls, solemn as judges, throughout the Communion Service.

At Ripon, the Wakeman doing his rounds looked up into the sky and was taken aback to behold the Trinity, bathed in glory. Less fortunate was the watchman of Ely who peered into a hole left by some workman, and beheld the Devil prodding a damned soul in a most painful manner. But it was, of course, the great vision seen by hundreds of respectable citizens of London that caused the most interest (and, when considered in the light of later events, the most wonder): the great Palace of Westminster, shrivelling and toppling in the holocaust of a January sunset.

Nevertheless despite these warnings, and to everyone's great surprise, the year proceeded quietly. Only the Catholics were really unhappy, because the fines for recusancy had suddenly become crippling, and they did not trust this Scotsman not to take more painful action against them. So the more extreme intensified their plotting, while the rest went on playing the good old English compromise game, invented for them by Elizabeth, of attending the required number of Church of England services, and slipping off quietly to Mass when nobody was looking.

This was Annette Peyre's method. She was no bigot. She was simply a good Catholic, and a loyal Englishwoman. And it seemed to her that if Paris was worth a Mass to the French king, peace of mind was worth a Matins to her.

But had she peace of mind? Had she been wise to let her husband's old friend use her house so freely? No. The question of Robert Catesby was a constant torment to her, had been for many months. Could she suspect her husband's greatest friend of treason? It was unthinkable. And yet, deep in her heart she knew. He and his friends were meeting whenever they could – sometimes even in her house – to work the State no good.

She had no illusions about what happened to those who harboured traitors. But – loyalty to old friends, lack of proof, a feeling (which she knew would be false) that her ignorance of her doings would save her, even a certain loyalty to her faith – all these had kept her silent.

She went over the old arguments: Robert was seldom in London. And he was a good man, he would do nothing outside the law. Yet these friends of his? What did they discuss so interminably? Suddenly, the remembrance of their sibilant whisperings was unbearable. No, she was no fool. She knew what they were doing. She had known for a long time, and had simply refused to face it. Now, with the courage and decision that characterised her, she did face it, if not for her sake, then for Matthew's.

Not a moment to lose, now her decision was made. She fastened a hooded cloak at her throat, pulled the hood over her sleek hair, and set off for Puddle Wharf.

She walked briskly. She was jostled, of course, and jeered and whistled at, and forced at times into the muck of the central kennel. But she was never molested. There was something about that determined figure that saved her from the coarser attentions paid to women rash enough to walk alone.

She came to the unsavoury South Bank, with its cut-throats and harlots, with its bearpits and brothels and theatres (yes, there was Master Shakespeare's Globe).

She found Puddle Wharf. She crossed herself under her cloak, praying that Master Catesby would be here and not at home in the Midlands.

It was a place of rotting timbers, of oily, sinister waters, of tumbledown wooden buildings. Certainly no place for a woman on her own, she was thinking, when a voice above her and behind her said, 'Why, Mistress Peyre, what are you doing here?' The voice was not unfriendly, but it was suspicious.

She spun round. And discovered Robert Catesby towering over her, his face unsmiling and tense.

It was not easy to say what she had to say. 'Master Catesby, my husband honoured you. I too honour you. But – ' She smiled pleadingly, laid a hand on his sleeve. 'I have come to forbid you my house.'

His face showed no emotion, but he removed his arm from under her hand. He said, 'Is this the way you serve your Church?'

She was no longer smiling. 'How do *you* serve your Church, Master Catesby?'

'With my life, if need be,' he said simply.

'And by taking other lives?'

'If need be,' he said again.

She knew a terrible fear; but her voice was level. 'You came to my house for the holy Mass, you and your friends. I was afraid, but that was any Catholic's duty. But afterwards you talked. And you have used my house for writing I know not what. But I think you have betrayed a trust, sir, and put my son and me in great danger.'

'To die for the Faith,' he said, 'should be our longing and our desire.'

'But not to kill others,' she said quickly. 'Nor have I any great desire for death, either for Matthew or myself, Master Catesby.'

He looked at her with contempt. 'It is fortunate that not all Catholics are as eager for *this* life, mistress.' He added cruelly, 'I thank God your husband did not live to hear you speak thus.'

She was stung bitterly, but let it pass. 'To kill others,' she said again. 'It is against the commandment of God.'

'Not when the object is to save a million souls from the torments of Hell,' he said quickly. 'Besides, the Holy Father has offered a full dispensation to any who kills a heretical king.'

She looked up at him in horror; recognised in the soldierly face, for the first time, the bitter lips, the inward-turning eyes of the fanatic. 'You – would kill the King?' she whispered.

He looked at her in silence, with, she thought, hatred. ' "He that is not with me, is against me," ' he quoted. He swept her a bow. 'We shall not trouble your house again, Mistress Peyre.'

'I am sorry,' she said. 'And – what you have just said – is safe – '

'I am glad to hear it, madam; for, mark my words, treason *has* been spoken in your house. Your neck is as much in the noose as ours, Mistress Peyre.'

'You have certainly served me well, sir,' she said wretchedly. And turned away, hoping for a word of friendship, or even farewell.

None came. Once she looked behind. He was standing there, watching her, straight and still as the wooden bollards on the wharf.

She turned back. He regarded her coldly. She said, 'Sir, do not take the lives of the innocent. It *cannot* be God's will.' She stood, hands clasped. 'For *all* our sakes, as well as theirs,' she said.

He went on staring at her. He almost spat out the words in his contempt: 'Get thee behind me, Satan.' He turned on his heel, and strode away.

She was afraid. She had come to Puddle Wharf, a woman who thought her house *might* be being used for treasonable purposes, and who was determined to stop it.

She returned home a woman who knew that her house *had* been used for treasonable purposes; and that this made her, in the eyes of the State (which was not over nice in such matters), a traitress. She, Annette Peyre, who like almost all Catholics had trodden most conscientiously a path of loyalty to her religion – traitress!

Well, she had stopped it. But she knew that would not save her – or Matthew. If Robert Catesby and his friends were caught in some dangerous folly, she and Matthew would be in as great peril as the others. Oh, why had she not acted before? Yet she knew that even that would not have saved her. She had been doomed from the moment when Catesby and her late husband had become friends.

There was worse. From now on she carried the terrible burden of knowing that it was in Catesby's mind to kill the King. Anyone who had such knowledge and did not divulge it immediately to the State, made himself one with the killers of the Lord's Anointed. She ought to go straight to Cecil, tell her suspicions. As a last possible chance of saving her own skin (and Matthew's) she ought to do this. As a loyal subject of King James she ought to do it. In an attempt to save innocent lives and to save her fellow Catholics from hate and detestation she ought to do it.

But she knew she never could. Her whole being rejected the thought, out of hand. Rashly she had told Catesby his secret was safe with her. But even without that, she could never betray someone both she and her husband had once called friend. In such a welter of conflicting loyalties, this one stood supreme.

She had walked so purposefully to meet Catesby. Returning, she walked bent, hugging the houses, her hands clasped tight across her stomach. She was trembling so much that she could walk but slowly. Such was the effect the very thought of the State, merciless and vengeful, could have on a serene and brave woman.

If only there were someone to turn to! But by its very nature, this problem could be discussed with no one. Not even with Matthew. Yet Matthew, obviously, had his own suspicions. There again was danger. A young boy was not always remarkably discreet. And she, having assured him nothing was wrong, was in no position to warn him of danger. A chance word to one of his fellows at the Children's Company he had now joined, and it could all begin: the questioning, the interrogations – something that would not end until the scaffold had had its fill of blood.

So oppressed was she that she did not even notice she was passing the Globe; until gradually it sank into her consciousness that someone had spoken her name.

She started, guiltily. She made herself look up. There, smiling at her thoughtfully, yet making no move to approach, stood William Shakespeare.

So great was her relief that she cried, 'Will!' and hurried over to him.

They had always been Master Shakespeare, Mistress Peyre. That sudden 'Will!' showed how she really thought of him. 'Annette!', he said, striking while the iron was hot. He clasped her shoulders with comforting masculine hands, gazed at her with concern. 'But Annette, you are troubled.'

Her smile was forced and drawn. 'A headache. It is nothing.' But oh, those hands, clasping and supporting. If only she, frail and anxious woman, could feel them there for ever!

He said again, as though she had not spoken. 'You are troubled, Annette.'

She hung her head. How she longed to lay her fears on this kind man's shoulders! But that could never be.

It distressed him unutterably to see her so wretched. Tenderly he put an arm under hers. 'Come into the Globe. The players are all gone. I will find you a cordial. And you can tell me your woes.' His smile was so compassionate, so understanding, she was hard put to it not to weep.

Gently, she withdrew her arm. 'I have no woes, sir. What troubles me is a matter concerning my Church. It would not be seemly to discuss it with one who is not of our faith.'

'Forgive me.' He was all contrition. 'I would not for a moment –' Yet all the time he was moving towards the theatre. There must be some way he could help this distressed and lovely woman.

And then, they were in the deserted Globe, in a room with a long table and a dozen chairs and, as in every room in the theatre, a clutter of swords and pikes and wigs and lutes. 'This is where we hold our sharers' meetings,' said Will as he bustled about mixing a cordial; saying it not because he thought she would be interested but because he yearned so desperately to take her mind off its secret cares. He carried a glass over to her. 'And how is the boy?'

'Your training has served him well. He is with the Children of the Queen's Revels. Master Evans tells me he thinks highly of him.'

In the belief that troubled persons are helped by finding that others also have troubles, he said, 'I miss the knave sorely, Annette. My evenings are lonely indeed.'

'It was a sad day for me when he left your care, Master Shakespeare.'

'Will?' he prompted.

She smiled. 'Will.'

Then they sat shyly, not meeting each other's eye, remembering their last meeting – and parting.

Will said, 'I have another cause for loneliness. Augustine Phillips – one of our number, you will remember him, Jaques in *As You Like It*, Horatio sometimes in *Hamlet* – is dead.'

'I am sorry,' she said.

'Of all our band,' he said, 'the best. He was quiet, and simple, and kind. Not like most of us actors' – he suddenly smiled – 'beating our chests and roaring.'

'You will have lost a friend,' she said.

'I more than most.'

'I am sorry.'

They were silent again, each striving desperately to send out waves of comfort to the other. He had achieved his purpose, diverted her mind, if only for a few moments, from herself.

She rose, moved towards the door. He followed. In both their minds was the memory of the time they had last walked thus, and of how two mature and strong-willed people had suddenly found themselves in a situation which neither had willed or planned. But she had learnt that the flesh, given an inch, will try to take a mile. He was a man torn this way and that by desire and guilt and compassion.

And it was compassion that won. He kissed her brow, tenderly. 'Can you not tell me the trouble that torments you, mistress?'

She shuddered. 'I can tell no one.'

'Except your priest?' he prompted.

She was silent. *Every* trouble, every sin, could be taken to the priest, and so lifted from one's own shoulders to the shoulders of God. But not this one. Even Father Grainger could not lift this burden from her shoulders. For Father Grainger, she feared, carried the same burden of knowledge as herself.

They agreed they would not meet again. It was unwise, it was wicked, it was a torment. Between London's most popular playwriter, and the elegant widow of a silversmith, stood the pleasant, homely figure of a Stratford housewife. For Annette Peyre, to yield to love for a married man was a sin that would make God turn his face away from her in anger, just at a time when she needed Him most. She *dare* not anger Him further. Yet, if they met again, could she trust her flesh not to betray her into the hands of the Devil? *I am a virtuous woman*, she had boasted to Matthew. Could she really be sure of that, alone with Will Shakespeare? So. 'We must not meet,' she said, full of tears.

He sighed. 'No,' he said. 'I have a wife, daughters.' He sighed again. And added, more out of politeness than conviction, 'Yet for myself I would count all well lost –' Then went on righteously, 'But not for them, or for you. No. We must not meet, Annette.'

And she thought: all our lives, from now on, empty. Both growing old, apart, with never a smile, a touch, to soften the bleak loneliness.

Not knowing that fate might have other plans; that already, though it was yet only May, Master Catesby had now divulged to his friends every detail of his monstrous plot. And the conspirators were already scattered in the country, awaiting the fogs and the mystery – and the holocaust – of November.

# CHAPTER 16

## THE SHEETED DEAD
### DID SQUEAK AND GIBBER IN THE ROMAN STREETS

They did not meet. The summer days crept by, and the lonely summer evenings, with the swallows darting outside his window, and the shouts of children at play, and the chatter of women, catching the last of the sun on their doorsteps. Loneliness! He had never really known it. Always before, his characters had been company enough. But now – no boy, singing, or muttering over his books, looking up occasionally with a tired shy, tired smile. No Annette. Only a pale ghost, flitting with easy grace in his dreams, to fade like gathered flowers at waking. Only a shade, to be clasped as one might clasp the wandering wind.

Augustine Phillips, kindly as death in life, had intensified the loneliness by leaving Will a thirty shillings piece in gold. Will had wept. Poor Augustine! Gentle, unassuming, yet always ready in a crisis to take a quiet lead. A man who had never let his obvious respect for Will the writer hold him back from offering comfort and advice. He was the first of that brilliant band to go. Death, why do you choose always the best and loveliest, Will asked of his quiet room.

They did not meet. The summer days crept by. Annette dusted her house, and weeded her garden. The apple blossom scattered, like summer snow, the apples plumped, the apples hung among the leaves, as mellow golden as the autumn sun.

Perhaps, she thought, Catesby will not act. Perhaps I imagined more in his words than were there. It never occurred to her to think: perhaps he will act successfully, and restore Catholicism to England. Too many plots had ended in incompetence and failure, with nothing to show but a few squalid deaths and a mountain of suffering, for her to think in that way.

Perhaps he would not act; but she was never one to leave fate to follow its own course. Father Grainger was defying banishment, flitting, a black bat, in the dusk, spending his days walled up with his vestments and communion vessels in some great house. To him she talked long and earnestly, for she felt he had the ear of the conspirators even if he was not one of them himself. She talked of the sin of murder, even of that of a heretic; she talked of the folly of pitting oneself against the State, of the need for Catholics to live quietly and unobtrusively in a Protestant land. She spoke, trembling, of the power and the ruthlessness of the State.

To all of which Father Grainger listened, watching her coldly. Then, with copious illustrations from the history of the Church, he refuted all she had said, showing that without the constant witness of martyrs, and the struggles of its warriors, the Church would have been trampled underfoot a thousand years before. Then he upbraided her for her lack of faith, and courage, and ardour, and besought her to examine herself most carefully for the corruption in her soul. The name of Catesby, the words 'plot' or 'conspiracy' were never mentioned. But each knew exactly what the other was talking about.

And Annette was left comfortless.

Perhaps Catesby would never act. But soon after her first conversation with Father Grainger she looked from her window and saw a man, leaning in a doorway opposite; a cloak and hat, despite the summer's heat, hid his features. The next day he was there again, at the corner of the street. Two days later, returning from shopping, she looked behind her. He was there, loping along, squeezed against the houses.

Her chin came up. She turned back, walked quickly towards him. She would soon find out whose man he was! But he faded into an alley. By the time she reached the mouth of the alley he had disappeared.

She was home, trembling.

There were three possibilities. He was one of Cecil's men, and already she was suspect.

Or Grainger and Catesby were concerned that she knew something of their intentions, and were satisfying themselves that there was no communication between her and Cecil.

Or he was Catesby's man, and was waiting his opportunity to kill her before she betrayed them all.

He was too open, she thought, to be Cecil's man. State spies were like woodworm, burrowing away unseen. But one could never be sure. So, though he frayed, relentlessly, at her nerves, yet she played her own game, with him running from the house suddenly to catch him (though never succeeding), or taking long walks through the London streets, an exercise she enjoyed and he, with his shambling gait, clearly did not; or even standing in her window and toasting him, gaily, in a glass of wine.

But she did not feel gay. And at night she would barricade the doors, and sleep with a knife under her pillow, and often, waking, would rise and stare down into the shifting shadows of the streets, wondering and fearful.

The summer days crept by. That fateful year crept by. The summer clouds, white and burnished, sailed over London, the Thames ran sweetly, the chestnut flowers burned out, like candles, the chestnuts nestled, silky-smooth in their spiked shells, the birds ceased their singing in airless summer eves.

Annette Peyre waited, in her quiet house, for the news that would destroy her. It didn't come. Peaceful England busied itself with summer sports. The twang of the bow, the hiss of the arrow, the laughter of children: these were your summer sounds.

Yet some men saw little of the bright days. Their work was in cellars, digging through walls, receiving, checking and storing heavy barrels, amassing coal and faggots and bars of iron. So – dedicated, fanatical men – they wasted the last sweet summer of their lives.

There were others who saw little of the sunlight: the Children of the Queen's Revels, rehearsing and acting from dawn to dusk, whipped if they forgot their lines, reviled if they spoke them ill, cuffed if they appeared other than joyous and contented on stage. Henry Evans, their master, was a tyrant. They could do nothing right for the explosive Master Jonson, who wrote most of their plays. Matthew Peyre cried himself to sleep most nights, thinking of those happy, far-off days with Master Shakespeare. His one thought was to escape from Master Evans, and return to the King's Men.

And yet, the tyrant Evans brought him out, goaded, mocked, maltreated him into a tense, high style of acting he would never have learnt from the gentle Shakespeare. Within a year he became Evans' most valuable actor. And, as such, was kept virtually a prisoner at the Blackfriars.

There was no doubt about it. Nicholas Fox was doing well. Shakespeare didn't like him any better than he had done. In fact, the youth had grown even more supercilious and arrogant. But he was getting the stature for the Egyptian Queen, and the command. And his limp was almost gone. When the time came, he would not be overshadowed by Burbage's Antony.

And the play was going well. Through that hot summer, despite all his other preoccupations, Will was ankle deep in Egyptian sand. Fascinated, entranced. Too involved to go to Stratford *this* summer (poor Anne!). But once let him get Cleopatra off his mind, and into production, and he'd be away. It might not be this year, of course. But there were other summers.

He wrote; carried away, inspired, drunk almost with the beauty of words. He had never used language like this before. Rich in colour, like a tremendous tapestry. Lordly in music, like a great consort of viols and curtalls and hautboys in a high cathedral. As wide and deep in imagination as the ever-changing sea. Never before had he (or any man, he suspected) written with this spate of imagery. It swept him on like a great river in flood. And it had a sunset splendour, thought this man of forty.

What demon, he also found time to wonder, drove him on to write thus. Was it a desperate searching for a refuge from his loneliness? A tumultuous compensation for his arid renouncing of Annette Peyre? A deep envy for Antony who could cry, 'I must from this enchanting queen break off', yet brought his world down in flames because he would not? Who, he wondered, was really the stronger, nobler character? Antony, with the courage to let himself knowingly be transformed into a strumpet's fool? Or careful, cautious Will, safe and smug in his little nest of marital fidelity?

It wasn't true. He too had known what it meant to be a strumpet's fool. And that had brought *his* world about his ears, a bitter shame spoiling the sweet world's taste. A long time ago, but *he* had soon learnt his lesson. No. You needed courage to be an Antony; a wild, uncaring courage. And this Will would never have; for the first time for many years he thought of himself as a shopkeeper, and the son of a shopkeeper.

But at least he could write. And *was* writing. Something, or he was much mistaken, that would make the groundlings wriggle. 'Let Rome in Tiber melt, and the wide arch of the rangèd empire fall!' He could hear Dick flinging *that* up to the galleries, and out to the back row of the yard. His spine shivered, his scalp prickled. Never, not even with *Hamlet*, had he so longed to hear a play performed. Well, it would not be so long, now. Late autumn, perhaps. Fox would be at least adequate, Burbage magnificent as always, Charmian, Iras and Octavia difficult, there were no boys to be had anywhere, but the King's Men would manage. He wiped his pen. Enough for tonight. 'Now boast thee, death, in thy possession lies, A lass unparallel'd,' he murmured. His eyes filled with tears. He had moved himself with the splendour of his own writing. He felt he could not wait to see the performance. But oh, if only it had been young Matthew he had been teaching through the long hours, instead of this insufferable Fox. That would have been happiness indeed.

The summer days crept by, piling up day after day a great store of heat so that London became like an oven. Some young men were even known to take off their ruffs, appearing half naked before their shocked fellows. Old men boldly risked rheums and agues by leaving off their furred gowns when at home. Annette Peyre sought each evening the coolness of her garden. She found the heat oppressive, unbearable, a physical complement to the fears that oppressed her mind.

And yet, despite the August heat, there was already a touch of autumn sadness. Outside the city walls, the shaven cornfields gleamed and glinted in the sunlight. On the Thames, proud swans pecked irritably at a scatter of yellow leaves. Soon, now, would come the first mists, the shiver of frost. The great winds of October would come, like bustling servants, to sweep away the mess of summer; the early, foggy dusks, the bonfires of autumn; and – the Lord being with us, thought some – the greatest bonfire of them all, destroying for ever the rotten wood, the withered branches, the cankerous growths of the tree that had once been Protestant England.

# Chapter 17

## Your ladyship is nearer to heaven by the altitude of a chopine.

Being so short of boys, they put on *Romeo and Juliet*. Fox could take the lead admirably, and the other women in the play were all old. Lady Capulet, having a thirteen-year-old daughter, could well have one foot in the grave, and no one would complain if the Nurse, who had suckled the child eleven short years ago, entered on a couple of sticks and clacked like a goose. As for Lady Montague, dead in the last act just to keep things tidy –? Any of the men could play these parts.

Will Shakespeare was taking the pennies at the door. It was a sweltering afternoon. In they came, sweating, guffawing, eager; prentices in their woollen caps, carpenters in leather aprons, butchers, their hot faces glowing like rising suns, stonemasons grey as the carved saints they worked upon, everyone with a penny clutched in one sticky hand, and in the other a bottle of beer, or the tools of his trade, or an apple. From somewhere near at hand came the sounds of the bear baiting, which had already begun – the sharp intake of breath into a thousand throats, the deep roar of satisfaction as a mastiff made his mark, the howls of execration at a dog showing cowardice. It sounded, thought some, like a good baiting, and they slipped away to spend their pennies there instead. But most stayed with Verona. There would, if they knew their King's Men, be as much blood on the stage as in the bear pit, and it would be human blood.

Also there would be a story, some of which they might even be able to follow; and even if they couldn't, they felt dimly, there would be a high intensity of poetry and conflict which would make them forget, for a spell, their hot, itchy, uncomfortable bodies, their peevish masters, their little narrow lives.

Will Shakespeare watched them file in, slap down their pennies, then rush to get as near the front as possible. He'd seen it all before so many times and never failed to wonder how he and his fellows, with a sword or two and a few cloaks, and his scribbling, could transport a thousand of the common sort for a whole afternoon to the palaces of kings, to Verona, to the courts of Oberon.

Not, of course, that they were all of the common sort. There were Inns of Court men, who would pay another penny at the inner door for access to a twopenny room with seats, or even a third penny at a third door for a room with *cushioned* seats. There might even be Court gallants who would pay for the private rooms at sixpence or a shilling.

For instance, this old gentleman, white of hair and pendulous of nose, tall, stooping, venerable, in a furred gown – surely he would choose the comfort of the cushioned seats for his old bones. The old gentleman drew nearer. To his utter astonishment, Will recognised Philip Henslowe.

Astonishment, for two reasons. Theatre owners did not visit other men's theatres. If they wanted to steal their current plays, they sent spies with tablets. And secondly,

Master Henslowe was never one to spend a penny in visiting someone else's theatre, when he could get into his own free. Therefore, reasoned Will, Philip Henslowe must have some very pressing reason indeed.

The one-time hired man regarded his old employer warily. But tried not to sound too suspicious. 'Why, Master Henslowe. This is an unexpected honour.'

Henslowe beamed, and put his penny firmly on the table. 'I have long wanted to see your most lamentable tragedy, Master Shakespeare.'

Should he let the crafty old fox in? He couldn't want to steal the play – it had already been published twice – yet reason, experience, intuition all cried out no. 'I cannot admit you, Master Henslowe,' he said firmly.

Henslowe went on beaming. 'Why? Is my penny bad?'

The first trumpet sounded from the roof. The crowd behind Henslowe, which had been pushing and shoving as a matter of course, became downright abusive. Will looked at Henslowe and, despite the beam, met a steely, determined eye. He beckoned Henslowe in.

The old gentleman gave him a glittering smile, and went and took his place with the groundlings. That penny had hurt. The King's Men weren't getting any more pennies out of him for their precious galleries. He pulled a chicken leg out of his gown's pocket, planted his feet firmly on the ground, and settled himself to enjoy the play.

Will said, 'We had an unexpected visitor, today. Master Philip Henslowe.'

Burbage, removing grease paint, glared. 'And you let him in?'

'I don't quite see how I could have stopped him. The first trumpet was sounding.'

'You should have told the old devil to wait for the *last* trump. Did you question him?'

'Yes. Smooth as ever. Wanted to see "your most lamentable tragedy, Master Shakespeare".'

'H'm! We shall lose something. God. I wish I'd been there, Will. I'd have kept him out somehow.'

The implied rebuke did not hurt as it would once have done. He was growing a skin. 'How, Dick? With a broom staff about his pate?'

The men roared. Everyone knew the story of how the young Dick had once used a broom handle to defy a Chancery Order withal; boasting afterwards: 'They came for a moitie; but *I* have delivered them a moitie with *this*, and sent them packing.' It was one of the King's Men's favourite stories.

Dick grinned. Will grinned. The laughter went on.

But Philip Henslowe, plodding home through the dusty evening, was not laughing. He had gone to the Globe to see for himself. Prince Henry's Men *had* to have Nicholas Fox.

Master Henslowe pondered. It was no use offering more money to the boy's avaricious mother. It saddened him too much to see human greed in action, though he might have found the courage to face this if he'd thought there was any chance of succeeding. So he must try the boy. But it would need more than money; he felt sure of that. A leading boy with the King's Men had a bright future.

Could he offer a brighter future with Prince Henry's Men? No. Bribery would get him nowhere with this promising youth. And what was the alternative to bribery? Threats!

Philip Henslowe put his thinking cap on. And went to visit his friend the Bishop of Winchester, the tenuous link between whom and Philip was the fact that Henslowe's brothels abutted on to his Lordship's Palace.

The summer days had passed. Now it was autumn.

In the cellars under the Palace of Westminster, the Grand Design was taking shape. No one, surely, was going to notice these stacked barrels, these iron bars, this heap of faggots and coal! Or, if they did, feel any alarm? And anyway, Master Fawkes was there to put any enquirer's mind at rest. There was nothing like a soldier, late of the Spanish Army, lurking with a dark lantern under the Houses of Parliament, to inspire confidence in any casual enquirer.

It was autumn. At the Blackfriars Theatre they were preparing for the winter: more plays in rehearsal, more performances with the darker evenings, for the Blackfriars had a roof, and could indulge in the luxury of plays by candlelight.

Matthew Peyre, at the end of his tether, was planning his escape. Or so he told himself. But with bars at his dormitory windows, and with his every movement watched by the wily Evans, he knew in his heart that he had no chance. And even if he did get away from the building, Master Evans had been more concerned about articles than were the cheerful King's Men. He had dotted every i, crossed every t. Staying out would be as difficult as getting out. Matthew gazed through the bars of his window – at the free sky and the sun and the shining roofs of London. He thought of his mother's house, and the garden. (It would be half in shade now, cool, but if you climbed one of the trees you came again into the sunlight. And you could pluck an apple, warm with the sun. He felt his teeth biting strongly into the firm flesh. It was a long time since he had tasted an apple.)

His face was forlorn, as a child's face should not be forlorn.

Nicholas Fox stood before Philip Henslowe. The fact that he was flanked by, and had been brought here by, two men of brutal appearance, did nothing to lessen his arrogance.

Henslowe waved him courteously to a seat. Nicholas sat down, scowling.

Henslowe sighed. 'Sin, Master Fox, is the canker at the heart of our great city. Would you not agree?'

Nicholas was silent. What was the old devil after?

Henslowe waved a paper. 'My Lord Bishop of Winchester is very diligent against sin, Master Fox. It is a foul stink in his nostrils.'

Nicholas waited. 'Lately,' went on Henslowe more chattily, 'his lordship has been making a tally of lewd and sinful women in this city, so that they may be whipped through the streets on a hurdle at a cart's tail. In this, his lordship shows a truly Christian zeal, would you not say, Master Fox?'

Nicholas licked his dry lips. 'Yes.'

Henslowe peered at the list. 'Among these lewd and sinful women, I find the name of Mistress Helen Fox. Would she be any relation, by any chance?'

Nicholas had leapt to his feet. 'How *dare* you?'

The two men of brutal appearance pushed him back on to his stool.

Henslowe said sweetly, 'His Majesty, who is also zealous for the Lord, might not be overpleased to find that the – er – mother of one of his King's Men had been whipped as a common harlot.'

Fox was on his feet again. 'My mother is *not* a common harlot.'

'No. Not common. I agree with you there, Master Fox.'

Fox said, 'Why did you bring me here?'

'Out of an earnest desire to help,' Philip said with engaging frankness.

'Help? How?'

Philip sighed again. 'Alas! That is difficult to say. Had you been one of Prince Henry's Men, of course, it had been easy. But – '

'Why easy?'

'Because I have the ear of my Lord of Winchester. For my sake, he might well have second thoughts about the degree of your mother's sinfulness.'

'You want me to join Prince Henry's?'

'My dear young gentleman, I would not think of suggesting such a thing. What, rob my old friends Dick Burbage, sweet Master Shakespeare? Besides, your own loyalties – '

'Loyalties?' cried Nicholas. 'Loyalties be damned. What are the prospects?'

Philip Henslowe looked at him with approval. A man after his own heart. 'Excellent, Master Fox, excellent. Now see – '

Crabbed age and youth put their heads together. It did not take them long to reach a decision…

'I *told* you we should lose something,' stormed Richard Burbage. 'But by God I never thought it would be our only boy.'

Will said glumly, 'What about his articles?'

'Not worth the paper they're written on, against a Shylock like Henslowe. Damn it, Will, it's all your fault. You lose one boy, and then you let that – that fox into the farmyard to steal the other.'

'I did engage both boys – against your wishes,' Will said humbly.

Burbage snapped, 'Look, Will, this is no time for pretty quibbles. It's desperate, can't you see?'

'Of course I can see. My Cleopatra –'

'Damn your Cleopatra to hell. How can we put plays on without boys? What about young Peyre? Can't we get him back?'

Will was silent. 'I could try,' he said at last.

It was no time for niceness. With his hat pulled well down over his eyes (like some Popish plotter, he thought wryly) he went and hung about the Blackfriars, where the Children of the Queen's Revels acted their plays. This was the sort of thing that was happening all the time in the world of the theatre, he reminded himself: stealing plays, stealing players, stealing boys. But it was not the kind of work Gentleman Will would have chosen to do himself. But he had a conscience. He supposed it *was* his fault the Company was so short of boys, and he was curiously excited at the possibility of seeing young Matthew again.

But there was no sign of young Matthew. Nor would be. Young Matthew was behind bars. He was a valuable property.

So the King's Men remained at their wits' end for boys. An impossible situation! Nevertheless, they had that combination of four parts ability, five parts hard work, and one part luck that never fails to bring its rewards. And, curiously, in this situation their saviour was Philip Henslowe!

Prince Henry's Men had gained a brilliant leading boy. But, like the King's, they were still desperately short of young actors.

So the indefatigable Henslowe put his hat on and attended a performance at the Blackfriars.

229

He had no plans. As was his wont, the pious gentleman just went along in the sure and certain hope that the Lord would provide.

And the Lord did.

Philip watched the play with interest. A pleasant enough comedy, about apprentice life. But he hadn't come here to enjoy himself. He watched, eyes narrowed in an intensity of concentration.

And it wasn't long before that most loyal of all the King's subjects, Philip Henslowe, was feeling shocked to the core of his being. The authors of the play, those lewd fellows Jonson, Chapman and Marston, were actually poking fun at the Scots!

Philip had to force himself to sit still and listen to these vile sneers at his Majesty's compatriots; written by Jonson and his fellow wits, put on by Master Evans, acted by these innocent little children. It was monstrous! To risk hurting the feelings of the Lord's Anointed for a few paltry pounds! It only bore out the truth he had always so sadly known: that love of money was the root of all evil.

The moment the play finished he was out of his seat, out of the theatre, and stumping back to his office as fast as his old legs and his silver-headed stick would carry him.

He climbed the stairs, panting. He flung himself into the dark little office, seized a quill and a sheet of paper. 'To The Hon'ble Robert Cecil, The Lord Salisbury: My Lord... '

Master Henslowe was not one to let lewdness and frivolity flourish if he could help it.

It didn't quite finish the Children of the Queen's Revels; but King James was understandably hurt by these jibes at his countrymen, and sent Chapman to prison, where the impetuous Ben insisted on joining him. And the Queen's patronage was withdrawn from the Children, audiences fell off mightily (the more cautious citizens feeling some delicacy about attending a theatre that had incurred the King's displeasure), and Henry Evans soon found he had more boys than he needed. The King's Men took some. Henslowe bought up a number, and sold them to Prince Henry's Men at a very satisfactory profit. 'Blessed,' he wrote in the account book in which he recorded this profit, 'bee the nayme of the Lorde.'

The splutter of a quill, the flutter of a candle, the peaceful muttering of the first fire of autumn: things had not changed in the rooms above the tire-maker's shop in Silver Street.

There was a knock at the door. The door opened. Will looked up.

A tall, personable young man, pale and grave, who stood silent.

Will stared. Then he was out of his chair, embracing the boy, weeping, surprised at his own emotion. 'Matthew!' He clasped him by the shoulders, held him at arms' length, studied him gravely. 'Why, how you have grown! Master Evans has made a man of you.'

Matthew smiled shyly, hung his head in mock penitence. Will was touched. It was a characteristic gesture. The boy said, 'Father, I am no more worthy to be called your son. Make me as one of your hired servants.'

'Nay, boy, we'll have a fatted calf, an mistress landlady can provide one.' In his joy he had relapsed into a country way of speech, something that seldom happened with Gentleman Will. He bustled out to the top of the stairs, called down for Mistress Mountjoy. *This my son was dead, and is alive again.* He came back, rubbing his hands. But surely, one part of his mind was thinking, I am growing old, all this pother and sentiment over a boy who cares nothing for me. Very well. He *was* growing old. There were streaks of grey in that trim beard. So he would allow himself the luxury of age: to show a fatherly affection for one he had longed to set in his dead son's shoes. 'So,' he said, 'you would come back to the King's?'

'If they will have me, sir.' The smile was direct, friendly, confident. The boy had become a man. Well, that wasn't surprising. He must be fourteen, at least. One did not remain a child for ever. Will said, 'What thought you of Master Evans?'

'He beat me, sir, and kept me prisoner. Yet he taught me to act' – he grinned ruefully – 'simply by whipping me when I acted ill.'

Mistress Mountjoy bustled in with wine, cold beef, bread, cheese, the inevitable pickled herrings. While she prepared the table the man and the boy sat beside the fire, gazing at the logs, every now and then stealing quick glances at each other. How good it is to be back, thought Matthew. Everything as it was. And he is – yes – he *is* like Father. Kind, understanding, a man to take one's troubles to. And Will thought: he *has* become a man. He has an authority, a gaiety, even. *Could* he play my royal gipsy? After supper he shall read the part.

They came to the table. And, now that they were alone again, the question he had wanted to ask ever since the boy arrived: 'How is your mother?'

The boy looked down at the cloth. 'Well, I thank you.'

It was an answer that did not mean what it said. 'But – ' prompted Will.

The boy looked up, suddenly scared. 'But – nothing, sir.'

Will said, 'Oh come, boy. Something is wrong, by your looks.'

'She is troubled, Master Shakespeare.'

'Still?' He remembered her fears when they had last met. Something to do with her Church, was it not? Some question of shriving, or not shriving, as like as not. Well, he couldn't imagine Annette Peyre had any sins heavy enough to bear her down to Hell.

But Matthew, it seemed, had decided to transfer the burden to this understanding person's shoulders. He said, 'There is a man of our faith, a Master Catesby, who came much to my mother's house. I do not know why, but it is because of him that she is troubled.' He concentrated on his cold beef.

Although of course he did not love her, Will knew a sudden, vicious stab of jealousy. She was beautiful, and, he had to admit, a secret woman. The fact that she appeared to have a sentimental attachment to the popular actor Will Shakespeare meant nothing. Most of the King's Men, at one time or another, had had some woman swooning for them. But it hadn't lasted. They were shadows, all of them. Take away the grease paint and the hollow crown, and what was left?

The boy said, 'They are not lovers.'

Will felt such a surge of relief at this statement that he drank a whole glass of wine at one gulp. But then he thought: if they are not lovers, what then? Why is she so troubled because of this man?

Matthew said, 'It would be pleasant if you would sup at my mother's house, Master Shakespeare.'

'Thank you, Matthew.' Pleasant, indeed. 'It is not seemly,' she had said, but with this boy between them at the table, what harm could there be? Not as much harm as some men would like, he thought wryly. Then he remembered that Hell fire was forty-one years nearer than it had once been.

No. No more adventures. No more roving. William Shakespeare, Gentleman, Groom of the Chamber, had become a foolish, fond old man.

After supper Will tossed a heavy manuscript on to the table. 'My new play, about the gipsy Cleopatra.'

Matthew opened it, began to read. Will said, 'Do you think you could play my gipsy? After,' he could not resist adding, 'Master Evans' training?'

'I would much like to try, sir.'

'Good. Now. Read this scene. Then we will try it. I will be Antony, you Cleopatra.'

They sat, one each side of the fire, Will in the great carved chair, Matthew on a stool. Oh, it was good to have the fire lit again, and the curtains drawn, no longer to be tormented by the click of the bowls, the happy sounds of summer. Good, best of all, to have this son back with him, this son who shaped so well, so tall and straight of limb, so direct of eye and speech, this son who had grown from a rather tiresome boy to a well-balanced man of fourteen summers. A son who, with his help, would play the greatest woman's part he had ever written.

# CHAPTER 18

## HELL IS MURKY...

Autumn days. Great clouds towered motionless in a sky of powdery blue; everything was soft, diffused, as seen through a gauze. Yet the days were retreating, and a waspishness was in the air at morn and eve, the skirmishing parties of cruel winter.

Annette Peyre was less afraid. Any day now, winter would launch an attack; and one day of winter could close the roads, cut off towns and villages, drive men into near-hibernation. Surely, if Catesby had been going to act, he would have acted before now. Surely a murder, even of a king, was of no use without a country-wide rising of the Catholics? And for that one needed the long, clear days of summer. So she was less fearful. Before her lay, she began to hope, a peaceful winter, with the fire dancing in the hearth, the candles lit, and Matthew safe back with Master Shakespeare.

At the Globe they were rehearsing *Antony and Cleopatra*. It was going well. Burbage, though he did not even try to hide a certain good-natured contempt for Matthew Peyre, nevertheless appeared entirely besotted by the character the boy was playing. And Matthew, though his Cleopatra lacked the lady's fishwife quality, made him a seductive mistress, a royal queen. Will hugged himself. If things went well, they should be able to put on a performance by early November. He would see the play that meant more to him than any play since *Hamlet*! And he would not see it from the stage, or the tiring-room. He had no part, and his work as guider would be virtually finished. He would see it from the sixpenny room, high in the gallery. With, dare he hope, the lovely Annette Peyre sitting at his right hand. (Surely she could not refuse to join the author to watch her son play the leading part in his new play!)

It was the happiest time of Matthew's life. No Nicholas Fox to goad and mock him; working closely and eagerly with his idol Shakespeare, whose feet of clay he had quite forgotten; spending at least one evening a week with his adored mother (oh, how wonderful it would be if plague carried off Master Shakespeare's wife in Warwickshire, he thought with the heartlessness of youth); happy above all with the exaltation that came from living on friendly and easy terms with men he had once terribly feared.

Robert Cecil, Earl of Salisbury, saw little of the autumn skies, for all England's doings appeared on his desk. And, in addition to everything else, he had all the arrangements for the meeting of Parliament to confirm. The date had been fixed: November the fifth. But there were a thousand and one decisions that only he could make. The King and Queen would be present in the House of Lords; so would their eldest child, Prince Henry. But what about the weakly Prince Charles, and the Princess Elizabeth? What about the ambassadors? The great Lords of the Council would be there; in fact, *everyone* would be there, from the monarch downwards. Even the travelling arrangements were a nightmare, for there was the question of protecting them on the way from madmen with pistols, Papists with knives, witches with the evil eye. The responsibility made even the cool Robert a trifle anxious; to lose a coachload of royalty now would mean starting all over again on the succession problem – just when he thought he had everything nicely arranged.

He begged an audience of the King, and pointed out the dangers.

King James was never one to take dangers lightly – especially when they concerned himself. He commanded that the troops lining the royal route be doubled. He also had all the known London witches quietly rounded up, and set a watch on the more hot-headed Papists, though he was relieved to learn that many of these seemed to be living quietly in the country. He also had some of the less reputable houses on the royal route searched for weapons and powder. 'There, my Lord Salisbury,' he said. 'These measures, added to the fact that God is not likely to let His Anointed One be brought to the dust, should protect me mightily.'

'Yes, your Majesty.' Salisbury coughed. 'I had in mind, also, if your Majesty will permit, the safety of your Privy Council, your great Ministers of State, your Lords and Members of Parliament.'

But the King's attention was wandering. 'Och, my dear Salisbury, ye canna expect me to deal with *all* the minutiae of these occasions. But ye needna' fash. I've considered very carefully, and there's naething else *could* go agley.'

A plot to blow the entire royal family, *and* the entire Government, sky-high with a few barrels of gunpowder, has a simple, direct, grandeur that almost disarms criticism. Given success, it would have been a bloody and horrible deed, rivalling the Bartholomew Massacre. Given failure, it towers head and shoulders over all the other monuments to human folly in English history.

And it nearly succeeded. Even Lord Suffolk, wandering through the cellars under the House of Lords on the afternoon of 4 November, and coming upon Master Fawkes with his barrels and his dark lantern, seems to have gone away somewhat reassured by Fawkes' warm, Yorkshire accents. And had not one of the conspirators, with more family affection than sense, written to one of his relations suggesting he find some reason for not attending that Parliament, Guy Fawkes might have applied his slow match and been well on the way to Gravelines before the flame reached the powder.

But someone *did* write to Lord Monteagle. Monteagle took the letter to Salisbury, who took it to the King. And the King realised that something *could*, after all, go agley.

The State went into action. Guy Fawkes was seized, the conspirators were chased across England, and either captured or killed. The inevitable trials began. James wrote his own version of the affair, ordered thanksgiving services in all the churches, and personally thanked the Almighty for thus confirming His interest in His Anointed. He also commanded the Bench of Bishops to devise for the condemned a death so hideous that no one for evermore would dare try to kill the Lord's Anointed. (But their Lordships, despite earnest and fervent prayer to the Holy Ghost for inspiration, could suggest nothing better than that good old standby, hanging, drawing and quartering; a sad commentary, many felt, on the intellectual and spiritual limitations of the Church of England.)

But if a failed plot has an element of farce, there is no humour in its aftermath. There is only suffering, and squalid tragedy: for the guilty, and for any who have known them.

Annette Peyre was taken in for questioning at four o'clock on the morning of the sixth.

She was not asleep. She had heard yesterday's rumours, and was awake and fearful.

She heard the tramp of armed men in the street. She heard the clatter of arms, shouted orders.

She heard them smash down her front door, and come clattering up the stairs.

She did not die. Fear seldom kills. She rose, pulled a gown about her shoulders, straightened her hair, and waited for them.

When they burst in she appeared to them pale, composed. Yet her limbs were palsied with fear. They had to drag her downstairs. She began to scream as they took her out of her house, into the menace of the raw November morning.

'Sir! They have taken away my mother.'

'Who? Where?' Will looked up from his everlasting writing.

'I don't know; but she is a Catholic. The Powder Plot! I am fearful for her, Master Shakespeare.'

Will had heard the rumours. He and Matthew looked at each other with a long, agonised surmise, each remembering Annette's fears, remembering the name Catesby, not that that name was mentioned in the rumours; so far, except for someone called Fawkes, the public had heard no names. For all they knew, the Pope himself might be at the bottom of it.

But Will was on his feet. 'Where have they taken her?'

'I don't know.' It was almost a wail. Matthew was white, shaken, yet with a wild, determined gleam in his eye. 'I found the door smashed in. And the neighbours say armed men – dragged her – ' He was silent.

Will was not a man of action; besides, with a Popish plot, what more natural than that the State should take Catholics into custody for a few days, even for their own protection? She'd probably be back safe in her own house within a week.

No. He could not slough off his duties like this, much as he longed to. It was this boy's mother they were talking about, Annette Peyre, the scent of whose hair still lingered in his nostrils.

There was only one possible way to help Annette: petition the high and mighty. Whom did he know? Mary, Countess of Pembroke, my Lord of Southampton (not much help in *that* quarter, he greatly feared), the King.

Yet to plead for a Catholic, on the day following the Powder Plot, was surely to place one's own neck in a noose!

He did not care. He, who had so often let 'I dare not' wait upon 'I would', was not afraid. Or, anyway, not too afraid to try to help this loved son, that respected friend his mother. He put his arm round the boy's shoulders. 'I shall do what I can, Matthew. In the meantime, do not go out, boy. The streets are no place for a Catholic tonight.'

The boy threw him a look of gratitude.

He changed into his best, russet-brown doublet, his plum-coloured breeches, fastened his mustard cloak at his throat, clapped his tall hat on his head, buckled on his sword, and set off.

In his anxiety, he almost ran. The streets were quiet. One or two known Catholic houses were going up in flames, but the authorities were not encouraging this. With all those timber houses, anyone setting fire to a couple of Papists might well finish up burning a thousand Protestants.

He hurried on. Pray God the Countess was in London. He could never reach Wilton in time to save Annette.

He reached the Pembrokes' town house. He ran up the steps, knocked. The door was opened. The servant would enquire whether her Ladyship would graciously receive Master Shakespeare.

She greeted him with her own warm, ample friendliness. Yet she was not helpful. 'My dear Will, do you know what you are asking? To plead for a Papist?' Her voice was kind, concerned; but appalled.

'But, my lady, she is an old friend. And the mother of the boy who is to play my Cleopatra.'

'Ah.' She looked at him shrewdly. 'So if we do not save her, there will be no Cleopatra.'

'That is not why I ask, Countess. I ask because she is a noble and good woman, and entirely innocent in this matter.'

'How do you know she is innocent, sir? Are you privy, then, to the Papists' plans?' But she smiled down at her jewel-encrusted fingers.

'No, my lady. But she is not a woman who would shed blood – anyone's blood.'

'Yet she is a Papist. And has not the Bishop of Rome stated that any who kills a heretical king does God a service?'

'She would not believe that.'

'What? Not believe Christ's Vicar here on earth? She must be a strange Catholic, Master Shakespeare.'

Was she playing with him? Or testing him? Knowing her kindness, and her cleverness, he suspected the latter. He said, 'Lady Pembroke, will you help this innocent woman?'

She was silent. Her great bulk slumped in its massive chair. Then she said, 'No. I *dare* not. It would not help her, and would endanger me and mine. The King is beside himself with rage. And I am already out of favour.' She added wryly, 'Once is enough, Master Shakespeare.'

He was rebuked. It was no use arguing. When Lady Pembroke said no, she meant no. And she confirmed this by giving him that wonderful smile of hers and saying, 'I'm sorry, Will, for your Papist. But not even silver-tongued Shakespeare could persuade me to broach the King on this.'

'Thank you, my lady.' He kissed her hand, bowed, withdrew. Sick with despair. If this stout-hearted woman thought it was hopeless, it was hopeless indeed.

# CHAPTER 19

## THE QUALITY OF MERCY...

Another audience with the King? 'About what?' demanded
Southampton. Will said wretchedly, 'To plead for a Catholic
woman, wrongfully arrested.'

Southampton looked at him sharply. 'Wrongfully? How
do you know, wrongfully?'

'She is innocent,' Will said stubbornly.

'In the King's eyes, and in the eyes of all loyal subjects, no
Catholics are innocent. Nor are those that plead their cause.
Do as you wish, Shakespeare. But I warn you.'

They looked thoughtfully at each other. Will sighed. 'I
would still like an audience of his Majesty.'

'Very well.' He was not one to waste his time saving a fool
from his folly. Especially when the fool was William
Shakespeare. 'I will inform his Majesty,' he said. He even
smiled.

The smile glinted like ice under a winter moon.

Southampton had been right. Jamie was indeed
overwrought. He twitched uncontrollably. His right eyelid
was down over its eye like a broken blind. His other eye
stared unblinking at Will. His words tumbled over one

another. 'Ah, Shakespeare! Have you finished that play about Banquo yet? Ye have? Aye, we must see it sometime. But gunpowder, mon! Gunpowder, against the Lord's Anointed!'

'A terrible sin, your Majesty.'

That one round eye went on staring. 'They took gunpowder to my faither, ye remember.' He sighed, deeply. 'Aye, that was a sair unhap, Master Shakespeare. But this Banquo. 'Tis finished?'

'Yes, your Majesty.'

'Good man, good man. Master Shakespeare, do you not see the hand of the Lord in the unveiling of this plot? Foolish, wicked men, to imagine that the Lord would let His holy one see corruption!'

'Your Majesty, I come to plead your mercy for a woman wrongfully arrested. As a Groom of your Majesty's Chamber, as one of your Majesty's Players, I will stand surety for her innocence.'

That round, unblinking eye was unnerving. 'You would plead with *me* for a Papist, sir? You are a brave man, Master Shakespeare.'

'But she is innocent, your Majesty.'

'A Papist, innocent?' The King's laughter was like the clatter of fire irons. 'Then maybe she knows some who are not so innocent, sir.'

'No, your Majesty.'

'Ye seem to know a great deal about it.' That single eye grew cunning. 'Maybe my rackmaster would be interested in *your* story.'

Will felt the blood drain from his face. His mouth was so dry he had to make two attempts to speak. 'One of your Majesty's Household? A Groom of the Chamber? A true Protestant?'

'Burrowing worms have been found in the royal wainscot before now, Master. And moths devouring the King's bed linen. And, mark me well, Master Shakespeare, traitors in the King's bedchamber.'

There was no doubting the menace. The King might be overwrought, but he could tell a hawk from a handsaw. He knew how to summon the Guard. He knew how to give his orders. He knew exactly who this foolhardy petitioner was. Will licked his lips. He said stiffly, 'If his Majesty doubts the loyalty of his most loyal subject, let him send for the Guard and have him taken to the Tower. Will Shakespeare would rather die than be thought of as a traitor by the King he loves.'

It was the sort of thing people said in his plays, though they usually said it in twenty lines of iambic pentameters, he thought wryly. Well, it often seemed to work in his plays, but it had never occurred to him that it could work in real life. Yet here, to his amazement, was James clapping a hand on his shoulder and saying, 'Och, Shakespeare man, dinna fash. I don't doubt your loyalty. It's just – I'm a wee bit overwrought, ye'll understand.'

'Overwrought? Sire, most princes would be prostrated by your ordeal. Yet here are you, your Majesty – if I may say so – cool, judicial, unruffled as always. No one, sire, looking at you now could believe that you have but yesterday felt death's hand clutching at your shoulder.' Oh God, am I overdoing it? he thought desperately.

Evidently not. James was preening himself. To a coward, praise of his courage and coolness is a heady wine indeed. 'Ye're a clever man, Shakespeare. 'Tis not everyone appreciates my scorn for danger.'

'Some men,' Will said sternly, 'are strangely lacking in perception, Majesty.' He paused. 'About the woman, your Majesty?'

'Aye. Ye say she's innocent? And had no knowledge of the plot?'

'I do.'

'Verra well, Shakespeare. I'll give the order for her release. And ye say ye've finished the Banquo play? Good, good! But powder – powder to the Lord's Anointed, Master Shakespeare!'

Will bowed almost to the floor. 'If your Majesty will forgive me. In one of my plays – a piece about mercy. "It becomes," I said, "the throned monarch better than his crown." '

The King was looking better already. The blind over the right eye had been drawn up a little. 'What play is that?'

'*The Merchant of Venice.*'

'We will have it performed. At Whitehall. Once we have dealt bloodily with these traitors. It will do no harm to remind the Court of our princely virtues.'

Will was still bowing. 'The woman's name, Majesty, is Annette Peyre.'

The King called the Captain of the Guard. 'Annette Peyre, one of the Papists, taken up this morning. Have her released, unharmed, and returned to her own home.'

The Captain saluted. 'Majesty!' He withdrew.

Will, with yet another deep bow, and with heartfelt thanks, also withdrew. The King, he decided by this time, wasn't the only one who was overwrought.

Southampton, knowing the King's mood, had assumed that Will would leave the presence under armed guard, on his way to the Marshalsea. He hid his astonishment, but his lip curled. 'Well, Master Shakespeare, was your wish granted?'

Will inclined his head. 'I am more grateful to your lordship than I can say.'

He passed on. Southampton glared at that sturdy back. Daniel, leaving the lion's den, could not have caused him more amazement.

# Chapter 20

## O, You are men of stones…

Will hurried back to his lodging. The boy heard him coming up the stairs, was at the door, waiting, quivering with eagerness. 'Well?'

'Well indeed. The King has given orders for her release.'

Matthew half reeled back into the room. 'Oh, sir. You have the order?'

'No.' Will would have preferred to have it in his own hand. But one did not quibble with princes in their moments of clemency. 'He instructed the Captain of the Guard, in my presence, to return her, unharmed, to her own home.'

'Oh, sir.' To Will's embarrassment the boy wept wildly. He flung himself down on his knees, seized Will's hands, kissed them. 'You went to see the King himself, for *our* sake?'

'Get up,' Will said, almost roughly. He approved of sentiment, but he liked it kept seemly.

Matthew struggled to his feet. He wiped his eyes. 'I only wanted – to thank you, Master,' he said piteously.

'You can do that best by going home and preparing for your mother's coming.' He added, more gently, 'She is a strong woman, Matthew. But she will have been afeared. She will be in need of all your care and love.'

'She shall have it, Master.' There were tears in the boy's eyes again.

Will smiled. 'Of course.' Then he became stern. 'And remember, in the morning the final rehearsal of *Antony and Cleopatra*; and on Saturday the performance.' He crossed over to his desk, picked up the manuscript almost lovingly. 'If you *really* want to thank me, Matthew, you can do it by playing my gipsy with all your mind and heart and spirit.'

The final rehearsal. It had been called for eight o'clock in the morning. It was scarce light. A few candles burned on the stage where men, at this wan hour, flitted like shadows. Except for the tiring-room and the stage, the Globe was a pit of ghostly grey.

Everyone was nervous, stretched, like runners before a race, each one knowing that he had the power to hold the play down to the boards, or lift it to the sky.

Will was there as guider; eager, fresh as paint, studying with a candle the plot that hung on the tiring-room wall. Burbage was there, muttering his lines. Though he would never have admitted it to the author, he was as eager as Will. What a part! A noble, tarnished ruler of the world, prepared to ruin that whole world for love of a whoring gipsy!

The hired men playing Demetrius and Philo were there. The Soothsayer and the boys playing Cleopatra's attendants were there. Enobarbus was there. The biggest cast they had ever assembled was there.

But where in God's name was Cleopatra?

Burbage was predictably furious. Will was strangely uneasy. But he had too much on his mind to concern himself unduly with *why* Matthew was not here. The important fact was that Matthew was *not* here.

They sent a lad off to look for Master Peyre, and if necessary go to his mother's house. In the meantime they rehearsed some of the Roman scenes.

The lad returned. Will broke off in the middle of a scene. 'Well? Did you find him?'

'Yes, Master Shakespeare. He is at his mother's house.'

'And he did not come?'

'No.'

'Why not, in God's name?' demanded Burbage.

'He – he would not say. I – I think he is ill, sir. And he asked that Master Shakespeare visit him when he is able.'

'God's teeth! That boy has brought us nothing but trouble. And now he expects one of the sharers to go running after him. Ill! And what about Saturday, forsooth?' Burbage was beside himself.

Will said quietly, 'I fear something is wrong, Dick. I will go when we have rehearsed what we can.'

Dick snorted. A sharer, at the beck and call of a boy player! He turned to Heminge. 'John. We had best prepare an alternative for Saturday, in case my lord Matthew does not feel like honouring us with his presence. Something without boys, blast them. *Caesar*? Can we do *Caesar*, John?'

'We have the parts, and the costumes. If we rehearse from now until Saturday – '

'Right! To hell with *Antony*. Find the parts for *Caesar*, John. And the plot. We'll start now. And you'd better go and see your ailing, wailing boy, Will. Tell him from all of us to go back to the Children of the Revels. We want men in this Company.'

Will went, furious. Really, Richard could be impossible at times. He strode angrily through the streets, angry with himself now for trotting off like a pet dog if Matthew but whistled. Angry with Matthew for ruining his Cleopatra, for being the cause of his humiliation. Yet, above all, filled with a dreadful premonition of evil, of what he would find when he reached the house of the silversmith's widow.

The doorway was a gaping hole where the soldiers had smashed their way in.

Matthew met him on the threshold.

And spat in his face. 'Come in, Master Protestant,' he said. His voice had the quality of vitriol. His face had a translucent pallor; his eyes a black intensity.

Patiently, Will wiped the spittle from his beard, and followed the boy in.

Matthew quietly opened the door into the parlour. It was dark inside. The curtains were drawn. 'She cannot bear the daylight,' said Matthew.

Will stood in the doorway, like one hesitating at the gates of Hell.

The boy's cruel, mocking voice said, 'Go in, Master Protestant; see your Protestant handiwork.'

Will took a few steps into the room. He could see nothing.

The boy said, in a voice now wonderfully soft and gentle: 'See, Mother, Master Shakespeare has come to visit you.'

Now, in the darkness, he could see a white face, a form lying on a couch, fingers clawing at his wrist. And a voice he would not have recognised as Annette Peyre, a high, dragging, urgent voice cried, 'Oh sir, what would you have me tell you? I will tell you anything, everything, only do not – Yes, Catesby, it was he, and Master Winter, and Father – '

Her voice fell to a babbling, rose to a sudden scream, fell back to a babbling and a desolate moaning.

'It seems you were too late, Master Shakespeare,' said Matthew in a cold, clear voice.

Will stumbled from the room, groped his way to the door, almost collapsed into the thin November sunlight. He began walking, anywhere, nowhere, leaning heavily on his cane, dragging his legs like a drunken man.

Matthew stayed in the darkened room with his mother.

Pain. It was a fact of life: toothache, bellyache, the stone, the rack, the fire – all part of life, as inescapable as death. He had never given it enough thought.

Now he felt it, for it was past thought. His world was built on pain. Spider and fly, cat and mouse, fox and bird, hunter and hunted. The shriek of the night owl was enough to set his mind running on beak and claw, on tearing, shrinking flesh; so that one creature might live, a dozen others must die in torment.

But that men – He had written of men as though some were noble, some evil, most betwixt and between. Now he saw them as the devils of this world, lusting after another's pain, hunting, destroying. He saw the world (which he had so loved. Oh, the meanders of Avon, the song sung to the sweet lute, the still, September days!) he saw the world as a sulphurous hell where men were the devils, endlessly tormenting, stabbing, burning. The bright, dancing loveliness of his world had been destroyed for ever. That darkened room where Annette Peyre lay, the utter desolation of her cries, had put out the light of the sun, and stilled the world's music.

He came near to madness, shutting himself in his room, sometimes flinging himself on to his couch and howling at the evil and the cruelty of the race of which he, God ha' mercy, was one. Yes, surely he was as evil as the rest. What had been done to Annette had been done in the name of *his* country, *his* God.

He ought to try to help Matthew, Annette even, though God knew she was past help, he thought bitterly. But a lethargy lay on his limbs and mind so heavy that he could do nothing.

Except, as always, write. A dark tale in Holinshed, an old, crazed king, villainy, bloodshed, heartbreak, stark evil cankering the minds of men. He would make of this play a great cry of outrage and horror at the monstrous evil of the world. Only with this could he purge his mind, only with this could he hold at bay the madness that threatened him.

So he worked, and brooded, shaken and weakened by ague fits, drained by long periods of despair, while England dipped into the sunless valley of winter. Sometimes he lay in his chair, staring at nothing. Sometimes he wrote. Sometimes he *was* the crazed old king, bellowing about the room, 'Blow, winds, and crack your cheeks! rage! blow! You cataracts and hurricanoes –'

Mistress Mountjoy assumed he had been bewitched, a common enough complaint. She took him his food, and left him alone, which was what he wanted. When his friends from the theatre visited him, he greeted them with gentle civility (which was what they were used to from sweet Will) and got rid of them as fast as he could. There was only one visitor he wanted, and he knew he would never come.

But he did. Still white of face, still with that black intensity of eye.

Will went to embrace him. But the young man held himself so stiffly that Will checked himself. 'Matthew,' he said. 'How is your mother?' His mouth was dry. The words were a whisper.

Matthew crossed himself. 'Our Saviour Christ has taken her into His peace.'

'Oh thank God,' cried Will. He sat down, laid his head on his desk, and wept.

The young man stood and watched him.

Will recovered slowly. He looked up at Matthew. 'And you? How is it with you, boy?' He rose. That suffering had been with him night and day. To know that it was at last over filled him with a curious, rather light-headed peace. 'Matthew. A glass of wine?'

'No thank you, sir.' Still that stiffness. 'Sir, I – treated you offensively at – my mother's house. I beg your forgiveness, sir.'

'My dear Matthew! Come, a chair.'

'I would prefer to stand, Master Shakespeare. I must not stay.'

'But Matthew, this is your home. I had long thought – ' He looked appealingly at this tall, unbending youth. 'I had hoped – I had a son, once, Matthew. I had hoped – you might take his place. Even, perhaps, my name.'

He sounded, he knew, pathetic. An old man, desperately begging a youth to take something the youth scorned.

Matthew shook his head.

Will said, 'I have only daughters. My family's Grant of Arms will lapse. I had hoped – '

The boy smiled. At last he smiled! He said, 'I do not need a Grant of Arms where I am going, Master Shakespeare.'

It had an ominous sound. Will said, humbly, 'Where is that, Matthew?'

The boy was still smiling. 'Douai, sir.'

'Douai?'

'The Seminary at Douai. I have to avenge my mother, sir. Not as a Protestant would avenge. But by saving a few English souls for Christ, Master Shakespeare. In a few years

I shall return to England a priest. And with God's help we shall still take England back to the fold of Catholicism.'

Will had been staring at him with a kind of fascinated horror. Then, suddenly: 'You're mad,' he snapped.

Arrogantly the boy stared at him, eyebrows raised. 'Mad, Master Shakespeare?'

'Mad! Your mother, Catesby, Fawkes, a hundred others all died horribly for this – this *quibble*. And now, *you* would throw your life away.'

Matthew was smiling confidently. 'It is no quibble, sir. Everlasting Life, eternal damnation are no quibble.'

Will said, 'You really think, don't you, that if a man do not believe as you believe, he is damned.'

'Of course. You, Master Shakespeare, you are a good man, a kind man. My mother respected you, I – loved you. Yet you are damned to everlasting Hell. Unless, of course, you repent.'

Will was no fanatic. His God, if he had one, was a pitying Christ who had known human suffering in its most hideous form; or, in some way he never troubled to define, the Beauty that informed nature from the meanest petal to the panoply of the stars. For the rest, he was prepared to accept the words of the wise old Queen:

> 'Twas God the word that spake it,
> He took the Bread and brake it;
> And what the word did make it;
> That I believe, and take it.

He said bitterly, 'So you would throw your life away.'

'Not, perhaps, before I have saved a soul or two.'

Will sighed. It was no use. He knew fanaticism when he saw it. But he said, 'You would have made a fine actor.'

He looked at the young man in amazement. He seemed to have grown in a moment. His eyes shone. Even his face seemed to glow with an inner radiance, with an unearthly joy such as Will had never before seen, even imagined. 'I may yet appear on the stage, Master Shakespeare. But it will not be the Globe, or the Blackfriars.'

He was moving towards the door, out of Will's life. Will's voice was the voice of an old man. It said, bleakly, 'What stage *will* it be, Matthew?'

'Tyburn,' cried Matthew in the high, ringing voice of the victor. And was gone.

The room was very empty. The fire burned low. He threw on a log. Another. He crossed to his desk. Books, manuscripts, thoughts. What did they all amount to, compared with the nobility, the monumental folly, of man? They were like the imaginings of a child, the scribblings of a diseased brain. He picked up a thick manuscript. *Antony and Cleopatra*. Suddenly his gipsy whore, his bloated warrior revolted him. He carried the manuscript across to the fire. That was the only place for his debauched lovers. The ice-cold flame of Matthew's fanaticism had taught him that.

The logs were beginning to burn. Flame licked around them, died, flickered more strongly.

But it was at this moment that William Shakespeare, the careful man of business, who all his life except for the past few weeks had kept such a tight rein on Will Shakespeare the poet, re-asserted himself. One did not destroy property. He carried the play back to his desk, tossed it in a drawer. It would not be acted in his lifetime, he would see to that. These bawdy creatures would be an insult to the memory of Annette and Matthew. And no one, he knew, was likely to be interested in it *after* his death. He had no illusions on that score.

Yet he could not bring himself to destroy it. Waste not want not. A man did not destroy property.

# EPILOGUE

'Hamnet Shakespeare. Born 1585. Died 1596.'

A small stone for so small a span. A short inscription, for so short a life.

But Will was adding to it. 'Matthew Peyre. Born 1590. Died –?' Matthew would have his years of study. He would be ordained. Then: the pale, black-clad young man smuggled back to England (disguised, perhaps, as a merchant or a scholar) the few months, or even years, walled up by day in a corpse's solitude, then, by night, bringing comfort and instruction and the Body of Christ to the faithful. Until, inevitably, the informer, the arrest, the trial, the cruel death on Tyburn tree.

The river mists still prowled, grey ghosts, in Stratford churchyard. Will turned away. On the first of the spring days he had taken fast horses for Stratford, changing horses every ten miles, covering seventy of the ninety miles on the first day. The next day he had been in the saddle long before dawn, riding like a man with a devil on his back – a devil of madness. He wanted air, Warwickshire air. He wanted, not London cobbles, but the breathing earth under his feet. He wanted Anne, their daughters. He wanted something he had needed in every crisis of his life – the quiet benison of trees and grass and wayside flowers. To this he would always return, as a hurt child to a mother.

He left the churchyard. He had saluted the dead – and those about to die – uttering his sad '*pax vobiscum*'. Now for the living.

By the time he reached Chapel Lane, the sun had dispelled the mists, and shone with all the brilliance of the spring. He passed the cottage where once he and Anne had lived, when the world was young and he as yet ignorant of its cruelty. He came in sight of New Place, its diamond panes glittering in the sunlight, its brick red and warm and welcoming.

He came nearer. Now the sun struck straight into the room. He could see them at breakfast. Two grey heads, Mother and Anne, a dark head, Judith, a head golden as the sunlight, Susanna.

He saw Anne look out of the window, saw her troubled frown as she watched the lurking stranger. Saw a dawning incredulity, for he had come on an impulse, unannounced.

She rose, groped her way round the table, for she did not for a moment take her eyes off the stranger. She passed out of his sight.

The door opened. She stood on the step, a housewife of nearly fifty, plump, rather shapeless. She held out her arms. In her face was an overwhelming love, an overwhelming joy. He saw her lips open, and wonderingly speak his name.

Cruelty, folly, hate, deliberately inflicted pain. This, he had come to believe, was mankind's contribution to the world. Why, even the God that men created for themselves made the same contribution. And now, suddenly, his whole dark hell of a world was illuminated, was *redeemed*, by the love shining from the face of an unlettered countrywoman. Could it *really* be so?

'Anne!' he whispered unsteadily. And ran to take her in his arms, in the bright morning of this new day.

# Eric Malpass

## The Lamplight and the Stars

Nathan Cranswick's third child comes into the world on the day of Queen Victoria's Diamond Jubilee. Whilst the Empire celebrates, Nathan's concerns are about his family's future. A gentle and wise preacher, he gratefully accepts the chance to move from the dingy, cramped house in Ingerby to the village of Moreland when he is offered a job on the splendid Heron estate. Anticipating peace and tranquillity for his wife and young family, his hopes are cruelly dashed when their new life is beset by problems from the beginning. A family scandal and the Boer War menace their whole future, but finally it is the agonising choice facing his gentle daughter which threatens to tear the family apart...

## Morning's at Seven

Three generations of the Pentecost family live in a state of permanent disarray in a huge, sprawling farmhouse. Seven-year-old Gaylord Pentecost is the innocent hero who observes the lives of the adults – Grandpa, Momma and Poppa and two aunties – with amusement and incredulity.

Through Gaylord's eyes, we witness the heartache suffered by Auntie Rose as the exquisite Auntie Becky makes a play for her gentleman friend, while Gaylord unwittingly makes the situation far worse.

Mayhem and madness reign in this zestful account of the lives and loves of the outrageous Pentecosts.

# Eric Malpass

## Of Human Frailty
### A biographical novel of Thomas Cranmer

Thomas Cranmer is a gentle, unassuming scholar when a chance meeting sweeps him away from the security and tranquillity of Cambridge to the harsh magnificence of Henry VIII's court. As a supporter of Henry he soon rises to prominence as Archbishop of Canterbury.

Eric Malpass paints a fascinating picture of Reformation England and its prominent figures: the brilliant, charismatic but utterly ruthless Henry VIII, the exquisite but scheming Anne Boleyn and the fanatical Mary Tudor.

But it is the paradoxical Thomas Cranmer who dominates the story. A tormented man, he is torn between valour and cowardice; a man with a loving heart who finds himself hated by many; and a man of God who makes the terrifying discovery that he must suffer and die for his beliefs. Thomas Cranmer is a man of simple virtue, whose only fault is his all too human frailty.

# ERIC MALPASS

## THE RAISING OF LAZARUS PIKE

Lazarus Pike (1820–1899), author of *Lady Emily's Decision*, lies buried in the churchyard of Ill Boding. And there he would have remained, in obscurity and undisturbed, had it not been for a series of remarkable coincidences. A discovery sets in motion a campaign to republish his works and to reinstate Lazarus Pike as a giant of Victorian literature. This is a cause of bitter wrangling between the two factions that emerge. For some, Lazarus is a simple schoolmaster, devoted to his beautiful wife, Corinda. For others, who think his reputation needs a sexy, contemporary twist, he is a wife murderer with a deeply flawed character. What follows is a knowing and wry look at the world of literary make-overs and the heritage industry in a hilarious story that brings fame and tragedy to an unsuspecting moorland village.

## SWEET WILL

William Shakespeare is just eighteen when he marries Anne Hathaway, eight years his senior. Anne, who bears a son soon after the marriage, is plain and not particularly bright – but her love for Will is undeniable. Talented and fiercely ambitious, Will's scintillating genius soon makes him the toast of Elizabethan London. While he basks in the flattery his great reputation affords him, Anne lives a lonely life in Stratford, far away from the glittering world of her husband.

This highly evocative account of the life of the young William Shakespeare begins the trilogy which continues with *The Cleopatra Boy* and concludes with *A House of Women*.

# ERIC MALPASS

## THE WIND BRINGS UP THE RAIN

It is a perfect summer's day in August 1914. Yet even as Nell and her friends enjoy a blissful picnic by the river, the storm clouds of war are gathering over Europe. Very soon this idyll is to be swept away by the conflict that will take millions of men to their deaths.

After the war, the widowed Nell leads a wretched existence, caring for her husband's elderly, ungrateful parents, with only her son, Benbow, for companionship and support. But Nell is a passionate woman and wants to share her life with a man who will return her love. Meanwhile, Benbow falls in love with a German girl, Ulrike – until she is enticed home by the resurgent Germany.

This moving story of a Midlands family in the inter-war years is a compelling tale of personal triumph and disappointment, set against the background of the hideous destruction of war.

## TITLES BY ERIC MALPASS AVAILABLE DIRECT
## FROM HOUSE OF STRATUS

| Quantity | | £ | $(US) | $(CAN) | € |
|---|---|---|---|---|---|
| | AT THE HEIGHT OF THE MOON | 6.99 | 11.50 | 15.99 | 11.50 |
| | BEEFY JONES | 6.99 | 11.50 | 15.99 | 11.50 |
| | FORTINBRAS HAS ESCAPED | 6.99 | 11.50 | 15.99 | 11.50 |
| | A HOUSE OF WOMEN | 6.99 | 11.50 | 15.99 | 11.50 |
| | THE LAMPLIGHT AND THE STARS | 6.99 | 11.50 | 15.99 | 11.50 |
| | THE LONG LONG DANCES | 6.99 | 11.50 | 15.99 | 11.50 |
| | MORNING'S AT SEVEN | 6.99 | 11.50 | 15.99 | 11.50 |
| | OF HUMAN FRAILTY | 6.99 | 11.50 | 15.99 | 11.50 |
| | OH, MY DARLING DAUGHTER | 6.99 | 11.50 | 15.99 | 11.50 |
| | PIG-IN-THE-MIDDLE | 6.99 | 11.50 | 15.99 | 11.50 |
| | THE RAISING OF LAZARUS PIKE | 6.99 | 11.50 | 15.99 | 11.50 |
| | SUMMER AWAKENING | 6.99 | 11.50 | 15.99 | 11.50 |
| | SWEET WILL | 6.99 | 11.50 | 15.99 | 11.50 |
| | THE WIND BRINGS UP THE RAIN | 6.99 | 11.50 | 15.99 | 11.50 |

ALL HOUSE OF STRATUS BOOKS ARE AVAILABLE FROM GOOD BOOKSHOPS
OR DIRECT FROM THE PUBLISHER:

Internet: www.houseofstratus.com including author interviews, reviews, features.

Email:    sales@houseofstratus.com please quote author, title and credit card details.

Order Line:  UK:    0800 169 1780,
             USA:   1 800 509 9942
             INTERNATIONAL: +44 (0) 20 7494 6400 (UK)
                        or +01 212 218 7649
             (please quote author, title, and credit card details.)

Send to:  House of Stratus Sales Department          House of Stratus Inc.
          24c Old Burlington Street                  Suite 210
          London                                     1270 Avenue of the Americas
          W1X 1RL                                    New York • NY 10020
          UK                                         USA

# PAYMENT

Please tick currency you wish to use:

☐ £ (Sterling)  ☐ $ (US)  ☐ $ (CAN)  ☐ € (Euros)

Allow for shipping costs charged per order plus an amount per book as set out in the tables below:

CURRENCY/DESTINATION

|  | £(Sterling) | $(US) | $(CAN) | €(Euros) |
|---|---|---|---|---|
| **Cost per order** | | | | |
| UK | 1.50 | 2.25 | 3.50 | 2.50 |
| Europe | 3.00 | 4.50 | 6.75 | 5.00 |
| North America | 3.00 | 3.50 | 5.25 | 5.00 |
| Rest of World | 3.00 | 4.50 | 6.75 | 5.00 |
| **Additional cost per book** | | | | |
| UK | 0.50 | 0.75 | 1.15 | 0.85 |
| Europe | 1.00 | 1.50 | 2.25 | 1.70 |
| North America | 1.00 | 1.00 | 1.50 | 1.70 |
| Rest of World | 1.50 | 2.25 | 3.50 | 3.00 |

PLEASE SEND CHEQUE OR INTERNATIONAL MONEY ORDER.
payable to: STRATUS HOLDINGS plc or HOUSE OF STRATUS INC. or card payment as indicated

STERLING EXAMPLE

Cost of book(s):...................... Example: 3 x books at £6.99 each: £20.97
Cost of order: ...................... Example: £1.50 (Delivery to UK address)
Additional cost per book:.............. Example: 3 x £0.50: £1.50
Order total including shipping:........... Example: £23.97

## VISA, MASTERCARD, SWITCH, AMEX:

☐☐☐☐☐☐☐☐☐☐☐☐☐☐☐☐☐☐☐☐

Issue number (Switch only):

☐☐☐

**Start Date:**          **Expiry Date:**

☐☐/☐☐          ☐☐/☐☐

Signature: _____

NAME: _____

ADDRESS: _____

COUNTRY: _____

ZIP/POSTCODE: _____

Please allow 28 days for delivery. Despatch normally within 48 hours.

Prices subject to change without notice.
Please tick box if you do not wish to receive any additional information. ☐

House of Stratus publishes many other titles in this genre; please check our website (**www.houseofstratus.com**) for more details.